Thank you to everyone who has listened to this story and these ideas
with positive encouragement over the past decade or so.
Thank you public library system.

THE WINDOWS AROUND

Part One

Chapter One

As the rain beat an illuminated symphony on the streets and buildings below him, Bill Kepstein stared out his office window at a sky and streets that he had seen day after day, year after year. A tall man with jet-black hair, he wore a finely tailored suit and matching vest, a gold Swiss watch, and Italian leather shoes. He moved with distinction, and while only in his forties, the silver streaks in his hair and pencil moustache created the appearance of a man closer in age to fifty or fifty-five. It was six o'clock on a Friday night.

Kepstein wandered over to his office mini-bar and poured himself a large rum and Coke. Returning to the window, he downed his drink and remembered the unmarked letter that had been hand-delivered earlier that afternoon. Returning to the mini-bar, he poured himself another drink and picked up the letter that had been relegated to the top of a stack of unfinished business. Setting his glass on the stand next to the window, Kepstein tore open the envelope and half-sighed.

Bill,

If you are reading this, I am dead. If I have assumed correctly, you will either be reading this in the late evening after work has ended and you have not gone home, or three days after my courier has delivered the letter. I am, indeed, writing to you from the grave. My funeral was today — the date of this signing — and preserving the last semblances of pride I could muster before passing on, I prudently neglected to invite you.

Further assuming that you would concern yourself more with my character, rather than whether or not your wife had any say in this decision, I won't digress into trivialities. I have my wife and I have my daughter. These are the only two constants in my life, and you have reduced one to zero. My daughter leads an idle life that does not even amount to a base of anguish and certainly not a glimmer of happiness. You have led her into an insufferable existence of neutrality.

Your fear of exposing yourself to anything outside of a pre-planned reality has led you to a numbness that no man of my standing or history can understand. You know very well the fortunes and failures of my family and myself. You are able to observe the natures and characters of good men and you value rather highly the noble expressions of daring decisions and calculated risks, but you, Bill Kepstein, are a coward.

I'm not writing this letter to you out of vengeance — the true one-sided argument from a dead man. I am writing this as a last request for a change; a humble request from a man who was unable to express humility in his life. If not for my daughter, then for yourself, Bill, do something worthwhile with your life. None of us are responsible for the limitations we were born with.

2

We are only responsible for what we create. By this logic, you are one of the most irresponsible and uncreative men alive. Take hold of your life. Take hold of my daughter's life or set her free — just do something. Even from the grave I cannot express any love for you. I can only offer hope you will heed what I say and do what's best for Rebecca.

Canton Bristle

Kepstein read the last line — the man's signature — out loud with a subdued air of disgust. His eyes traveled mechanically from the bottom of the letter to the skyline. He felt cold and removed from the news of his father-in-law's death. He took another swallow of his drink and folded the letter into a small square, almost smiling at the thought of his father-in-law's last words, now creased with fold lines, the ink bleeding through the paper, creating a physical closeness that was not meant to exist.

"Talk more to us, Bill, interact more with us, don't be so stiff — you're always so serious." Kepstein recalled his wife's words.

Maybe if you hadn't raised your daughter to be as deaf and dumb to the world around her as you were, Canton, your cute little request might amount to something. You think I'm lazy? At least my lack of significance bothers me — you people wear it like a badge.

Kepstein stuffed the letter into the breast pocket of his jacket, where it rested alongside the two cigars he had packed earlier, just in case he went out after work. That was now a necessity. He had no goal in mind,

3

no special plan to have an affair or meet new people. He wasn't seeking anyone to solve his problems, but wanted to find solace in drinking and talking with strangers. At least they wouldn't condemn him.

* * *

Pulling into the alley behind McArthur's, Kepstein enjoyed the sound of the Mercedes engine rumbling against the old brick walls and felt lucky to find a good parking place on a Friday night. As he entered the bar, he realized that there would be a wait for a pool table, which he expected, and that small talk would be useless amidst all the noise. He sat down at the bar and ordered a whisky and a tall glass of beer.

The bartender knew him, and like any good bartender, she was good at offering just enough friendship to keep the patrons drinking, but not enough to offer solution to their problems, or to suggest they go home. Kepstein, in his role as patron, appeared to her to maintain an air of positivity — the look of a man enjoying a blessed existence. Closer inspection, however, revealed much less stability, and it was clear to her that this sad man was going to work on his sorrows for one reason or another, and that he would need a steady stream of attention. She read his face and saw features that remained unchanged after each drink, but said to her, nonetheless, "Go ahead. Ask me a question. I have stories to tell."

* * *

Jack Shales could be best described as simple and lucky. He was twenty-nine- years old and stood almost six feet tall, but he appeared shorter because of the way he walked, always aiming his face either

4

downward towards the ground or upward towards the sky. He was a handsome man who, whether intentionally or not, set his mouth tightly at the corners regardless of the tone or subject of conversation, as if to remain unmoved by news, be it good or bad. In spite of this, visible lines of joy could often be seen branching outward from the corners of his eyes, and at times it was possible to see these signs of kindness extend down his cheekbone, coming to rest in two large dimples.

Jack entered McArthur's with an air of purpose. He was scheduled to meet his friend, Lenny Manzarec, a recent graduate from a film school in New York. As far as Jack knew, this was NYU; Lenny had always been reluctant to talk about his training. Usually he would give a broad description of a project in which he was involved in letters that were short, hurried, and self-effacing. All Jack knew was that Lenny was heading to Richmond for the Easter holiday and that he wanted to stop through Baltimore to catch up with his old friend. Lenny promised to call when he was close to town.

Jack sat at the bar, one hand in his pocket and the other pulling up his left sleeve so he could look at his watch. He didn't actually want to know the time — this was just a habit. The bartender knew Jack well and asked if he wanted vodka or beer. Jack opted for vodka, as he'd been drinking beer most of the afternoon.

Sipping his drink, Jack noticed the man next to him at the bar. He could tell for certain from the man's appearance that he was successful and much older, but Jack also sensed despair in his eyes. Jack could also detect detachment in the man's face, an objective and observing mental state that some people maintain when they are on the road for long periods of time.

"I'm very happy to hear John Coltrane playing on the jukebox on such a busy night," Jack said to the man. The stranger seemed lost in the moment, engulfed by the opening of Coltrane's *Naima*.

"I put five dollars' worth of jazz in the juke about half an hour ago — you'd better let the bartender know you like it before they hit the skip button," the man said, smiling, then returning to his trancelike state.

"Jess!" Jack yelled in the direction of the bartender. "Don't skip the jazz. We like it — a lot."

"You two are the only ones, but you got it, honey," Jess said, winking.

"It's not jazz — it's music, my friend," the man said begrudgingly. "John Coltrane never really made music — he created environments. Do you know what I mean?"

The man's deadpan stare and the point-blankness with which he asked the question caused Jack to stop short. He thought about the comment for a moment.

"I think some people listen to John Coltrane — or jazz in general — like some people listen to the ocean. Some plant themselves in the ocean's presence, but without any real understanding. They have no Descartes-like impression of the 'I am here, therefore I enjoy' mentality." Jack exposed a few crooked teeth. "Others smile at the turn of phrases, and enjoy jazz as they enjoy the ocean's presence— as a background melody."

"That's a valid point you make. And which type of jazz enthusiast are you?"

"The vibrant kind!" Jack answered. "I let the music carry me, pick me up, and drop me wherever it pleases. I let the music *talk* to me — how about yourself?"

"Same."

Jack was happy to speak with someone interesting. Usually, he found himself drinking alone, listening to music alone, and moving about in the city alone, always surrounded by people, but not "real" people. Because he typically was attracted to, and sought out, thinkers, he now relished, in some sense, Kepstein's self-awareness.

The conversation was interrupted by the sound of Jack's cellphone.

"Hey Jack, it's me — Lenny."

"Lenny! How's the drive?" Jack answered excitedly. He hunched down, placing himself closer to the bar so he could hear better and not appear rude.

After Jack and Lenny arranged to meet at McArthur's, Jack swiveled in his bar stool and stared blankly at the crowd. He had a pretty good buzz and was glad his friend was coming to visit. He began to realize that he should plan something for the evening. Too often, he thought, people came to visit, excited by the thought of a big night on the town, only to return home with a distaste for spending money and riding in cabs, or even worse, being upset with *him* for one reason or another. He didn't want that to happen tonight, so he decided to keep it simple. They'd have a few beers at McArthur's while catching up on what's been happening in their lives, and with a bit of luck run into some old acquaintances, or better yet, girls.

Chapter Two

After twenty minutes of waiting for Lenny to arrive, Jack started to get restless and began to prowl, cat-like, through the crowd. Suddenly, he spotted Lenny leaning against the side of a pool table, his hands clasped around a mug of beer. With a shrill, piercing cry, Jack called out, "Lenny!"

Lenny jerked away from the side of the pool table and turned toward the source of the loud noise, his glass of beer crashing at his feet as Jack enveloped him in a bear hug. Lenny, shoes covered in beer and glass shards, cracked a wide smile and returned Jack's second hug. "You son-of-a-bitch, you're still the same wise guy, aren't you?"

Jack laughed as he released Lenny and stepped out of their warm embrace. "Yeah, and you're still drinking too much caffeine, you spastic fucker. How the hell are you, Lenny?"

"Good, man, let's just get another beer, I'm dying here. It's cold as hell outside and my shoes are soaking wet — I didn't bring a spare pair inside."

"Why *would* you bring in a spare pair?" Jack asked, moving right past his friends' odd conversation patterns. "Anyway, I've got a couple of seats over here, next to a very interesting dude I was chatting with earlier."

As they threaded their way through the crowd, the men shared small talk about Lenny's trip: how long he'd stay, the weather, and so on. Jack wanted to reserve important conversation for the more relaxing atmosphere of alcohol and living room music, but Lenny was only going to be in town for one night and told Jack he didn't want to spend it in an apartment. He wanted to see all the old bars he remembered from earlier years, and maybe, with a little luck, see an old girlfriend or two.

They sat themselves next to the man Jack had spoken to earlier that night. Patting Lenny's back, he said to the man, "This here is my old friend, Lenny. He used to be my roommate in days of old, but he moved up to New York. Oh, and by the way, I never introduced myself. My name is Jack, Jack Shales."

"Bill Kepstein. Glad to meet you."

"Yessir, I'm Lenny" Lenny quickly added, shaking the man's hand. "Just stopping by to see ol' Jackie boy, here — on my way to Richmond for the holidays."

"Well, it's very nice that you fellas are staying connected — it's important not to lose contact with old friends," Kepstein said, realizing that he was saying this both for them and for himself.

"It's easy for us." Jack eyed the friend he hadn't seen in years. "Lenny writes screenplays and works in film. I write articles for newspapers and magazines, and also try to dabble in the arts from time to time . . . so we're both story tellers and talkers in our own ways."

"Lenny, what exactly do you do in the film industry?" Kepstein asked, rotating slightly in his seat so he could face him more easily.

Lenny detested talking about his work to strangers, as he felt it was just their polite way of asking if he knew anyone famous. He found that they would listen for however long he rambled on — he'd actually tested the length of time someone would idly listen—before asking which stars he'd worked with. This time, though, something led him to believe that the man asking the question was a little different. "I like to write screenplays, but they haven't been able to pay my bills, so I do whatever else I'm needed to do at the school's production house. Mainly camera work and the background stuff, you know, editing, etc."

"That's great to hear. I've always had a passion for the arts myself, especially for film. Since I was a boy, I've watched, studied, and always been on the lookout for good films. Say, why don't we grab a few drinks and shoot a game of pool, boys," Kepstein suggested, tossing a fifty on the bar and standing up.

The men shot two games of nine ball, then Jack and Kepstein played a game of eight ball while Lenny tried his luck with a cute brunette standing nearby. They eventually returned to the bar, where Jack and Lenny continued to scan for familiar faces or an evening's romance. It was late and everyone ordered another shot and two beers from the always flirtatious waitress. When another Coltrane song came on the jukebox, Jack saw Lenny smile.

"When did you put this in, Jack?" Lenny yelled above the noise.

"Actually, I didn't — he did," Jack said, pointing to Kepstein.

"No shit? Do you have any idea how much Jack loves his Coltrane?"

11

Kepstein turned to Jack. "Jack, do you have a favorite place in town to see live jazz?"

Jack turned his eyes toward the ancient panel ceiling and paused before answering. "Yes, I often go to Elbows over on the Westside — the place is falling apart, the drinks are cheap, and they let the players go all night long. How about yourself?"

"I know Elbows well. In fact, I've been good friends with Sonny Mitchell, the bartender, for years. He's got the right attitude. And what about you, Lenny? You ever make your way into Birdland or any of the *historical and fantastic* hangouts in New York?"

"I've seen one show there, but only when Jack was visiting. Quite a while back, but I recall it was amazing"

Kepstein laughed. "I remember seeing Miles Davis play in the early eighties at the Hollywood Bowl — now that was a show." He was trying hard not to reminisce, but he felt comfortable with the younger men. "And those were the days, too. I could hop on a plane or take a cross-country road trip with no goal other than to enjoy the party."

"I've done something like that a few times, taking road trips out to Utah to catch the Sundance Film Festival," Lenny interjected, "but . . . I'm a movie guy, what can I say?"

"I flew to Mexico last fall for the Day of the Dead festival," Jack chimed in. "Yes, seeing the big parties is important!"

The men were having a good time telling stories and continued to talk about jazz, music, and women — always returning to women — before Lenny started to chat with Jack in private. "I can't imagine where this night's going man, but it's going in my direction! What do you think about this fellow, Kepstein? He seems quite sad, wealthy, wise, or detached, or maybe all of those. I can't figure him out."

"I can't seem to figure him out either, but I think you're right, it might be all of the above."

As Jack and Lenny talked, Kepstein took a cigar from his jacket pocket and lit it. He puffed slowly, casually observing the people around him. He had immediately liked Jack and Lenny. They reminded him a great deal of himself when he was their age. Except for the gap in social status, he thought he and Jack were similar in many ways: well-educated, insightful, yet obviously a bit different — but in a good way. He felt a common bond with Lenny, in that both were avid theatergoers and experts on cinema.

As the evening flowed into the early a.m. hours, Jack looked at Kepstein. "I'll tell you what. I don't think there is anything in this world that I hate more than closing time. They turn on those damned bright lights and cut the music so abruptly that all you can hear is a bunch of individual conversations no one is listening to anyway."

"That always gets me too," Kepstein said. "It sneaks up on you and always happens too early. You figure, it's only one thirty and half the people have been here for a few hours, and the other half less than that. Everyone's just getting really loose."

"That's exactly how I see it. Usually you don't meet anyone until after you've been at the bar for an hour or so, and if it closes at two then there really isn't enough time to get to know anyone. And, after all, that's the reason to go to the bar anyway, isn't it? — to meet people?"

"Usually," Kepstein said as he extracted another cigar from his pocket and began to light it. "I never really know anymore. Half the time, I just end up at the bar. No point, no purpose, no plans."

Seeing Kepstein suddenly stare at the door and then look down at the floor, Jack changed his tone, deciding it was one of those occasions when it's best not to comment further. He glanced at the crowd, aware that he and Kepstein were making exactly the kind of small talk that he despised. Jack always thought his ability to recognize and understand the ways of the night was both a gift and a curse: it was satisfying to know what others were thinking, but at the same time, he wanted to enjoy himself without intensely observing or commenting on what was happening. Sometimes he just wanted to be normal.

After another half an hour, one bathroom break, a few kisses from the women lingering around, and another round of beers, Jack was very drunk. He looked at his newly-found drinking partner.

"I wish there was some sort of afterhours bar, Bill . . . and I know what you're thinking — there are tons of them in this city. But that's not what I'm talking about. Not clubs with plush chairs shaped like flowers, or lingerie-wearing waitresses, or whatever else, not a club with cheap shitty music played low enough so that no one notices, and not a club with loud dance music playing to a crowd of people trying to relax. I'm talking about a

14

place with some good live jazz, or at least a little lounge music — just a decent club open till maybe four or so in the morning, but not overbearing." Jack could tell by the look on Kepstein's face that he had hit the mark, but asked anyway, "You know what I mean?"

"Know what you mean!" Kepstein exclaimed. "I know more than what you mean, I know *the* place. It's called Betriebsnacht. It's extremely comfortable. An old German opened it years ago. He's a jazz enthusiast, but his sons are usually running the place and they play a lot of newer music. Still very good though. Betriebsnacht is a rough translation of 'plant night' in German. The place is covered wall-to-wall with plants of all shapes and sizes. It's basically an indoor terrarium."

"I can't believe that I've lived here all my life and never heard of the place." Jack paused, a stunned look on his face. "Where is it? Is it in the area?"

"Yes, but definitely off the beaten path." He looked off into the distance, as if to conjure up an image of the building he was describing. "It's on the corner of 11th street and what I believe is Taylor Ave. — you know where all of those old abandoned broadcast buildings are? It's in the old Erickson building, sort of in the basement, I guess you could say."

The street came into razor-sharp focus for Jack. He remembered walking around the area and being intrigued by the height of the buildings. He'd found the emptiness and abandonment of these structures intriguing and almost eerie. They were a testament to the passage of time in a big city where families were raised for generations under the watchful eye of

15

corporations, but now there was nothing to show for it, only a late-night bar that Jack had never seen or heard of.

"Well, Jack, Jack, Jack," Lenny said, shaking his head from side to side. "Stop salivating and ask the man."

"Can we go?" Jack asked, blushing slightly.

Rising from his seat, cigar in his mouth, Kepstein stood, looking to Jack like a handsome, more slender version of Winston Churchill.

"Well, Jack, I'll tell you what. I'm having a rare good time tonight. I'm not going to lie to you, the day started off sour, but it's turned into something sweet. The night's young, life is a mystery, the music must keep playing, and I would love to treat you both to a cab to Betriebsnacht." He stumbled over the name with a purposefully bad German accent.

Chapter Three

Kepstein, Jack, and Lenny piled into a cab and rode to the club like men who knew how to live without care. With each drink from the flask Kepstein grabbed from his car on the way out of the bar, their inhibitions were burned behind them. Lenny was grinning from ear to ear as he dangled his cigarette out of the cab's backseat window. He felt that everything was going better than expected for a one-night visit. Being a poor boy from Virginia, he never had a chance to rub elbows with money and he knew that this would probably be one of his only opportunities to at least see what the moneyed-people did and thought.

Jack was far more drunk than he'd allowed himself to be in the past six months, but despite his state, he could tell that this night was different than most other nights of hanging out at a bar. This night was special; it was exactly what he had been looking for and exactly the kind of experience he believed he needed. He had a wide grin and a knowing, mischievous gleam in his eyes as the cab came to a screeching halt in the alley next to a rundown building with a large, sliding steel door and no markings. The entrance was around the back.

"Hey Mica, how about a round of beers," Kepstein hollered as the three men entered the bar.

As soon as he went through the bar door, Jack felt himself transfixed by the music and the atmosphere, especially the lush plants that were illuminated by extravagant lighting, each light reaching a leaf in a particular way. The place reminded him of a hidden oasis, a rainforest in the middle of a cement jungle. He found the music to be finely-tuned to the taste of late-nighters, just upbeat enough to keep someone awake, but also at a volume low enough to allow for conversation. As he sat at the bar waiting for their drinks to arrive, he grinned from ear to ear when he realized that the music was coming from huge speakers mounted in a circle at the top of the bar and from smaller ones throughout the flooring at his feet.

The bar itself was a large oval with a pinch in the middle, made of brushed aluminum, with a stained-glass countertop. It served two purposes: ordering drinks or suggesting music, but other than that, the lounge was really the place to be. It was set below the rest of the bar and resembled a sort of basement within a basement, with dozens of tiny, strategically placed speakers hidden among the foliage. It was crafted for enthusiastic alcoholics with lots of money to spend who loved good company and late conversation. After a few moments in the club, it would seem apparent to anyone that this was the only way to set up a place for this kind of patron.

Leaving the bar area, the men made their way down seven steps to the lounge, palm trees on both sides tickling their heads as they passed. The lounge consisted of four tables, each surrounded by a circular couch, two pieces missing on either side so people could get in and out. The furnishings were simple enough, just as Kepstein had said, but clean and comfortable. As with the bar, the tables were made of brushed aluminum and glass tops, and each couch was made of dark green leather, the color of chloroplast.

Drinks in hand and smiles on their faces, their heads slowly and unsteadily bobbing, the men made their way to a couch in a corner of the lounge.

"Man, you weren't kidding, this place is ama-a-a-a-zing," Jack said, awestruck, surprising himself by his comment.

"Not too bad, eh?" Kepstein agreed, settling into a couch and putting his feet on the table in front of him. He relit his cigar and momentarily closed his eyes, reveling in the events of the evening.

Jack arose from the couch. "I would like to make a toast. To this evening, to new friends, and to all the beautiful plants." He waved his arm at the scenery and smiled. "Thank you very much for inviting us here, Mr. Kepstein. You're right, the night is still young. We were smart to leave the bar early, and it's only two o'clock! Let's have a drink and another round — cheers!"

Glasses chimed, drinks went down the hatch, and before their glasses could hit the table, a waiter was standing over them, taking fresh orders. "Hey Andreas, these fellas have never been here before. Do you have any more of that old German beer — the thick black stuff?"

Dancing to the music, one hand carrying his notebook and the other placed on their table, the waiter replied in very loud broken English, "Oh yes, we just got case of them yesterday. Is very, very good beer, I think you guy will like very well."

"Sounds good, Andreas. We'll have three of those." Kepstein looked at his companions with an approving smile. "It's not bad, more like a loaf of bread than a drink though."

"It sounds good to me. I figure when in Rome, . . . you know," Lenny joked, making it obvious he was happy to be along for the ride.

"Lenny," Kepstein said abruptly, "I want to talk to you about making a movie."

Lenny spit out most of his beer, and nearly sprang out of his seat. Everyone laughed like schoolboys, and when their hysteria subsided, it was Kepstein who spoke first. "I'm serious."

"Mr. Kepstein, what do you mean by that?" Lenny asked meekly.

"Call me Bill, Lenny. And I mean just that. I want to make a movie. I told you how much I have always loved movies, and so it is my passion. You guys may have noticed that I have plenty of money. But I can assure you it has brought me no great pleasure."

"Have you really always wanted to make a movie, Mr. K—er, Bill?" Jack asked. "If you were serious, Lenny would be the best guy in town to talk to — even if it's only for one night."

"Cool it, Jack," Lenny said, grinning. "Bill, it is really great that you have an interest in making a movie, but so many factors are involved. You mentioned finances — do you want to finance a movie? Or get involved with producing?"

"No, no, Lenny. I want to be involved with everything from day one. I want to put my own thoughts into a picture — I want to *create* something." Kepstein appeared to his two companions to become distant and lost in the moment as he recalled the letter from his late father-in-law. "My wife's father was buried today. He neglected to inform me of his pathetic death, aside from a crass letter delivered this afternoon — post-mortem."

"Wait," Jack said. "Your father-in-law wrote a letter to be delivered to you after he was dead? And you were not invited to the funeral . . . on purpose?"

Jack and Lenny quickly realized they were not dealing with just any ordinary businessman who was drinking a late night away at his favorite club. Kepstein clearly wanted to talk. "That's correct, Jack. My marriage has not been one you'll find winning any awards for being the most pleasant. In fact, the only distinction you'll find within my marriage is the lack of love, and the degree of outright hostility that it embodies. I'm afraid this is mainly my fault. I feel I've wasted a good portion of my life and I've allowed this feeling to become part of my character."

There was a heavy silence at the table.

"You see," Kepstein continued, "I don't just *want* to make a movie. I don't just *want* to create a film — or any work of art really — I *need* to. The majority of my life has been wasted, and I am reaching a point where I am beginning to understand the significance of such a squandered existence."

"That's pretty heavy-duty stuff, my friend," Jack said.

"And a pretty convincing backdrop for needing to work on a creative endeavor," Lenny added emphatically.

"You two are not psychologists, and I am not seeking counsel. However, I must say I have a lot of burdens. I've come to the conclusion that there is no way to get rid of burdens except by building something new. One can either bury one's burdens, trying to hide or avoid them, or one can take a burden and shape it into something new — a form of personal liberation."

"I couldn't agree with you more," Jack said with woozy sincerity. "We all want to *do* something we're proud of. Whether it's building a monument, having children, or promoting positive social change, humans want to leave some piece of themselves behind."

"That's true, Jack, but it's not enough for me to leave a legacy behind. I will leave a large bank behind with a few public outreach programs, some public parks I've helped create through my donations, and so forth, but that's not enough. In order for something to matter, it has to be deemed self-fulfilling. You know what I mean?"

"Yes, I do. It has to be something you, personally, find value in," Jack said while thinking about his own past. "Value for yourself. And if it's something you're not proud of, it could backfire and become a burden."

"It's not possible to speak for all men, but I would venture to say, with some room for consideration, that each of us have similar desires," Kepstein said, clasping his hands.

"I agree with you there," Lenny said, his eyes tired and a weary smile on his face, "and my desire right now is to get some rest."

The men laughed at the shared sentiment. The night was coming to an end. They finished their drinks, hoping this would not be the last time they talked to each other.

"Why don't you fellas take my business card and get hold of me next time you want to have a drink at this place, or make a world-famous movie," Kepstein said, winking at them.

"I'll do that," Jack replied, reaching into his wallet, "and here, take one of mine." *Jack Shales. Freelance Observer/ Freelance Writer.*

Lenny couldn't pass up the opportunity. "Yes, Mr. Kepstein. As you can see, my very professional friend, Jack here, would be a great benefit to your organization, in the event you need any professional observing to be done!"

Kepstein laughed heartily and placed a hand on Lenny's shoulder. "And where are your business cards, Lenny?"

"Ok, Ok, I don't have any," Lenny admitted, blushing.

"So Jack wins the business! In fact, I may be in need of assistance with both observing and writing. Jack, I'll ring you up some time soon. Lenny, keep your mind sharp and make some contacts in case I'm not just a drunk fool blowing smoke."

Chapter Four

As Jack Shales was waking up with a morning hangover, Milo Elpmis was entering the freeway in his rusted-out Chevy Malibu, heading toward downtown. He was drumming the steering wheel as fast as humanly possible, trying to hit the high notes along with Johnny Rotten. "God save the Que-eeeen." Milo was king of the road, champion of the weekend warriors. Living a life of routine boredom as a corporate electrician for the past five years, he was always happy when the weekend arrived, as he was able to shed his "yes boss" and "right away sir" for two days. He kept those days sacred and swore never to allow his weekend mornings, middays, or afternoons to become anything less than sheer happiness.

It was still too early that Saturday morning for the overcrowded metropolis that was Jack's neighborhood to empty itself of its guests' cars, so Milo found himself parking nearly six blocks away from Jack's apartment. A light rain fell. For almost anyone else, the morning would have been ruined, but not for Milo. He walked through the cold streets, black snow piled high on the sides of the road. He was a thin man wearing blue jeans and a ragged sweatshirt that barely met his belt. Milo had blonde hair that blew wildly in the wind, momentarily covering and uncovering his large blue eyes. He walked briskly, carrying a freshly baked baguette in one hand and a bottle of cheap champagne in the other.

"Milo! You are not going to believe what happened last night," Jack exclaimed as he opened the door for his friend.

"Is that a fact, Jack," Milo said, pushing through the door and tapping his friend on the shoulder with the crispy loaf of bread.

"What in the hell is that — well — I mean, I can see it's a loaf of bread . . . but why do you have a loaf of bread?"

"That's not a loaf of bread, man, that's a freshly-baked baguette." Milo went into the kitchen and began fixing mimosas, using the champagne and orange juice concentrate. "So, what's the big news? Did Lenny ever make it into town last night? Where is that guy — how's he doing?"

Just as he had done on countless Saturday mornings, Jack accepted the mimosa from his friend. "You will not believe what happened last night!"

"Yeah, you said Lenny was in town— did you guys have a good one?"

"Yes, of course, but beyond that, I mean way beyond that, we met this guy —Bill Kepstein — he's some sort of big shot downtown at Fidelity Sworn. Hell, I think he runs the place, the way he talks. But anyhow, we meet this guy at McArthur's and start talking jazz, you know, and next thing you know, wham!" Jack clapped his hands together like an on-looker describing a speeding car, "and off we go to Betriebsnacht where we spend the rest of the night talking about philosophy, and the world, and —."

Jack paused for effect.

"And what?"

"And making a movie!"

"Making a movie?" Milo repeated, appearing very uninterested as he walked into the kitchen for a refill. He was yelling and pouring at the same time. "You might want to settle down, my friend. You know just as well as I do, one night of drinking with a rich old man seldom leads to anything good. They'll promise you a future until it conflicts with their — or their partners, or their shareholders, or the wives, or their *friends* — or whoever it is — plans. They're savages, man."

Milo returned to the living room and, as he spoke, he stared at Jack intently, continuing before his friend could reply. "You're smart, Jack. Either take a cold shower or have a few more mimosas. One of them is bound to get you back on track, but I worry that you might be chasing a pink rhinoceros or something like that."

Jack couldn't resist laughing at Milo's complete lack of couth when it came to using figures of speech. "Right, I don't want to be setting off on a wild moose chase, or anything . . . Milo, relax man. This Kepstein fella is a stand-up guy. You'll see when you meet him. As for Lenny, that guy is dying to find a break. I mean he is dy-y-y-y-ing to find a break. He's excited to meet just about anybody with a little bit of money in the bank."

Milo was unfazed by Jack's rationale. They were best friends and had been for a long time. Milo counted on Jack to be a sort of sensible stability in his life, as Jack was always calculating, always able to look objectively at the risks and benefits of any situation and provide advice to his friends when they needed it. Milo was uncomfortable with the role reversal, having to warn Jack of his seemingly hasty behavior. After a few drinks and discussion about their mutual friend, Lenny, and his recent activities, Milo decided to let Jack cool down from the previous evening's excitement. He left the apartment abruptly, cutting his visit shorter than usual.

* * *

Bill Kepstein opened his eyes, immediately roused himself, and began to think about the day. This was his usual morning pattern. The first thoughts he had this morning were that his father-in-law was dead and that the previous night his wife had been at home alone thinking about her father's death while he had slept on his plush leather couch, high above the city.

He prepared a pot of strong drip coffee at his office bar, brushed his teeth, and ran ice water through his hair, patting some under his eyelids, then sat at his desk, preparing to read his emails. The sun had been up for nearly an hour and Kepstein was happy to welcome another day, regardless of his circumstances. He always liked the way his stomach felt empty after a night of drinking and he had a lack of appetite the next morning. Having coffee and no desire to eat gave him a sense of health. Getting thirty minutes' worth of work done on a Saturday morning, and walking down the steps from his office to the parking garage instead of taking the elevator, furthered his sense of activity.

As he neared his house in the suburbs, Kepstein was in a good mood. Then, turning into the driveway, he felt a sense of despair, a grotesque contradiction to the pleasantness his home was meant to possess, a pleasantness represented by a freshly cut lawn, white picket fence, and Victorian trimmings.

27

Hearing her husband's car, Kepstein's wife, Rebecca, peered through the second floor bedroom window. She was aware of feeling a sense of revulsion, for she thought that her husband looked happy; he had that same forced spring in his step he always did, as if nothing could knock him down.

"It's so good to see you, honey," Rebecca said, casting her eyes down and allowing sarcasm to mingle with desperation. She was sitting on a small stool at the vanity table that occupied the center of their bedroom and, one leg crossed over the other, was delicately manicuring her toenails. She did not budge as her husband removed his shoes and set his jacket inside the closet.

"It's very nice to see you as well, Rebecca." He glanced briefly toward the vanity's mirror in an effort to catch his wife's expression. "Have you had a fruitful morning?"

"The eulogy was really something, you know." Rebecca was still looking at her toes. "It reminded me a lot of you, actually, Bill. The eulogy part, I mean, the dead part — kind of like a description about a man who once was."

"Is that right? A eulogy, you say. Did someone die?"

Rebecca leapt from her stool, kicking it over by accident, and turned towards her husband.

"Yes, Bill, my father," she said coolly, staring into his eyes with disgust. "One of two people responsible for bringing me into this world and for raising me, loving, and caring for me, died two days ago. I'm fortunate, as a woman, not to rely on your sympathy to get through a tough time. God knows how disappointing that would be."

"I don't feel sorry for you, Rebecca, and I think it's pretty sick not to inform your husband of his father-in-law's funeral. It's disturbing."

"It's *disturbing?* Go take your shower, I don't want to keep you from your *important business.*" Rebecca sat back down on the stool, taking the file to her toenails. "In fact," she said quizzically, looking straight ahead, her eyebrows scrunched as if she were struggling with a complicated thought. "I don't want to see your face, I don't want to hear your voice, and I'm going downstairs to have some privacy."

When Rebecca retreated to the first floor, Kepstein let warm water run over his head and, like Macbeth, no amount of washing could remove what was on his conscience. He could almost hear his wife's anguish as he asked her, "Did someone die?" He replayed the words in his mind, envisioning his snide and sinister expression as he said it. *What's wrong with me? What is going on here?* he asked himself. It was getting to a point where he knew that the vilest of Rebecca's words were his fault. He used to trick himself into believing Rebecca was a vindictive person, but now it was clear to him that if he fought back, he was only fighting against himself, while if he said nothing, he was allowing his own apathy to affect them both.

As his wife drank a cup of coffee and cried, Kepstein went through his bathroom rituals. He could smell the coffee, but it did little to encourage his spirits. He had never been a cruel man. He didn't like the current state of affairs in his marriage, but he felt unable to talk to his wife. He would listen to her as she harangued him about how much he worked or how he never laughed enough, or how little he paid attention to her. She would often talk about how differently her father had treated her mother, how different her friends were with *their* husbands, and how men were *supposed* to behave. She would point out his many flaws, finding none with herself. If he asked her how he could improve, she would tell him it was too late — it was just his personality. If he asked her what she wanted, she would tell him she wanted a husband who cared for her. When he asked her why she thought their love was broken, she would explain that it was because he was a cold and callous man. There was no room for improvement in their relationship, and certainly no way to dialogue.

They had never seen a marriage counselor because Kepstein felt above asking for help. His wife had never asked him to change on a fundamental level because she believed he was unwilling to and she could not consistently insist that he do so. For his part, Kepstein hated conversations with his wife more than with any other person he'd ever met. He found her to be illogical and unable to reason and, as a result, he found himself unable to discuss anything serious with her.

Kepstein was looking out the bedroom window, examining the cold, winter lawn, and thinking about his marriage. His relationship with his wife left a bad taste in his mouth. He had long thought that a change was needed. Now he felt that it was needed soon, for the years he once took for granted seemed suddenly to be fleeting. He wanted to do something he would enjoy, regardless of what others thought. He believed that his wife was not going to leave him, regardless of what he decided to do, and perhaps it was that conviction that allowed him to have these thoughts. Something had to give; he just wasn't quite sure yet what it was.

After putting on a fresh pair of pants and a clean shirt, Kepstein slowly made his way down the wooden staircase, running his hand along the banister. He made sure to alert his wife by putting pressure on the creakiest of steps. Entering the kitchen, he sat silently for a few moments on a stool at the kitchen island, then asked his wife if there was any more coffee. Rebecca nodded silently, pretending to rub sleep from her eyes.

"I'm sorry about what I said this morning, Rebecca. That was inappropriate. I do feel quite strongly for your family, and your father was a good man who will be dearly missed."

"Don't ever bring up my father again," Rebecca said matter-of-factly. She often felt the moral high-ground was hers after an argument.

"Ok." He felt a burning sensation in his veins and heard a rising buzz in his ears.

"I know you never got along with my father, but that's beside the point. I've just been comparing the two of you in my mind over the last few days, and I don't know who you are anymore. I don't know how we ended up here together . . . in this." She waved her hand at the room.

Kepstein felt himself pulled into another one of his wife's fruitless arguments. There was nothing he hated more; no greater waste of time could befall his day. "Yes, you've been dealt a very raw hand in life, indeed,

Rebecca. I've always been amazed at how well poised and calm you seem amidst all the horrible stress in your life — it's a true gift!"

Against her will, she slapped him in the face. "Fuck you, Bill."

Against his will, he smiled. He was never the best for arguments, and like a child, he typically retreated into a nonsensical smile when confrontation arose. "You're a weak woman, Rebecca. When your little brain cannot handle big thoughts such as death, your own personal limitations, and this pathetic home we share, you resort to lashing and striking out like a cave person. You wear your scarves and hats like some kind of industrial-age socialite, but you crumble into this state as soon as you're behind closed doors."

She turned away from him, tears in her eyes, tears of despair, but not due to her husband's vitriol. No, Rebecca felt almost broken down. She'd almost given in to the abject lack of happiness in their lives. As she began ascending the stairs to their second story, she turned to face Kepstein, still standing at the kitchen island, his hands upon the counter in the center of the room.

"It truly bothers me to the core to say this, but I wish I were with my father at this moment. Dead. I wish there were words to explain to you how much I hate you, how much I hate living with you, and how truly sad I am that you've brought me to this point."

"Yep." Kepstein said, feeling confident that a symbolic lack of response was better than digressing into another fruitless argument with his wife.

Rebecca stood and looked at her husband in a way she'd never done before, as if he had become weak in her eyes. "You know, my father might not have been as successful or as wealthy as you, but do you know what he had that you will never have, Bill?"

"What's that?"

"He was able to die in peace, with a life unclouded by corruption. He made bad decisions, but not like you. His choices never followed him through life, and he never hid from his past like a coward. My father was a real man, Bill, not a shadow of a man, but a real man — flesh and blood. You are a coward."

Kepstein said nothing. He stood up and left the kitchen, retreating to reading and watching TV for the rest of the weekend. He and Rebecca walked past one another in the hallways, but that was the extent of their closeness. It was a sad state of affairs and the negativity of it all was buzzing violently against the sea of positive change that Kepstein sought for himself. He found the relief he was seeking Monday morning, finally safe again in his office high above the hive of activity on the streets and in the buildings below.

* * *

Seated at his familiar perch by the large office window, Kepstein decided to contact Jack Shales. He took his cellphone from his pocket, found the number, and began dialing without knowing what he'd say.

33

"Hello — is this Mr. Kepstein?" Jack answered, surprising the man calling him.

"Yes, yes, greetings, Jack," Kepstein replied quickly. "But please call me Bill —you make me feel like an old man calling me 'Mr.' How are you, Jack?"

"I'm doing very well today — finally recovered from Friday night! How about yourself?" Jack replied, trying to sound nonchalant.

Kepstein laughed briefly, hoping to get past some of the awkwardness. "And the same for me. It was quite a big night, Friday — Monday always comes around sooner than expected. Anyhow, Jack, I know this is short notice, but I wanted to see if you had plans this afternoon. I was thinking of grabbing some lunch at a place I like downtown."

"No plans today," Jack answered, slightly embarrassed not to have a busier schedule when talking with an important financier. "What's the name of the place?"

"It's Alameng's Tavern, on 3rd. They have the best lunch in town. Would you care to join me around 1 o'clock?"

"I have never had lunch there, but I know the place. It sounds great — shall we meet there?"

"Meet me here at the office, Jack," Kepstein said and gave Jack directions to his office.

After the phone call, Kepstein felt his heart racing and he didn't know why. Usually he operated within his comfort zone, but his contact with Jack felt outside that limit. Jack wasn't sure what to make of the request either, but he knew he couldn't pass up the opportunity. In fact, he lived for these moments, moments when the mysteries of fate provided a chance to say yes or no, to go or to stay.

Chapter Five

Jack walked a few short blocks to Fidelity Sworn bank. Reaching the front steps, he entered a revolving door and stopped at the main desk, where the receptionist directed him to the executive suite. After stepping out of the elevator on the top floor, he was greeted by Kepstein's personal secretary, a very attractive brunette about his own age.

"Good afternoon sir, my name is Jolene. Is there anything I can get you while I let Mr. Kepstein know you've arrived?" she said as she stood to shake his hand. She had an interesting spin on a long-lost southern drawl.

"No thank you, Jolene, you've been too kind already. I'll wait here," Jack said, removing his coat and sitting on one of the two oaken leather chairs that faced the secretary's desk. He was enjoying the view.

"My pleasure, honey. I'll let Mr. Kepstein know you're here."

Jolene paged her boss via an intercom, and within seconds the foggy figure from a few nights earlier came back into Jack's life. Jack was once again impressed by the man's solemnity, juxtaposed by what Jack considered to be an outpouring of kindness.

"Good to see you again, Jack." They shook hands as Kepstein ushered him into the office and addressed his secretary, "Thank you, Jolene — if anyone calls, please let them know we'll be stepping out for lunch and I'll probably be returning around 3 o'clock."

"I'm glad to see you made it home Ok and survived Friday night," Kepstein said, laughing as he approached his desk chair. Jack sat on the other side of the expansive desk, facing Kepstein.

"Likewise," Jack replied. "Lenny and I couldn't recall all the details of how we made it back to my apartment, but it seemed to work out alright . . . and it appears you survived as well — that's good news." Jack was at ease and ready to see where the conversation was going.

"I always manage, Jack, but only by the skin of my teeth. I actually slept right over there." Kepstein pointed to the couch along the far wall of the office. "A home away from home, I guess you could say, but the drive is shorter."

Jack looked over his shoulder. "Not a bad view either. I bet your wife gave you an earful the next day!"

"That's a long story, my friend — come on, I'll tell you all about it and more over some lunch. Let's get out of here."

As the details of their prior meeting abruptly flooded his memory, Jack regretted his comment about Kepstein's home life and he was eager to change the subject and place of conversation. He quietly followed Kepstein through the door of the executive suite, into the elevator, and onto the city's busy streets below. After a short walk they settled into a small booth in the back of a quiet Polish tavern where Kepstein ordered strong beers for them while they opened their menus.

"I want to thank you for meeting me today, Jack." Kepstein offered a smile as they briefly chimed their beer glasses. "You are probably wondering why I called you this morning, what my intentions are, and how they might involve you."

"Yep," Jack agreed, matter-of-factly, "and thanks for the invite — it's my pleasure."

"Thank you, Jack. I'm sure you're busy, as am I, and I've always found small talk one of the unnecessary trivialities of our daily routine. So, I'm going to cut right to the chase." Kepstein took a long pull from his pint glass, then set it gently on the table. "As I mentioned to you fellas on Friday night, my wife's dad died and they had his funeral that same day. I was not invited. When I returned to my wife on Saturday morning, it was more of the same — a never-ending battle of words and ideologies. My assumption is that my wife is completely irrational and, I believe, mildly incompetent."

"I see," Jack said, his mind reeling. He began to feel uneasy.

"Please, relax. I didn't invite you here for marriage counseling. In fact, I'd prefer not to speak of the subject at length. It's just this — I'm at the point in my life where a man has the chance to think about his legacy. My marriage is in bad shape, and I'm not pleased with the lack of progress I've made on other fronts either. Whether it was imagined or not, I felt hopeful for change when I met you and your friend Lenny the other night, and for whatever reason, I felt an immediate stirring — it's as if it were now time to alter my course." Kepstein took another drink and tried to gauge the meaning of Jack's silence. "Many men my age will have a midlife crisis, not unlike what I am experiencing, but I feel that I have a different calling.

Perhaps my work obligations make my situation somewhat unique, but regardless, I want to make a dramatic outward change — to leave an impression on the world — not simply an inward change, you see. Perhaps that's why I find the discussion of creating a film so intriguing."

Jack had been listening to every word and was visibly excited. "You know, I was wondering if you'd remember all that showbiz talk, or if you might bring it up today. Were you serious about that?"

"You'll find, Jack, that I am serious about everything I say. I would be very happy to learn more about Lenny's involvement in the business. And as for you, you mentioned that you also create screenplays at times? Do you have a local business here in Baltimore?"

"It's somewhat complicated," Jack said, readjusting his position, "but I think you might find my hobbies more exciting than what I actually do for a living."

"That's what I was hoping you would say, Jack!" Kepstein exclaimed, offering another "cheers," his beer glass an ambassador to tumultuous social waters. "I knew the minute we met that you'd have things to say — things to talk about. I was hoping you could tell me more about yourself — you know, your background, and hobbies, your business, and so on. I don't mean to pry, but it just makes conversation immediately more fruitful. You understand?"

Jack could sense the man's genuine curiosity, but he was still somewhat intimidated by their different stations in life. He felt Kepstein was in a position to approve or disapprove of his thoughts and theories as he saw fit. He also knew there was no room to retreat or escape Kepstein's desire to know more about him; it was time for Jack to lay his cards on the table.

"Well, I blackmailed the police a few years ago, and it afforded me enough money so that I don't have to work anymore. Now I spend my days studying and trying to master the tools of communication and dialogue," Jack said, his heart racing. He could hear himself talking, but he wasn't sure if the words that he really meant to say were being said.

"Wow," Kepstein exhaled in obvious surprise, "that's not what I expected, but let's hear it — blackmailed the police, you say?"

Jack looked across the table and the men's eyes met for a brief moment, a silent pause, as if to convey the level of trust Jack was hoping for. "Well, I'm the product of luck — of being in the right place at the right time. Essentially, I've made my fortune through journalism."

"Ah, journalism." Kepstein laughed. "The most lucrative form of blackmail in America."

"Yes indeed!" Jack agreed, "So I'd been working for the *Baltimore Sun* for a few years, when they asked for an article about that dirty cop caught laundering money through a children's hospital. You may remember the story?"

"Unfortunately. It was shameful," Kepstein replied.

"It was," Jack agreed, and took a sip of his beer. "And unlike most criminals, he did not get into too much trouble, nothing more than a public apology, and community service. Anyhow, the story had been covered extensively by every news outlet in the area and interest had already peaked, but the *Sun* wanted a racy article about the various benefits that come with being part of the F.O.P. At first, the story didn't interest me much, but after a while I began to look at it differently. Around this very same time, I got pulled over after drinking and it cost me a boatload of money. I realized the hypocrisy, and I started thinking of the news story differently. It became my calling.

"I remembered an old friend of mine, Tim Donelson. His old man was a cop and a drunk, and I recalled going with Tim and his mom to pick up his father at this bar across town. It was where all the off-duty cops drank without worrying about getting caught drinking and driving — like a safe zone or something, out towards the end of Tennyson."

"I know the area, but I'm not sure if I know the bar." Kepstein was listening, but looked uneasy.

"I knew Donelson was the Chief of Police at the time, and thought I'd check it out. I stopped by the bar one evening and found him there. He was getting drunker than a skunk and then, sure enough, hopped into his jeep and drove himself home. I was still doing community service for my trouble, and here I was in the lion's den, watching a football game and trying to go unnoticed by the men I'd be spying on for the next few months." Jack grinned. "I was pissed off."

"I began collecting information on who was on the police force, when, and what — if possible — it was they drove. I studied each of the officers, obtaining license plate numbers, models and makes of cars, and how far each person would drive to get home. I'd sit with the men, counting how many drinks they'd have in a given night. It became a full-out campaign and I amassed numerous notebooks with detailed logs of misbehavior and the citations that went with each offense; men stumbling out of the bar to their cars, a few falls, a handful of key-droppings, and even one hit-and-run. I finally had enough dirt to put the entire force in hot water and went to confront Donelson on his way out of the bar while recording him."

"You actually had info on the whole force, not just Donelson?" Kepstein asked, intrigued.

"Right, on a *lot* of guys, but I figured it would be best to take it to the top man — I always thought he was a dick anyhow. So, I'm sitting in my car and I see him coming out. I get out with my camcorder in front of me, like so," he held his hands up, mimicking a camera, "and I start making my way over to Donelson. He was in shock and goes, 'What do you think you're doing, you son of a bitch!' waving both fists over his head. He finally notices I'm Tim's old friend and I tell him that he's in deep shit. And then... the guy sucker punches me across the parking lot. I'm lying in the gravel, a few teeth lighter, and I see Donelson peeling out of the place. I checked into the hospital that night, and woke up the next morning with Officer Henson, a nasally little ball of a man, handing me a check for half a million dollars for an agreement that I'll keep quiet!"

Kepstein was stunned into silence for the first time since he sat down for lunch. It was well past one o'clock and there was a stillness in the air for a few seconds as both men sat quietly. He raised his mug for a toast. "Jack, that is incredible. You stood up for what you believed in and you made it happen. You have to tell me, with all of that money, what exactly do you do with it? I mean, that is if you don't mind letting me in on the secret."

After chiming their glasses of beer together, Jack began explaining his case, but he was immediately cut short.

* * *

A woman appeared at their table. She was gorgeous and nervous; a Puerto Rican woman of petite stature but with a commanding presence, mastering the importance of designer clothing and friendly dimples, either of which appearing to work at will.

"Bill!" She exclaimed, stepping up from the hallway and onto the landing that housed their booth. She shifted her purse to the side as if to welcome a hug or some type of congenial greeting.

"Margaret Johns, how good to see you!" Kepstein responded, reluctantly stepping up from his seat to embrace her. "It's been quite some time, how are you these days?"

Margaret smiled, thanking him for the warm regards. She worked for Kepstein for many years. While not a personal assistant or secretary— or in any capacity requiring immediate responsibility to the man— she became part of the Kepstein's family over time. She was a middle-manager in the financial department and always went above and beyond to alert Kepstein when things looked off or suspicious. As such, she was good at her job and garnered tremendous respect from him and everyone else on the top floor of the bank. Unfortunately, not all suspicious activity was meant to be found.

"I am great Bill, how nice to see you here. And this must be—"

"Jack Shales, good to meet you," he said standing from the booth to shake Margaret's hand. "Please have a seat if you'll be a while."

There was a palpable tension in the air. A silence that was unavoidable, but unexpected by Jack. Margaret looked towards the booth, then to Kepstein as she began to move in that direction.

"No, that's quite alright." Kepstein said blocking the pass. "Margaret is always so busy, I am sure she's not able to sit down with us right now."

Kepstein forced his resolve with a quick glance. "Margaret worked at the bank for many, many years, Jack. In fact, she is a very good family friend of my wife and mine. And unfortunately, like all outstanding employees, she was eventually scooped up and left us for greener pastures."

Kepstein winked at them both, smiling and turning towards Margaret. "And Jack, here, is a man I recently met at my favorite haunt, Betriebsnacht. I am sure you remember this place?"

"Oh indeed! I remember it quite well, and must admit I don't find it surprising you still go there."

Kepstein laughed, "Old habits die hard, I suppose, they say."

"And old secrets die even harder," Margaret said smiling down at Kepstein as he sat back in the booth. She locked eyes with him and paused for a moment. It wasn't meant to be pleasant. She then turned her attention. "And Jack, what is it you do?"

"Jack is a free-lance writer and well-known for his craft covering all things interesting here in Baltimore and the region," Kepstein interjected, becoming visibly perturbed.

"That is great Jack! I believe I have seen some of your work—quite confrontational matter in some cases, if I am not mistaken."

Now Jack was standing out of his seat proudly with both hands resting behind him atop the black leather booth, and began to describe some of the works he'd penned in the past year or so. He was not ignorant to the awkward way Kepstein monitored the discussion. He was not unaware of the sweat building on Margaret's forehead or the redness about her neck. And Kepstein was not ambivalent to the vibe surrounding their discussion, nor of his influence upon it. Instead, he pushed the dialogue to the extent he was able.

"Margaret, where are you working these days?" He asked as he reached for his beer, tilting his head upwards towards her.

The redness that embodied her neck now began to infiltrate her cheeks. She stammered briefly, responding quickly, "I work at the County Clerk's office now Bill."

"Here in Baltimore?"

"Yes, indeed—just down the street, of course. In the first floor of the courthouse. It's boring as hell, but I enjoy the pace."

"The pace?" Jack interrupted.

"Yes. I guess by that I mean, the cleanliness of the job and the expectations. Unlike the bank there are not subjective or ethical decisions about what's right and wrong and there are no important people asking me to do something, or worse yet, *what to do*. It's just laid back. Everything is black and white, you know what I mean?"

"Yes, we know what you mean, Margaret. At any rate, we must be getting back to business." Kepstein said with finality.

"Oh, is Jack writing a piece on the bank?" she inquired.

"We really have to get back to our work now, Margaret, if you'll please excuse us." Kepstein was losing his temper.

"Well it was good meeting you Jack. And nice to see you again, Bill," Margaret waived meekly, turning on her heals as she left them.

Kepstein stirred in his seat for a moment deciding what to say next. He took a sip of beer and looked across the table towards Jack." Sorry I had to cut that short Jack, it's just that Margaret can be a bit of handful when she gets going. I'll be transparent with you. We worked together for nearly a decade, but there were some stressful events that took place and we needed to go our separate ways in what I must admit were unfriendly circumstances. I haven't seen her since, and that was a challenging situation to navigate."

Jack wiped a bit of condensation away from the beer glass, striking an arc with his finger through the frost. He looked over the bar and through the front window watching Margaret exit the building and disappear into the square outside. Thinking about their discussion and what had just transpired, he began to gather a sense of Kepstein's life. It was clear to him that there were notable differences in who they were and what they did. All the same, he took the situation with a grain of salt, and felt best to sit back and listen to what the man had to say.

Chapter Six

"Again, my apologies, Jack for the interruption. But where were we? You were describing what you do with your new-found wealth I believe. It's a unique situation you're in and I am dying to hear it honestly!" Kepstein was clearly a well-polished man, and not accustomed to being pushed off balance. Margaret's intrusion changed the timbre of their meeting immediately, but he was intent on moving it forward.

"No, no, there's no big secret or anything." Jack was chuckling nervously. He always did so when answering that question. "It's kind of sad really, but I don't do anything at all with the money. I just sort of have it."

"What do you mean? You don't spend it?"

"Yeah, I spend it alright, but only because I don't have a job. I don't buy extravagant things or live luxuriously by any means. When I got the money, I decided to keep living the same life, just without the work."

"That's a safe bet, and what do you do with all your free time then? Is this where those *exciting hobbies* come into play?"

"Exactly," Jack replied, smiling. "I spend my days studying the human canvas, testing a theory of mine that the common fabric of life is being held together by communication."

Kepstein folded one leg over the other, leaning in closer to the table. Since their first meeting, he'd been searching for the punchline of what he clearly knew was an unusual bond forming. He couldn't help but wonder if this was "it".

"Communication — in so far as . . . what?"

Jack was dead serious now. He knew his integrity as a rational and sensible human being was on the line every time he explained his peculiar situation. He felt Kepstein handled the blackmailing story well, and hoped he'd do the same when he heard how he used his time and energy since the settlement.

"Well, I believe in communication on an extremely high level, Bill. It is my opinion that it will be the leading force to propel the human race and our societies forward. All the new technologies, such as two-way video-calling and the various social media platforms, will become catalysts for changing how people communicate and these changes will take place very soon."

"Emerging communication technologies, you say," Kepstein asked, leaning back in the booth and slowly stroking his mustache, as if to further demonstrate his interest in the subject. "The first thing that comes to mind when I think about what you've just said is the Arab Spring and how Twitter and Facebook were used by the protesters to mobilize people for demonstrations. What I'm wondering, though, is what sort of communication are you referring to? With these tools — even in states where the freedom of expression is suppressed — people have the opportunity for open dialogues, don't they? But, also, that's not always a good thing. Don't you agree?"

"Yes and no. Yes, I agree we — and they — are able to dialogue, but no, I don't agree that it is always an open dialogue. Oftentimes, what is considered to be a dialogue takes place through official channels, such as the media, diplomats, or public relations firms. In most cases, we're seeing the world through the lenses of the two most powerful groups on our planet, governments — or at least those considering themselves as governments — and corporations."

"And this is bad?"

"I don't think it inherently ever had to be a bad thing, but, yes, I feel it has become that way. Everyone wants more transparency, everyone wants to know their basic needs are met, and their basic rights respected, but these days there really isn't any way to tell if that's happening or not."

"People do ask more questions now," Kepstein said. "I've seen this firsthand as people write about my bank on the Internet. What more could be asked?"

"I don't think it's enough to hope for — or ask for — dialogue. Unfortunately, I think it may be necessary to force it. By forcing communication and open dialogue among everyone — citizens, governments, corporations — those in charge will be completely naked to their citizens and customers. Those offering value will remain, and those who destroy value will be removed."

Kepstein looked closely at Jack, then replied, "That's an interesting point. Do you mean, like forcing a paparazzi-type presence on those in power? Or a Big Brother scenario with 24-hour cameras watching their every move? Don't you worry that if one person gets demoted or fired, or whatever, someone else will simply replace him and things will remain the same?"

"Not necessarily Big Brother . . . I don't think it's the means of obtaining surveillance that is the most important, but rather the desire by the people for this type of surveillance or information that will make a difference. The people in charge will get better at hiding, of course, but a simple mind shift by the people they're accountable to will make all the difference. Do you remember even as far back as five years ago now, the videos of the Chinese policeman beating up a citizen? Bystanders recorded the incident on their cellphones and spread the video within seconds across the Web. The country was enraged and the policeman was tried in court. Or think of the outrage in Ferguson, Missouri when the man was killed and half of the audience had video-cameras on their phones to catch the action. There is no more hearsay when everything is recorded. The people have this kind of power now, and when they use it, it makes a big difference."

Kepstein digested Jack's words for a moment, then said, "But how do you take into account the bad guys who get better at hiding, or what do you do when the bad guys are replaced with others like them? Let me use one example. Again, The Arab Spring movements have elicited a positive change in the Middle East, depending on whom you ask, but in some scenarios, the results have been catastrophic. What new regime will rise up in Syria when the civil war ends? Will it be better or worse than the current regime, and what will be the cost?"

"You're correct, Bill, and I think you bring up a good point. I really think those revolutions will be successful if the lines of communication remain open, and they will fail if the lines of communication are not. And I'm not referring to the power of democracy or the importance of free speech. In my opinion, freedom of speech is a moot point. I think speech is inherently free and if someone tells you it's not, record them saying it and post it on the Internet. It's all changing now."

"My only concern is that — and this is coming from a man that's spent the majority of his life in management— there are a whole lot of bad opinions out there. Furthermore, there are a lot of really dumb people. I mean, if you get enough dumb people with bad opinions together, it can sway the crowd to make a bad decision. I've seen this many times."

"And so you have uncovered my true nature as an optimist," Jack said, laughing. "The foundation for my theory is based on the *assumption* that the world is inherently good and that the good will outweigh the bad when individuals and their ideas are exposed to the societal litmus. Also, that change would require a desire for people to learn and to become engaged in the world around them."

"And that is going to be a major stumbling block, I can assure you." Kepstein took another drink of his beer and thought about his wife and what he took to be her inability to think constructively.

"You're right. The way I see it, those who don't have the desire to get engaged with the world around them will miss the sea change, and their current positions in life will either remain stagnant or worsen. That's just how it has to be."

"And if I might ask, have you been putting any of these ideas into action? I mean, a lot of these concepts we're talking about are huge global changes."

"Right. I can only do so much as an individual, of course, but if you like, I could tell you about a few projects I've been working on," Jack said.

Kepstein laughed. "Yes, please keep going!" He ordered a plate of oysters Rockefeller and two more beers.

"I guess you could say," Jack continued, relishing the attention, "that most recently, I've been on an exploratory quest to determine the availability of free information."

"Free information?" Kepstein briskly wiped a bit of beer foam from his lips with a napkin.

"Yes, first I develop a question, one that I want to have answered in depth, usually a question I can't completely answer by my own research. Then I determine the best available source to answer the question. Lastly, I ask the source for the answer."

"You really must have journalistic roots, Jack!" Kepstein laughed again. "How well does your method work for you?"

"Of course that background helps! For example, recently I wondered how many people worked downtown to collect and sort through all of Baltimore's taxes, so I went to City Hall and asked the receptionist for a tour and an explanation of the process." Jack paused, then continued, "She explained that there was no tour, but she invited me to a magnificent dinner at Le Pom where I learned more about the inner workings of the city and state tax systems than I could've dreamed of."

"The receptionist took you to dinner at a nice restaurant?" Kepstein knew the city's tax coffers well and knew they didn't toil in extravagance.

"It was a fortunate turn of events. One of her department heads had been asked to attend a meeting to review a new development project, and when he couldn't go, the ticket was up for grabs. She took me as a date and we had a wonderful time. In fact, when she introduced me to others at the table, explaining my request, the flood gates of information broke wide open!"

"That's incredible — who would think learning about the city's tax system could be so entertaining?"

"The most recent quest I've been on was really interesting. I was reading a novel by Tolstoy one afternoon and became interested in the Church's stance on nonviolence. I met with a local priest in Baltimore, and eventually the conversation led to the city's head diocese. I have to tell you, Bill, it was one of the richest conversations I've ever had — I mean to discuss a matter of faith with one of the more focused and learned men in the field is astounding."

Kepstein realized he'd probably spoken to many of the same people Jack had, but from an altogether different position, and for altogether different reasons. "It's obvious you've had many successes. Have you ever been denied when you've tried to request information?"

"Honestly, I've found that as long as I do my homework first and approach people with intelligent questions, they don't seem to refuse my requests. Perhaps it's their vanity or a passion to share what they know, I'm not sure, but I haven't been shot down yet . . . and then again, maybe I'm not asking hard enough questions."

Kepstein saw what seemed to be a mischievous smile on Jack's face. "I have to tell you, Jack, this is an impressive venture you've undertaken. It forces me to rethink the results of my life's work and compare it with something that has a very different purpose. I've always had a similar love for observation and dialogue, but you've taken it to the next level by actually recording the results of your requests."

As Jack and Kepstein finished their beers and conversation, it was clear to the both of them that jazz was not the only interest they shared: they both subscribed to the life-long pursuit of learning through attempts at open communication with others, a notion both simple and endangered in the present-day world.

As Kepstein drove home, he thought about his gift for conversation, but also that, without that gift having a sense of purpose, it had never amounted to much. He thought about his wife as he drew nearer to home, about all the things that they needed to discuss, and about all the years of mistrust that needed to be repaired. Today, he realized, he felt some degree of responsibility for Rebecca's emotional state and he was aware that while his spirits were improving, hers were worsening.

Kepstein passed through the iron gate and onto the long driveway that led to his home. Stopping his car in front of the garage, he turned off the ignition and rested his head on the steering wheel for nearly half an hour, then bolted from his seat, slammed the car door, and made a beeline for the house.

Chapter Seven

It was obvious to Kepstein that the kitchen light being on signaled that Rebecca was home. What he could not tell, but was hoping for, was that his wife would be in better spirits than she was the last time they crossed paths. He had a lot that he wanted to tell her, and he wanted to extend an olive branch — a long overdue gesture. His hands were beginning to sweat as he unlocked the door; it had been so long since he'd looked his wife in the eyes, let alone apologize to her for anything.

Rebecca was not in the kitchen and Kepstein began winding his way through the hallway into the main room, where he found her watching TV. As he approached the couch, she turned to face him, giving him a look that immediately paralyzed him. He saw in her eyes stern hatred, leaving him feeling physically incapable of carrying out his plan to begin reconciliation. Instead, he managed to offer her only a brief smile.

"Look at the smiling, red-cheeked lush coming home after a long day at the office," Rebecca said, looking again at the TV and speaking to Kepstein over her shoulder. "Did you need to have some drinks after work to calm your nerves so you can tolerate being in your own home?"

"No Rebecca, I had a few beers with a client at lunch. And now I'm here. I'm going to head up to the den to get some reading done."

"Don't care," she replied coolly, continuing to stare at the screen.

Kepstein walked up the stairs and splashed cold water on his face in the bathroom, then poured himself a scotch in the den. His life was a mess, and he had no clear and certain way to fix it. He fell into his overstuffed leather chair, its brown hues matching the mahogany of the room's interior. Looking out the window at their backyard, he mindlessly swirled the liquid in circles while he thought back to his discussion with Jack at lunch. He thought about what Jack had said about the importance of communication and the idea that communication could be the catalyst for change in the world, or at least the most important factor involved in making change happen. While Kepstein had always considered himself an excellent communicator and had always pursued a chance to speak with anyone who'd listen, this idea of communication as an agent of change was new to him.

He turned on the TV in the corner of the den. Silent images on the evening news showed jeeps filled with men touting guns and waving flags, one group or another pursuing change in one country or another in the Middle East. As he watched these images, he thought about how these groups used religion as a criterion for membership in the group, and as a way of radicalizing its members. He thought about the speed with which messages, photos, and videos of beheadings were shared and spread around the world through social media. Perhaps, he thought, Jack was onto something, and perhaps his ideas deserved more attention. Kepstein thought of calling him, but was stopped short by the thought of his wife, one story below, sulking on the couch in pain.

Kepstein refilled his glass, drinking the whisky a bit more quickly. He felt disappointed at the way things turned out when he reached home, his high hopes fallen by the tone in her voice and he blamed himself for not having the nerve to try in spite of her attitude toward him at that moment.

"What did you expect to happen?" he muttered. "*Hi honey, let's make up for the fight and the funeral thing — I'm feeling better now. How was your day?*" he thought sarcastically.

Kepstein then began to remember the night when he'd met Jack and Lenny and how he'd talked about making a film that could result in a lasting change in society, but that memory only intensified his feeling of failure. His mind was jumping all over the place as he remembered the events of the past week and alcohol was no longer helping, but only made things worse as it became harder and harder for him to focus on one event at a time.

Kepstein finished his second scotch, but couldn't bring himself to get another. He rested his elbows on his desk and put his head in his hands. He felt a buzzing in his ears, as if his thoughts were so intense he could hear them raging. As a long-time executive, Kepstein was always searching for solutions to problems and he was typically able to find them. The situation with his marriage, however, had been going on for nearly a decade, and it seemed to him to be a problem without a solution, an enduring stalemate.

Staring into the TV screen for a few more minutes — there was another mass shooting near home, the third of the year, at a holiday corporate potluck — and feeling helpless on multiple levels, a thought began to form through the fog of alcohol and emotion: Kepstein didn't try to overcome his wife's hostility that night because he wasn't expected to do so, and he wasn't expected to do so because his behavior had become predictable and unchanged over many years: he and his wife had created a self-generating cycle of hostility and inaction based solely on their expectations from one another. The more years that passed when they shared insults instead of dialogue, the harder it had become, then, to break the cycle.

It became brutally obvious to Kepstein at that moment that his life was in a rut for the same reason that his marriage was a disaster. Rebecca's father was right — he was a coward. He had never done anything he had really wanted to do, but instead he had acted out the expectations that others had for him since childhood. He had met others' expectations for so long now that no one expected anything different from him: people assumed that the person they saw and interacted with on a daily basis was the real Bill Kepstein, CEO of Fidelity Sworn. They assumed he was content with his role and unshakable from what they also assumed were his chosen path and goals. At home, he had lost the ability to communicate with his wife. Outside of home, he had lost the ability to communicate with the world. He couldn't explain to his employees, the city councils, the shareholders, and the media that the man they knew was not the man that he felt himself to be. He told himself that he did not have the skills to break free from the expectations he'd created for himself; he was his own jailor.

The following morning, Kepstein rose quietly, making it into the shower, out of the house, into his car, and to his office, avoiding any thoughts or feelings of being blindsided by his wife's hostility.

"Good morning, Jack," he said into his office speakerphone, "how is your Friday looking this weekend?"

"Hey there, good morning. I have no plans, what's in mind?"

"It has been a long week at home and I'm thinking it'd be a good way to finish it, making a stop at Betriebsnacht. If Lenny is still in the area, feel free to invite him."

"Yes, that sounds great," Jack said, forcing himself to project a sense of excitement, as he was still sleeping when the phone rang. "But, no, Lenny is back in NYC. I usually go out for drinks with my good friend and colleague, Milo, on Friday evenings. He's an extremely interesting person, I must say, and he'd be more than happy to meet up, if that is alright."

"That sounds great, Jack. Can we meet a bit after eight, then, Friday night?"

Chapter Eight

On Friday morning, following a quick shower and a strong cup of coffee, Kepstein left for work. He had the usual business to attend to, the same stack of papers that always accumulated, and the same desire to be doing something else. He spoke with Jack in the afternoon to confirm their evening plans. He hoped that it would be another long night at Betriebsnacht and he relished in the thought of not having to go home early. Jack and Milo would most likely be arriving at the club separately, so Kepstein thought it best to arrive early to make sure he could get a table for them.

"Heading home so early on a Friday, Mr. Kepstein?" Jolene, his secretary, asked in her unintentionally flirting manner. In the three years she'd worked at the bank, he had never left prior to five p.m.

"Indeed, Jolene. Heading down to the club tonight — I'm going to meet Jack, the fellow who stopped by here on Monday, if you recall."

"Oh I do, of course. Be sure to let me know if he's single," she said, winking at her boss as he buttoned his jacket and pressed the elevator button.

"Of course, I'll see what I can do." He smiled as the door was closing. "Have a nice weekend, Jolene."

Kepstein left the parking structure and began making his way home to shower and change for his night out. As he drove, he pictured Rebecca standing in the doorway, cursing him as he left to go out for the evening. He imagined the harsh words she'd surely hurl at him for being such an asshole. For being so predictable. The pattern had been going on for so long, there was no need for him to explain where he was going or what he was doing, but this time he wished he could share that information; he wished he could tell her that it was for a positive goal, even though he wasn't sure just yet what that goal was.

Imagining what would happen at home were he to arrive there, he turned off the highway and drove to the health club that was just a few miles from his office. He sat in the sauna for twenty minutes, showered, shaved, then had a deli sandwich in the lounge while catching the last of a college basketball game. It was nearly seven o'clock by the time he finished dinner and an appropriate time, he thought to make his way to the nightclub.

Kepstein parked his car behind the club. Walking down the alley, he hit the alarm button as he looked over his shoulder at his luxury automobile that shined like a neon sign in the darkness. Entering the club, he shouted, "Hey there, Mica!" as he approached the bar. "You are the best bartender — best DJ — in the whole city!"

Mica smiled, his thick Nordic lips stretching from side to side as he accepted Kepstein's compliment. Feigning surprise and raising his eyebrows and arms, he replied, "Bill, my friend. It has been so very long since I've seen you. How are you, old friend?"

"I'm doing great, Mica, thank you for asking. Meeting some friends here for drinks this evening. Has anyone asked for me?"

63

"Not yet, my friend. Can I get you something to drink, or something to listen to in the meantime?" Mica was bobbing rhythmically to the music, and it seemed to Kepstein that he was uninterested in the answer to either of his questions.

Kepstein ordered a beer and made small talk with Mica in between his various bartending duties and conversations with other customers. Sipping his beer, he felt a burst of energy coming from the club entrance. It was Milo Elpmis.

Milo drifted towards the bar almost instinctively, as it was the one place he'd always been able to call home, where he believed everything important was to be found, and where anyone important could be approached. Noticing Kepstein, he stopped short.

"I take it you must be Bill Kepstein," Milo belted out, giving Kepstein a strong handshake and a brief pat on the shoulder. "I am Milo, it's good to meet you — I've heard many great things!"

"Likewise, Milo, it's very good to meet you as well."

"Jack is parking and should be in shortly," Milo said, looking at Kepstein, then towards the bartender. He ordered a drink and finished it before Jack entered.

"Greetings, all!" Jack yelled, approaching Milo and Kepstein.

"Good evening, Jack," Kepstein replied as they shook hands, then led Milo and Jack to their table in the subterranean lounge.

"Well, this place just gets better and better," Jack said as he walked into the room and fondled a small patch of vines near the entrance. "You really have style, Bill."

"I know. I love it here — it's nice and relaxing. Any particular choice of music?" Kepstein slowly sifted through the digital music list. "That box on the wall has any song that has been produced by a major record label, which means any song you can think of . . ." Kepstein was rubbing his hands together and grinning. "But that's not it. We've all seen the jukeboxes plugged into the Internet and they are very neat, you can find virtually any song you'd like, yadda, yadda, yadda. But what we have here is altogether different — it is the future. The company that installed this box, who Mica has partnered with, has cameras stationed across the globe to capture virtually any live performance — in any location, at any time. If Bono is doing a fund raiser in Brussels, for example, we can watch it. If Norah Jones is playing a street fair in Greenland, we can watch it. If Neil Young is working his guitar and belting out 'Cinnamon Girl' in Milwaukee, we —"

"We can watch it," Milo said, laughing affably and genuinely impressed.

"I'm sure we can find something good, just don't let Milo start any Karaoke talk," Jack chimed in. "In the meantime, I'm going to flag down the waiter. I'm thirsty!"

After the three rounds of drinks and some general bullshitting, Kepstein thanked everyone for coming. "In addition to my gratitude, I'm sure you fellas would like to know why I wanted to meet up on such short notice, my ulterior motive for this gathering, you might say."

65

Milo looked at Jack while Kepstein reached for his drink. It was obvious to Jack that Milo was skeptical and that he found the situation surreal and confusing. There was no way either of them could imagine what Kepstein was going to say next.

"I have questioned my own recent, erratic behavior. What I mean is, I've had to examine my life and my plan. I've had to examine what I've done and what I plan to do, and it has become apparent unto me that Bill Kepstein is a very, very boring man. Boring in the most offensive sense of the word. I am a bore to myself and to those around me."

"Except for your fellow board members, Bill —no pun intended — but I'm sure they find you very interesting!"

"Yes, Milo, and that is exactly my point. The people who profit from me find everything I do interesting, and they always have. But unfortunately, my interest in that one-sided part of my life is over. I'm not getting any return on my investment of time — and I don't mean financially. I have to do something I want to do. It is time I do something I — me, Bill Kepstein — find worthwhile."

"You mentioned that your behavior has been erratic lately," Jack interjected. "But you also talk as if these things have been weighing on you for a long time. Is your behavior erratic only lately or has something been building up for some time?"

"Perhaps my behavior has seemed erratic to an outside observer, but no, not to myself. It is necessary for a change. Jack, if you recall, when we spoke this past week, I said that I believe I've pinpointed the cause of my recent behavior and my mood. You see," he said, shifting his position to ensure eye contact with Jack and Milo, "you were describing to me, Jack, what you do for a living, your personal hobbies, and so forth. Do you recall that?"

"Yes, of course," Jack replied.

"Right, we were talking about a theory that you feel strongly about. You have an almost academic interest in sociology, right? — social experiments, if you will —about how people act and work. At any rate, you brought up something that really hit me close to home, an interest we share."

"Academic!" Milo blurted, out slapping Jack on the back. "I like that, Bill, I like that a lot."

"Yes, yes, *almost* academic. Jack, you were describing the projects you'd been working on, studying, what I believe you called the 'availability of free information.' But what I didn't tell you at the time was that I've also been on a similar kind of quest in the past!"

"A quest for free information?" Jack asked, perplexed.

"Yes! About ten years ago I was with my wife in Argentina. I woke up one morning and felt like getting some fresh air. There was a small church across the street from the hotel and I decided to talk with the priest. I wanted to ask him what he thought about his geographical stance in global Catholicism." Kepstein smiled, feeling proud of the question he had asked the priest. "It was my notion that the answer to this question would be a more honest one as opposed to one I could come up with from hours of partial and biased research."

"His geographical stance?" Jack asked, intrigued by the idea.

"Yes. At the time, if you recall, 9/11 had just happened. The world was starting to be concerned about the consequences of radical Islam, terrorism, and so on. I asked the priest what he thought about it all, especially as he lived in a part of the world where Catholicism was the religion of the majority. Jack, he took me to meet one of the smartest scholars I've ever known, a professor of religion at a university in Buenos Aires — and all that, just for asking a question!"

"That's amazing," Jack said. "You're a decade ahead of me in these pursuits, and what a great question to ask! I'd never thought about it, and I'd be happy to hear what he said."

"Another day perhaps. What I really want to get at is your theory of communication. As I said, I've had similar interests for a very long time. While I've never been in a situation quite like yours, I've always enjoyed a good conversation. Imagine how boring my routine is: bankers talking to bankers about the various banking that goes on in their respective banks. It's never really been my desire to do banking, you see, and so I've escaped my office as often as possible so I could do the things that truly interested me, particularly striking up conversations with people who don't expect them.

"I've tried to engage the bank's employees as often as possible. Some folks have called that a 'hands-on management approach,' or as I recall one headline reading, 'An Executive Approach to Staying Down to

Earth.' People assumed this was some kind of heartfelt way for a busy executive to stay in touch with his staff, but I assure you my motive was more selfish. The truth is that I frequently need to talk to people with different viewpoints or else I become disillusioned."

"Do you ever talk to anyone else besides your employees?" Milo asked. "I do commercial electric work at a lot of the high rises downtown and I've noticed that the further up the building I go, the less friendly people are. By the time I get to the C-suites, guys look at me like I have three heads or something."

"That's a shame, Milo. Of course I talk to others at the bank. A large office building is really like a small city, and I've found that there are many, many commonalities shared by people, both at the top and bottom of the building. There was one time when I asked the elevator maintenance fellow how I could improve the bank. He taught me about the modern world of energy efficiency, an important topic I hadn't known about. After that discussion, I set some meetings, signed some papers, and we've saved thousands on energy bills since. And now the bank receives national accolades each year for being friendlier to the environment."

Kepstein furrowed his eyebrows, concentrating on his thoughts and enjoying the brief silence. "Jack, we share this interest and I have a sense of where you're coming from, but can you explain the nature of your foundation? I mean, what is your driving force here — what do you want to learn or change?"

"Sure I can. We're talking about how important communication is. I truly believe that many troubles in the world, from business to religion to politics, arise from a lack of communication." Jack spread his hands across the coffee table in front of him, making sure not to tip their drinks over. "I believe that when people aren't talking with one another, there's no room for growth, because when people don't really talk with one another, they don't know anything about the other person's beliefs and desires. They can't understand the other person's fears and point of view. If we don't know these things about one another, how can we expect to live in peace, and move forward as a society? So if that doesn't happen, it's just a matter of one group gaining power and another group losing it."

"You mentioned 'knowing things about others.' Are you talking about individuals or groups?" Kepstein asked.

"Communication has to take place on an individual level, but the collective effects of communication, or its lack, reaches all levels of society. All the major religions incorporate a form of communication into their worship in some way or another, and for this reason it helps create a sense of community. If there is a lack of communication, people split off into factions and differences that were once considered to be insignificant become altogether insurmountable, as seen when the Protestants split off from the Catholics, the Shiites from the Sunnis, and so on. Eventually, each religion becomes reduced to groups of orthodox, fundamentalists, and liberals who do not talk to each other, leading to all sorts of problems."

"Yes, you can see the same thing in politics as well," Milo chimed in, leaning forward, his elbows on his knees. "Those in power seldom speak to and for the people they govern, leading to national uneasiness. Then, as the men in power cannot overcome their egos and biases, they cannot communicate constructively with the members of other political parties, or even with others in their own party, resulting in the stalemates we've seen recently in Washington, for example."

Kepstein nodded, thinking of his own domestic issues at home, as Jack spoke. "Exactly. You have radical religious groups waging war on behalf of their constituents, and governments waging war on behalf of their citizens, for the sake of 'spreading Islam, protecting the Jewish state, spreading democracy, or ensuring regional stability.' The list of reasons goes on and on, but it's worth questioning how many of these religious constituents or citizens would be in full or even partial agreement with the activities carried out on their behalf. We don't know, because there's no open dialogue."

"I've often wondered that myself," Kepstein said. "I understand the need to secure oil and rare earth materials in the Middle East as our basis for war, but I wonder if the average US citizen has a grasp of this, and further, if they would willingly support our engagements? Or, as you mentioned, the Jihadist, acting out plots of terror. The Muslims they claim to act on behalf of are, instead, denouncing them and any affiliation with them."

"Exactly my point," Jack exclaimed. "And I think the idea of the importance of communication can seem to be a bit abstract when applied to issues such as religion and politics. It can be understood more clearly when it is applied to situations where people talk to each other in their everyday lives. As I said earlier, open communication is essential if people are to be kept from developing a negative view of the world, as open communication helps them from feeling isolated and voiceless. Instead, they can feel as if they are part of a larger community that shares their beliefs and views. And it's also a way of avoiding major disruptions, for if people are speaking with each other in an honest and open way on a daily basis, they can truly understand each other, even if they disagree in their beliefs. It's a way of promoting tolerance, rather than conflict.

"But there are also other important reasons why open communication is necessary for any society. For example, if there is open communication between parents and children, this promotes greater understanding by the parents of their children's needs and can also help the children develop empathy for others. Without being able to communicate with their parents, children go astray and become adults with destructive personalities. A lack of productive communication also lies at the root of most broken marriages, as one spouse wants one thing while the other wants another. Without each spouse discussing their needs, silence and secrecy can develop in the relationship, the commitment of one's partner to the relationship can be questioned, and the relationship can easily fail."

Jack stopped talking, his face reddening.

"Yes, my wife and I have had communication troubles in the past," Kepstein said, a somber look crossing his face. "And I always thought it was Rebecca's fault. For example, I assumed she would not have any knowledge or interest in the topics I wanted to discuss. Perhaps topics such as those we're discussing tonight. But now I see that there's more to it. Not only doesn't she try and bridge the gap between us, but I also don't give her the chance to do so." Kepstein paused briefly, then continued, "That's at the root of the problems we all face. With globalization and the presence of the

Internet in our lives, and this gigantic push for connectivity, somehow we're still not *engaged*. Hell, if anything there is more secrecy, more deals going down in backrooms, and war certainly hasn't ceased. Consider for a moment the power of social media — it led to a democratic upheaval in the Middle East — but today I hear nothing from those countries about the use of social media, and some of the same countries are even facing collapse. We could talk about the pros and cons of specific examples for hours, but what I would still maintain is that by forcing people to communicate, or at least making it more accessible for people around the world to do so, there is an enormous potential for positive change.

"But I never discussed politics, philosophy, or business with my wife because she doesn't know about these matters. If, a decade ago, I had only tried to teach her about these things, or had given her the chance to do so . . . I . . ."

Kepstein sat back in his chair and a heavy silence was felt by the three men. Looking up from his folded hands, he regained his focus and looked thoughtfully at Jack and Milo. "It is time we start discussing making a film," he said. "A serious film, one of great importance historically. Jack, Milo, your friend Lenny works in this field, and Jack, I know that you enjoy writing screenplays. Let's do this."

Chapter Nine

The sun rose above the Atlantic in a vain attempt to heat the streets and buildings under its jurisdiction, a fruitless venture in a Northeastern March. This was a day that was better suited for staying indoors. At least that was Jack's assumption. Milo lay on the living room couch, both men content to waste the day after a night of drinking.

As the morning fog drifted away, Jack remembered the events of the previous night and, as was his custom, he mentally recapped the evening play-by-play. He found this to be a convenient and effective method of remembering important details such as plans and names. It was also a useful tool for determining whether or not his tongue had gotten too loose. He never intended to say something foolish or offensive when drinks were dished out like they were that evening, but he thought back on the evening, wondering if he had spoken out of turn.

As he thought, too, about Kepstein and his aims, Jack had conflicting thoughts and knew he was going to have to talk to Lenny, for he needed to get a better sense of whether or not this film project sounded like something a reasonable person would consider to be a worthwhile undertaking: for example, how difficult it would be to make a movie and how much it would cost. Jack knew little about such things, except for what he had heard on tabloid television and read about in gossip magazines. He also knew that Lenny had been unable to raise the necessary money for his own movie projects.

Jack wandered into the living room. Milo was wide awake and throwing a baseball up and down above his head. Throw, catch, throw catch, over and over again, until Jack startled him.

"What in the hell are you doing up this early, Milo?!"

"I should ask you the same thing! Jesus, man, you could have made me drop this ball right on my face, sneaking in here like that."

"This is my apartment, if you recall, I can sneak anywhere I like."

"Alright, fair enough. But, seriously, what are you doing so bright-eyed and bushy-tailed this early?"

"I've got to call Lenny," Jack explained. "I've got to talk to him about what went down last night."

"Oh, c'mon Jack. You can't still be serious about all of this, can you?"

Jack was moving about the apartment quickly, oblivious to his friend's questions. "As soon as I find that damn phone of mine." He returned to his bedroom, searching for his cellphone.

"Lenny?" Jack blared, moving quickly through the living room, his phone pressed to his ear.

"Yeah, this is he." There was a tremendous commotion in the background. It sounded as if Lenny was in a bar.

"Lenny, it's Jack. Man, where are you?"

"Oh —" Silence. Thud! Silence. Thud! Silence. Thud! "Jack, are you still there?"

"Yeah, I'm still here! Man, what are you doing?"

"You don't need to scream," Lenny said, offhandedly. "Sorry about that. My phone is always on the fritz. I just have to smack the side a few times to get it up and running."

"Oh, I see."

"Can you hear me Ok now?" The background noise had settled into a tolerable rumble.

"Yeah, yeah, I can hear you now. Where in the hell are you?"

"I'm just down the street from my apartment getting a cup of coffee. What are you up to, old friend?"

Jack mused, resting his own mug on the table. "I was just sitting down to have a cup myself, brother."

"Ah, it is a fine morning to enjoy the bean, isn't it."

"It certainly is. It certainly is, Lenny."

"So, to what do I owe this extreme pleasure on such a fine Sunday morning?" Lenny asked with a mocked grandiosity.

"Well, it's a pretty interesting matter really. It has to do with your, uh, well, your business." Jack proceeded to describe their first meeting with

Kepstein, in case Lenny had forgotten, and the conversation he'd had with the man the previous night at Betriebsnacht. He also made sure to emphasize how excited Kepstein had been about the idea of creating a picture. Lenny was clearly dumbfounded by the news, and couldn't keep from interrupting Jack with excitement.

"I can't believe you find this so exciting," Jack said. "I feel the same way, but I don't know why—it's absurd!"

"I told you, man, I can't get a break out here. These assholes all expect you to get so excited that they're offering money to pay *you* to do *their* work. It's unbearable! You know I'm not a sellout, and I couldn't be, even if I tried — which I'm not — but you get the idea."

"I get it, Lenny, I get it, but don't you think it all sounds kinda crazy?"

"Crazy or not, I have no other options, man. I have to take any and every possible project seriously, or at least keep it in the back of my mind until it expires. Plus, I handpick people who I think are worth a damn in the first place, so it's not like I'm remembering hundreds and hundreds of conversations or people. Your friend Kepstein, for example. He seemed to be a standup, down-to-earth sort of guy, and I think that's awesome you still keep in contact with him, and even went out with him last night. I mean, do you have any idea who that guy is? I mean who he *really* is?"

"Yeah, I do — I mean, I think I do. He's the president, or CEO or something, whatever they call themselves, at Fidelity Sworn Bank."

"Oh Jackie-boy, Jackie, Jackie, Jackie . . . He's not just a wealthy banker. He's worth a bit more money than you may have previously thought, a bit more indeed!"

"Well, how much?" Jack exclaimed.

"Millions, Jack, millions and millions more than you can even imagine, I mean, this guy probably has breakfast with Merrill Lynch and dinner with Morgan Stanley."

Lenny went on to explain how Kepstein had made his fortune, how long he'd been making it, and how much of it he'd saved, invested, spent, etc. Jack was shocked that he'd been in the company of such an important man, and that the man could be so casual and normal. He was also a bit embarrassed about his own lack of journalistic diligence regarding Kepstein's history.

"I know it's amazing — I was blown away at first too. You can really learn a lot using the Internet these days if you know where to look. It's incredible really."

"I had no idea," Jack said quietly, still calculating the numbers in his head. "So I guess it goes without saying he'd be more than able to fund a film project?"

"To say the least, Jack. A producer usually only rents the equipment and staff. I mean, this guy could start his own production outfit with the kind of money he's saved — now I don't know why anyone would do that and I doubt he would— but I mean . . . the possibilities are endless."

Lenny went on to tell Jack what was involved in producing a movie: the equipment, the staff, the companies that provided both, as well as the costs and the importance of the payers' financial resources. He told Jack about his connections in New York who were in the movie business and how surprisingly easy the project would be once it was set in motion.

"It's just a matter of setting up a meeting with one of these agents, describing the details and expectations, along with the financials, and after that it's pretty much all fun." Lenny paused on his end of the phone momentarily. "What we need, Jack, for this type of thing to really come off is an idea, a plot. It's not enough just to approach one of these people and say, 'Hey, I have a shit load of money and I want to make a movie — yeehaw and hooray.' It's a whole process, and unfortunately a political one at that. The company has to be interested in the project. They have to believe it is worthwhile, and so on and so on. What we need is a really good idea, and for that —"

"Hold on a minute," Jack interrupted. "Let's not get ahead of ourselves, Lenny. I mean, we're really only talking about something that was thrown about during two extremely drunken evenings."

"I know. I apologize. I get carried away too easily, but also take into consideration that this is all I have to do with my time — sit around and think of the . . . possibilities."

"Yeah, well I guess you're right — we might as well look at this movie idea from all angles. I know I've seen and heard of crazier things happening." Jack slowly took a took a sip of his coffee. "But like you said, I wonder what kind of an idea a guy like Kepstein would have in mind. I mean, his view of the world is so drastically different from that of any normal human being, it would be hard to guess."

"That's the beauty of it, Jack. It would be very hard to guess. A man that rich, that powerful, that is still as easy to talk to as he is . . . I mean, who knows where he's coming from. Did you ever notice he doesn't even have his own limo driver, an entourage, a bodyguard, or anything? He just sort of carries on as if he were John Normal Doe."

"I suppose that does seem peculiar now that you mention it, but I never really gave it much thought. I mean, I assumed that a man who owns and runs an entire fucking bank does pretty well for himself, but, Jesus Christ, I assumed it was like another position to hold, you know, the top of the totem pole. I figured, too, there was some sort of cap!"

"For most of us there is, man, but this guy was not raised on Kellogg's cereal and union picnics in the summer. He came from some decent backing, and if I'm not mistaken, I vaguely remember reading about his father doing something quite similar."

"Yeah, I think his father may have either been a higher-up in the bank or the owner. I can't remember the details either." Jack stared blankly at the checkered pattern in the floor and fell silent.

"Something like that . . . so you really think, though, that this might be serious?"

"I don't know, buddy. Like I said, I've seen crazier things happen — we all have. But if it's a question of whether or not he would be serious about something like this, well the man definitely has the audacity to go through with it. He's got a lot of ambition and there's not much stopping him from pursuing it."

"You would know better than me, Jack, but like you say, it's obviously a long shot. I just can't help but get drawn in . . . You know, it's a real bitch getting your foot in the door with these people."

"Who?"

"The agents and companies I was just talking about. It's just such an ass kissing contest if you don't have any money. I can't stand the taste of ass, so it doesn't work too well for me."

Jack and Lenny broke into laughter. Jack ran his hands through his hair and cracked his back against the chair. Lenny set his empty cup of coffee on the table and shot his steely fingers into the pockets of his jeans in search of a cigarette.

"Well shit, Jack I just don't know. I mean I've met the man only once . . . You say you see him often these days?" Lenny asked, inhaling his freshly lit cigarette.

"Yeah, believe it or not — and now that I know all this I really don't understand it either. I believe," he paused, "I believe it is due to a number of circumstances. For one, I believe the man may be having a midlife crisis. I mean, he seems extremely eager to spend time with us, all, no doubt, younger than him, and he is certainly young at heart, plus there's this movie-making business. I think, too, that he may have had a shitty childhood and is now wishing it could be made up for in some way or another."

"Wait a minute. People who stay young at heart don't have midlife crises, and as for his childhood, I have no idea about that, other than that it was probably pretty damn stuffy. Why do you think his childhood was so subpar anyway?"

"No real reason or anything, but he mentioned pretty strongly, and on more than one occasion, a disinterest in what he'd been doing for so long, the bank I mean. You can tell he resents the establishment, as if running a bank were more an obligation than a choice that he'd made. I don't know, man, I just don't know."

"Yeah, well you're usually pretty good at figuring this type of thing out, Jack. Whatever he's got going on in his head is probably pretty interesting, and I for one would love to know what that is!"

"You and me both, brother, but you know some of the best things in life don't make a damn bit of sense."

"True enough . . . I wish I could come into town to check all this out for myself." Lenny snapped his fingers. "That's it — I'll plan a trip down there immediately!"

"I have better news for you, Lenny." Jack paused momentarily. "Kepstein and I actually discussed the possibility of taking a trip to New York. In fact, he was asking about you last night."

"Holy hell! That could be huge, man. We could all talk about it and maybe even meet with some people here in Manhattan."

"Yeah. But listen to us, making up all these ifs and maybes. We'd better find out the facts first."

"You're right, Jack. But as for me, I'm afraid I've already gotten my hopes up. There's no going back. So there's no sense in looking at anything but positive possible outcomes. All I want to know is what sort of idea he could have for a movie, if any."

Jack ended the call, hazily placing his phone on the countertop next to the coffee maker. Lenny's last question weighed heavily upon him. One part of his brain was overrun with abstract ideas, while the other half stayed busy counting linoleum tiles and sequences of alternating black and white squares. He had a vague sense that different parts of his life were coming together in a strange way.

"What's gotten into you, buddy?" Milo asked, leaning against the kitchen doorway. He'd been listening to the second half of Jack's conversation. "You've become smitten! Blinded by the light, my friend!"

Jack blushed. He was caught off-guard by his atypical lack of reserve. "Take it easy, Milo. You had no problem with the man last night, when you guys were making toasts every fifteen minutes. I'm sorry you're not going to New York with us, but it's probably because you're acting like such a Debbie Downer about this whole movie business."

"I think there's a fine line between enthusiasm and stupidity, Jack. I was making it very clear last night, and I will make it very clear again, that I think the whole concept is a waste of time and energy. What are you going to do when this guy snaps out of his midlife crisis and cuts you off? You'll be the red Porsche that sits in the garage or gets sold for cheap when the man comes to grips. He's got problems, I can assure you, but you better make damn sure what it is you're getting yourself into before you become some rich man's pet project."

Shaking his head, Milo walked to the refrigerator. He grabbed a beer and turned to his friend. "I just don't get it. You spend your whole life trying to be smart, trying to avoid all the world's traps, and here you are following money and fairy tale preconceptions on a trip with a stranger to New York."

Jack rose from his chair, brushed past his friend, opened the refrigerator, and took out a beer for himself. He leaned against the stove a few feet away from Milo and said calmly, "Maybe that's just it, Milo. Maybe I am sick of the constant pessimism. I've studied the human condition just as you have, but I'm tired of giving up on it. Your lack of interest in this possible project unfortunately goes along with your lack of hope for change."

"Ok . . ." Milo interrupted sarcastically, taking a sip of his beer.

"You're my best friend, Milo. We've seen a lot of shit, but so what? No one cares what we do, and I think they should. I think this Kepstein guy gets it. You claim you're wise, but by who's measuring stick? By what standard do you consider yourself wise? You have no college degree, no six-figure income, no published studies in scientific journals. Who would think you're wise?"

Milo pointed a thumb at himself.

"Yeah. You, me, and now this guy, Bill Kepstein. He thinks our interest in dialogue, conversation, and learning through the process of talking is remarkable. He does the same thing. It's not his fault he's the richest man in the city, and it's not my fault either, but if he wants to use his wealth to do something that might involve me — well, I'm going through with it come hell or high water."

"I don't think you need to worry about hell or high water, my friend. I just don't want you to change." Milo made his way onto the couch.

"That's just it, Milo. I *do* need to change. We all do. We need a major change, or it's always going to be the same for us all — complacency. I have all this fucking money, and of course it's a blessing, but it's also been a curse. I took a bribe, Milo. I silenced myself for money, and I'm stuck with that knowledge about myself. It's pathetic."

"You're going to complain about getting a half million dollars?" Milo jeered. "Donate it to charity if it's holding you down, man. Don't bring your fortune into this. They're not connected, and you know it!"

"You're right. I don't regret the money, but I'm also sincere when I say that it's time to change. I know this Kepstein guy has some serious skeletons in his closet, or his mind, or wherever it may be, and he's trying to find a way to clean them out. I'm doing the same thing, nothing less, nothing more. I don't know what to expect from all of this, but if it can lead to some sort of cleansing, I'm going to do it."

* * *

The following day, Jack and Kepstein agreed to travel to New York to explore the film business. Kepstein contacted Lenny directly. He wanted to better understand what Lenny did and who Lenny's business contacts might be.

"Lenny, this is Bill Kepstein. I met you and your friend, Jack, a few weeks ago here in Baltimore. Jack's mentioned that you'd be expecting to hear from me."

"Yes, of course, Bill! It's great to hear from you. I understand you and Jack will be traveling here this weekend. Right?"

"Indeed, Lenny. I'm an outsider looking to get involved in the film business and I need a little help learning the ropes. Do you have any contacts in the area of production?"

"Yes sir. Jack gave me some details about your interests, and I have to admit, I don't know exactly what type of film it is you're interested in, but I do have one very close friend who will be good to speak with."

"Right, Lenny. I haven't gone into any detail about the type of project I'd be interested in working on yet and I prefer to keep it that way . . . in an effort to avoid any preconceived notions about the project. You understand?"

"It's not a common way to do business here, I'm afraid," Lenny added, matter-of-factly, "but, as I said, this man is a good friend of mine."

"Understood, Lenny. What is your colleague's name, if I might ask?"

"His name is Cleveland Adams, but he goes by General Adams. He's an intriguing fellow, and if you go online, you can see some of the work he's done in the past. Even if you don't agree with his themes, I'd recommend you meet him . . . if nothing else, he can be your first contact so you can get a handle on the lingo and how these guys talk. It won't be a waste of time, I promise you that much."

"Fair enough. I sincerely appreciate your discussing this with me. We'll be heading up Saturday morning and arriving around lunchtime or a little after. If you can, please keep in touch with Jack about the details, and we'll see you soon."

"Sounds like a plan, Bill — see you soon, indeed!"

Lenny hung up and danced around his tiny apartment for a few minutes before calling Jack to tell him what was happening. "This is it! This is it, Jack!"

The old friends spoke for less than five minutes, but it was all the time they needed to share and understand the enormity of what was happening. After the call, Jack looked out his apartment window at the park and river below. He thought about how much he loved the view, and how that particular view was the reason he rented the apartment. He wondered what those kind of decisions would mean, now that he was getting involved with this project. Would they change? Would *he* change? He wasn't sure, and didn't even care about the answers. For he knew that his life had also become stagnant as well and he was ready to entertain fate.

Four days later, he climbed into Kepstein's Mercedes and they made the three-hour drive to Manhattan. They planned to get a hotel, have a few drinks, and have dinner with Lenny Manzarec and the man who called himself General Adams.

Chapter Ten

Jack and Kepstein stopped at their hotel at 43rd and Broadway. Doors opened for them and they exited their car under a canopy of towers that created a da Vinci-like study in converging lines. It was as if the buildings, closer and closer overhead, created a sanctuary for creativity. Stepping out of the car and onto the greasy, timeless streets of New York City, they had a sense that it was for some unknown purpose.

After a quick stop at their hotel, the two men hailed a cab and collected their thoughts at a local pub.

"We've got about an hour and half before we need to meet Lenny and Mr. Adams — I'm not calling him 'General,'" Kepstein said with a smirk.

Jack laughed. "Yes, I find the title he chose interesting. I must also say that I find that a few beers before a big meeting is always a good idea. This is pretty exciting!"

"Indeed, it is, Jack. A bit surreal in some sense, but without a doubt exciting."

"Do you have any idea what questions this guy is going to ask us? Or what kind of project you're planning to talk about?"

"You'd probably know better than I would, as this is my first foray into show business . . . but I think we'll do just fine," Kepstein replied with a grin.

After they finished their drinks, Kepstein and Jack left the tavern and walked a few short blocks to a small restaurant. They were in Hell's Kitchen, at the outskirts of the area's restaurant quarter. The restaurant was called Kimpo, named after its owner. Its menu was closer to Vietnamese fare than to anything else; this description, however, would not accurately describe the nature of the place.

Kimpo was an elderly man from Vietnam who had lived in Australia for nearly two decades, then in Holland for another two before landing in the basement of a music hall in New York City. He offered a restaurant experience quite unlike any other in the city, for it was not the food, but rather the atmosphere, that was desirable. The restaurant was really more of a social club, private in nature and catering to a very wealthy and very eccentric clientele.

Kepstein had reserved the loft in the back of the restaurant and he and Jack were sitting at their table when Lenny and General Adams arrived. General Adams looked like the man both Kepstein and Jack had expected him to be — stout and of modest proportions, with a kind of Southern Californian haughtiness that too many producers tended to assume. He wore wire-rimmed glasses and dark clothes that were made of heavy cloth.

"Greetings, Mr. Adams," Kepstein said, extending a firm handshake as he rose.

"It's a pleasure to meet you, Mr. Kepstein. Please call me General. I've had my name officially changed. *Generally* speaking, it's the way I prefer to be addressed, and is in no way a reference to anything military."

"Then please call me Bill, General," Kepstein said as he pivoted towards Lenny. "And Lenny, a pleasure to see you again. Thank you for arranging this meeting."

"Of course, Bill. It's great to see you, and you as well, Jack. This is my good friend, Jack Shales," Lenny said as he shook Jack's hand and introduced him to General Adams.

"A pleasure to meet you as well, Jack. Shall we?" General motioned back towards the table.

"Yes. Let's get started," Kepstein agreed.

Kepstein felt both serious and enthusiastic at that moment, but it was also apparent to him that no one else knew what to expect from the meeting, let alone what to say. He knew from experience that when he sat down for a business meeting, whether or not his reputation had preceded him, that everyone at the meeting saw him as the alpha male. And this was also the sense he had today.

"We haven't had a bite to eat all day. You guys will love the food here, and I hope you're as hungry as I am," Kepstein said after the formal introductions had been made and drinks had been ordered.

"I hadn't much of an appetite until a few moments ago," the producer replied, exclaiming further, "This food smells amazing — is it Vietnamese?"

"It is indeed, General, but wait until you see how they serve it . . ." Kepstein smiled. "Have you ever been to a restaurant where there are wine pairings with your meal, or in a brewery when there are bourbon or beer pairings — that type of thing?"

"Of course," General replied, the others nodding in agreement.

"It's even better here," Kepstein said. "Here they do *music* pairings with your food!"

"They do what?" Jack said, grinning. He was sitting on the edge of his seat, excited as he wondered what was going to happen next.

"Here is how it works," Kepstein continued. "We each get the same drink and the same meal with each course. The music is programmed so that it goes well with both the food and the drinks. Then there's a nice surprise at the end . . . But there's time for all of Kimpo's surprises, as you gentleman will see. For now, though, let's get down to business, shall we?"

"Yes, great idea!" Adams agreed, ready to sink his teeth into the mystery he'd been wondering about. "So, please tell me, Bill . . . I understand from what Lenny has told me that you're interested in putting together a film of some sort?"

"Yes General, that's correct, and that's why Jack and I have traveled to New York City and why I'm very grateful for your meeting with us."

"And I've gathered, too, that everyone here is as curious as I am to understand the nature of this project?"

"You're correct again, General, so I think it's time for us to begin that discussion."

92

General Adams nodded as Kepstein continued, "I want to make a movie, but I would contend that it would be more appropriately called a project, for its purpose is not necessarily to entertain. I've seen some of your work, General, and I understand that you are familiar with the idea. Judging from some of your documentary pieces, sometimes it's better to make something that goes beyond entertainment, isn't it? — something that engages the viewers and makes them think? Then if the project works as you hoped it would they begin to behave differently."

"I'm listening," General Adams said, leaning forward.

"I've been around the world and done business on many continents. I have observed the inner workings of many large corporations, banks, and governments. I have seen them work together, as well as separately. And I've spent time in the most luxurious of settings being treated like a king, knowing that the reason I was treated that way was because I could offer them what they wanted most — financing. On these trips, I've always found that I wanted, and had to, sneak away from my confines of luxury to the world of the worker. When possible, I would speak with these people as if I were just another passerby interested in understanding everything I could about them and their culture. I have also done this with people working at my bank. In fact, all my life I've been interested in understanding their views on work and their work world, and what I have learned is that at both ends of the socio-economic spectrum there are more similarities than differences. What I want to do in this project, then, is expose the common fiber that binds humanity together and show how we humans have lost our awareness of this commonality. Further, I want this project to depict the consequences that this loss of awareness has created and what the likely consequences will

93

be to our world, not only if this awareness is not regained, but also what the positive consequences would be if there were a strong, determined, and convincing world-wide recognition of this commonality."

No one spoke for the next couple of minutes, the sound of the down-tempo bass-heavy house music overlaying their thoughts about what Kepstein was saying.

The General spoke first. "You're a very smart man, Bill. You've had tremendous success, and no doubt you've had to be very calculating in order to achieve that success. I would also assume that you are too smart to want to do anything foolhardy, as well as a bit stubborn when you decide something you believe in."

"Perhaps," Kepstein offered, smiling politely and taking a sip of wine.

"This is a compelling topic you're addressing, though, exposing the common fiber that holds humanity together. How do you plan to do that through film?"

"Well, to be honest, that's why I wanted this meeting. I'm hoping that *you* can tell *me*. A smart man once told me that if a person wants the answer to a difficult question, he can begin by studying the subject in depth. But if an efficient person wants the answer to a difficult question, he will find the person who is best suited to answer it and ask that person. And I believe that's you."

"I agree . . . but I still need to know how you envision the film. Are you interested in approaching it as a documentary or as fiction? Or, perhaps, through a journalistic lens with commentary? Knowing what you have in mind will help me greatly."

"I completely understand, General. Thank you . . . I met Jack and Lenny about a month or so ago. What caught my attention when I spoke with them were their interests. Especially Jack. He has a comfortable amount of money to live on as a result of blackmailing the police. Now he spends his time and energy studying the human condition using the medium of dialogue. I, too, have started thinking about the importance of communication in human relations as well as the feelings that I have had for a very long time about that subject."

The house music faded into a sultry mix of dub, as the modern sounds of electronica gave way to old world temple drums and Vietnamese tribal chanting. The music careened through the back room and every noodle of Pho tasted and smelled to the men at the table as if they were eating in a small Vietnamese village.

"As we enjoy this main course," Kepstein continued, "I'll explain my thoughts more clearly so we can consider how they can be addressed through the medium of film. Follow me on this, if you will . . . While Jack and I were driving on the 95 to get here, I had this thought. When any person outside of the US — or inside for that matter — sees images of the American coastline, what do they see? Well, I think they see high rises, gorgeous men and women, wealthy yacht owners, in general, a very small minority of the US population. Their assumptions, biases, and ideas of this world come, by and large, from movies, television, and magazines. What they don't see, however, are the greasy boat mechanics and hotel maids who live forty minutes inland in their window-unit air-conditioned apartments, eating microwave dinners and raising poor, disease-plagued families. They also don't see the elderly man trying to keep his Mom-and-Pop grocery open down the street from the Wal-Mart. No one sees or hears anything about the tired, the poor, or the disenfranchised. And why would they? The media do not present these people in the same way they present the one percent.

"With the web and globalization, however, while the whole world has become connected, there still isn't a protocol such as the Internet that allows people to communicate on a world-wide basis. By that I mean that we expect people from different cultures, religions, and countries to work together — you make a product here, I'll buy it there — but not to talk with one another. It's absurd if you think about it. I know that on one hand politics can be seen as the reason for this problem, while on the other hand it can be assumed that politics is the only way to solve this problem. The dilemma we are faced with, then, is cyclical in nature.

"Political methods are sluggish and cumbersome, an embarrassment to enlightened people, and yet we've come to believe that they are the only means for accomplishing any changes on a large-scale basis. Politics is, indeed, a means by which societies' wants and needs can be communicated to those in power. There is absolutely no way, however, that communication can take place, in this arrangement, from the ground up. Grassroots movements are really just material for cynical jokes. What has to happen instead is that people have to stop begging for and asking their governments to allay their concerns. Right now we think that if we, as citizens, tell our representatives what we want and need, and they pass on that information to people at higher levels of government, then those needs will be met and things will change. In actuality, though, these so-called representatives don't even talk amongst themselves in a larger governmental setting such as Congress, but instead they talk together only in small fractionated groups. So why, then, would they talk honestly with the citizens they are supposed to represent? If people would simply speak with one another freely and often, then, I believe, this imbalance of power would change. Very simply, then, what I want to try and do is attempt to put in place a 'how-to' guide for communicating on a global scale."

"How?" Jack asked. "How can you make a film like that? Have you come up with any concrete ideas?"

"Well I've thought of a few ideas, but there still is a great deal of work that needs to be done. That's why I'm glad to be part of such a bright and enterprising group of people who can help the process along," Kepstein said warmly. "I've made a few notes, and I'd like to read them briefly before stepping away from my soapbox so we can enjoy my favorite part of this restaurant —" He took out a small piece of paper from his breast pocket during the momentary pause, "the after-dinner drinks, of course!"

Jack, and Lenny looked at one another with a mixture of concern and astonishment. When Jack looked towards General Adams, he was met with what he took to be a questioning glance.

"There have been many recent changes in our world. Chronologically speaking, in the past few centuries we have made more advances in the areas of science and technology than at any other time in human history. We are

social animals. We love, we care, we build, and we destroy. In one way or another, everything we do is done by and to other people, people with whom we share our planet. To ensure the ongoing vitality of humanity, and not its destruction, all the people on the planet have to engage, to some degree, in a form of dialogue and communication.

"Progress is difficult to achieve, and even more so to measure. It is not the means to an end, or even a goal. And with progress comes change that is not always positive. I believe that, along with the rise of technological progress and economic globalization, we have been losing an important aspect of our humanity in that the use of this technology has resulted in people isolating themselves into groups that are defined only by the commonality felt in these groups. This began with the advent of radio, then television, and then with the rise of the Internet. As a result, we are beginning to move away from knowing who we really are as people. We accept what we hear, see, and are told much too easily and willingly. Some say this is because there are too many of us and we have to get our information about the world via the mass media. If we do this blindly, though, without any examination of what is being told to us, how do we know if we are being told the truth? We rely on so-called 'experts' to give us information. But who, indeed, are those experts? If we only listen to and follow the opinions of 'official' groups, and have no way to determine the nature of these groups and their opinions, what then?

"I believe that the time has come to ask these questions. That is what I want this film to do. I want to pair the opinions of two people or two groups from clearly different vantage points and show how these people or groups share the same opinions and points of view. In doing so, I will make a mockery of our assumptions — a mockery of the timeless assumptions — that our gender, race, religion, income, or other defining characteristics make us different from, and separate us from, one another. This observation is obvious, but we have forgotten to remember it because of the reign of what is called, and valued as, 'diversity.' In the film, I will show what happens when this awareness is ignored and I will demonstrate that we can sincerely communicate with one another.

"I am not denouncing the nature of our social media. I am not denouncing blogs, social networking tools, or any other form of digital media. I recognize that they are important and, if utilized appropriately, can enhance the nature and quality of communication like never before. But let's not forget the uniqueness of face-to-face interactions, body language, and setting. If it's not possible for us to talk in person with each other, we can talk via video. If, due to its importance, a conversation or subject needs to be communicated globally, let's videotape it and broadcast it. If the topic is considered by any authorities to be illegal or dangerous, let's lift the veil and let the masses decide what is illegal or dangerous. Let them discuss things openly and not behind closed doors. Unless society has already been damned, I believe that choices that are positive and for the good of humanity will emerge through the process of dialogue. If you do not believe this, then you have lost hope in society at large, and why, then, should people even be communicating?

"With this simple cinematic effort, then, I want to lift the minds of the world out of, and above, the mire we are currently living in. Once there was a dark age, and now there is a digital age, where, as our immersion in information increases, our social awareness goes down. Join me in the effort to change this."

Kepstein folded up the piece of paper and placed it in his breast pocket. "This is, philosophically, where I am coming from. Whether or not we can distill these ideas into film, I'm not sure."

The General was the first to speak. "This is, indeed, a very important topic that you're attempting to distill into a film, Bill. From what you've told us, you want to demonstrate that there are commonalities between very different groups of people — opposite ends of the socio-economic or geographical spectrum, in many cases. Doing this would require filming real people, not creating a screenplay and filming it with actors. Further, I assume that the men and women who are at the top of the socio-economic spectrum would not care to be recorded in any manner, especially considering your intentions. So, I have to ask if this means that you're proposing the use of a candid/secret camera?"

"You know your craft well and you've got a good ear for details, General!" Kepstein said heartily.

"I like the concept, Bill. I really do, but I've got to warn you that this kind of film is in the style of the conspiracy-theory genre — which has really been dying as of late. And it also begs the question, what kind of reaction would we expect from powerful people being videotaped without their consent?"

Kepstein took a moment to consider Adams' concerns. Jack and Lenny also contemplated what was being said. Thinking of his history and the lessons he learned, Jack weighed in, "Perhaps we could simply ask the interviewees prior to filming them? There are any number of ways we could spin our purpose in order to make it more attractive and prevent a lot of red tape. I've had good luck in the past being straightforward with my requests for information."

"You have indeed, Jack," Kepstein agreed, "but we would potentially be recording very important players — think heads of corporations, governments, etc."

"We'd have to either ask them ahead of time — which carries its own pros and cons — or we'd have to undertake the entire process in secrecy," Lenny interjected. "If you start asking people if they can be recorded for your film, and it rubs someone the wrong way, there's a good chance the word is going to spread fairly quickly in certain circles."

"Let's take a step back for a moment," Kepstein offered. "I want to make sure we're all on the same page before we discuss this any further. General, first I'd like to clarify how the film could be potentially perceived . . . designed to expose conspiracies. I feel that conspiracies really operate one-dimensionally, that they simply expose the bad at the top of the social or governmental ladder. This film though, as I understand it, would go beyond that. It would illustrate the fact that there are desires and similarities that both those at the top and those at the bottom have in common. By demonstrating that many thoughts and sentiments that lie behind decisions made at the top are the same thoughts and sentiments as those that lie behind decisions made at the bottom, people may see that what are called 'conspiracies' are simply decision-making processes made on a larger scale than those made on an individual basis. Does that make sense?"

"It does from your description, Bill. However, I think it is right to be concerned with how this type of production would be *perceived*. It would need to be done very carefully to make sure that it is not seen as a typical conspiracy-genre documentary." General took a drink and continued. "On that note, though, before we go any further, let's go back to why we wanted to meet today, Bill. What do you desire from me — are we just bouncing around ideas, or is this a project that you intend to follow through on until it is done?"

"In all honesty, I intend to follow this project through, from inception to completion. This meeting serves as a gut check for me. If you are interested in the ideas, I'd like to ask you to help produce the film. If you are not interested, I hope we can have a clear discussion of what it is I am up against in making it a reality."

"You don't hold your punches, Bill Kepstein!" Adams said with glee. "I'd certainly be interested, but do you realize the amount of time and capital this sort of project requires? Have you thought of who will be investing in the film, if there will be partners? We'd need to discuss the desired timeline, how those participating in the movie are to be compensated, where the shooting would take place, how the shooting would be done, and how the end product would be marketed."

"To begin with, I think it would be wise to shy away from any outside funding. As for marketing, that topic can be reserved for the time when we are closer to completion. For now, I think it best to focus on the production of the movie . . . and to revisit the idea of outside investing briefly before we go on . . . It is important there be no mention whatsoever, by anyone involved in the project, of what I do for a living, nor any discussion about how I plan to pay for the film, and no mention of this film to anyone until I give the green light. I have a great deal at stake simply by participating in anything outside of what I do for a living, and for the word to escape that I am spending my time and money elsewhere would be devastating for my career, my current status, my family, and put the wealth that I have earned and have planned to use for the funding of this project at risk. If these conditions are violated, then the funding for this project, as well as the project itself, will end. Let's leave it at that. Agreed?"

The agreement was sealed with a congenial toast and a discussion of filming and directing options began. Where everyone but Kepstein had felt some trepidation about the project half an hour earlier, now the atmosphere was, overall, one of genuine enthusiasm.

"I don't really understand how you can plan to show two sides of the same story and expect to make people find it appealing," Lenny asked as the discussion progressed.

"Only real people will be in the film, Lenny," Kepstein answered. "We humans love comparing ourselves to each other. It's natural."

"Ok, but will we be recording them secretly or openly? Because from what I have come to see is that people behave differently in front of a camera and it's nearly impossible for them to be totally honest when they know they're being taped."

"It's like this," Kepstein replied. "The movie will begin with some sort of general explanation as to what will be happening, an introduction if you will, something about communication. The important part, though, is that we're not creating a documentary, nor do we want to make it seem in any way, shape, or form that we are creating a typical documentary. The film is going to be an exposé, with hidden cameras rolling as people describe their needs, wants, positions, and sentiments — some for the better and some for the worse. There will be narration in order for the audience to understand the setting and who's speaking at any given moment. Stylistically, the film will fall somewhere between direct cinema — as if we were a fly on the wall — and cinéma vérité, uncovering truth and meaning through real-world scenes of real-life conversations.

"It will begin with a scene almost reminiscent of the dystopian story, *The Giver* . . . you are left with the chore of bringing communication back to the masses. From there, the film will take place in the farmhouses of Illinois and the executive suites of Wall Street. Cameras will roll in the rice paddies of Vietnam as well as the frozen factories of Moscow. No locations or cultural perspectives will be left out. Documentaries, for example, have been made about the Sunni/Shiite battles within a nation, with the leaders of the nation as well as the leaders of the warring factions being interviewed, but there has never been a case where all the leaders were interviewed at the same time. We will be recording opposing viewpoints of people from all walks of life, and in so doing we will create one of the starkest, most vivid descriptions of how things are that the world has ever seen. You see, we will discuss the border with Mexican immigrants, healthcare with indigent single mothers, manufacturing with Chinese factory workers, religion with Islamic terrorists, finance with the head of the Energy and Finance Committee, alcoholism with the head of InBev, and love with Ted Kaczynski, the Unabomber. We will break down every single preconceived barrier to dialogue and communication. The point behind all this, however, and this is important, the point that will be next to impossible to achieve, will be the avoidance of politics."

"What exactly do you mean, 'the avoidance of politics'" Adams asked. "How can you discuss or even represent half of these concepts without invoking politics? I mean, the Energy and Finance Committee, for example, is a political bureaucracy."

"A bureaucracy indeed, General, and that is what we will make very clear in the film. So many people waste time and money describing the lack of progress made via government, but they also wish for more government when they ask for change. Why hasn't anyone created an alternative mode of change? Not from the ground up, like grassroots movements, no petitions, no waivers, and no public demonstrations for change — it's all so laughable when you think about it. We despise governmental sluggishness, yet we beg for more government.

"Instead of asking for more government, we will present different scenarios of real-life problems that need to be solved. People on both sides of an argument often want the same thing, but will never be able to achieve it because we make it too hard to do so. For example, we will film governors mentioning plans for reforms that their citizens have been speaking of for decades, and House bills the citizens wish for that never get sponsored because their representatives are afraid of not getting reelected or because their financial backers disagree. I've found that people discuss important matters all the time, but their voices may never be heard because they don't care for politics or have the money to influence the system. But for the first time, we will, in this film, demonstrate that there is an alternative to the sluggish embarrassment that is called 'political representation.'

"People do not need to talk to their governments and representatives, but instead among themselves. If many people talk to each other at the same time, significant change may take place for once. When there is a way of mobilizing so many people, you don't need a hierarchy of discipline. It's like when a group of small children sees another boy playing with a toy, they will all want to play with that toy because the boy is interested in it. The more he wants it for himself, the more the others want it, until finally, when he tosses that toy aside with disinterest, the group finds other means of entertainment. In a similar fashion, it's time we disregard the importance of our planet's governments and stop desiring the toy the child is playing with. It's time we shrug off this political pointlessness and say, 'We're not interested any more, we toss you aside, we have learned to talk to one another on our own, thanks. No middleman is necessary anymore.'

"I know many questions will come to mind about what I am saying. For example, without governmental intervention, will the lunatics then run rampant and destroy us all? I would answer that if there truly is universal communication among all the inhabitants of the world, then that would be impossible. With all-encompassing communication, psychotic plans for destruction would not stand up as long as day to day dialogue took place."

"Those are pretty fascinating concepts," Lenny said, interrupting what looked to him to be a feverish and crazed man. He looked at everyone at the table, quite confident that they agreed. "I mean . . .I hadn't ever

106

thought of that — I don't know who has . . . I'm sure someone has at some point in time, but this right now, it's . . . it's — "

"It's genius," said General Adams. "It's absolutely genius!"

Kepstein glanced patiently in the General's direction. "General, to answer another of your questions, you wanted to know where we might shoot this film. I want to spend a great deal of time in the cities and countryside. My reasoning is simply that I believe this is where my ideas are already taking place to some extent and I believe that this is where the changes will begin. If you watch the news, or listen to presidential campaigns, the demographic of interest is always the middle class, those typically living in the suburbs. Despite the possibility that the middle class is already extinct, the media portrays it as the majority of the people in the Western world. This is where the grumbling comes from and these people feed on it. They have nothing more to do than watch CNN and rant and rave at the direction this or that is going and how their almighty taxes will be spent. Unfortunately, the suburban middle class has been the target of outside influences for so long that it is unlikely that those people will be the catalyst for change. However, I believe that this project will reach them. I'll explain what I mean.

"Those living in the city are engulfed by their daily activities. They live for the moment. Like here in New York City, for example, you ride trains from point A to point B and people move with a brisk pace, always to the next event. There is no time in their busy lives to sit idly by worrying about everyone else's issues. From time to time, the mayor may enact a new law that will greatly affect them, but for the most part these measures go unnoticed, as there simply isn't the time to examine them and start a protest. Likewise, those living in the country typically farm for a living, and if they don't, they are still surrounded by miles and miles of land. They have their own way of living. They can shoot guns and have wild outdoor parties without first notifying the city planning committee. It's how they live and politics does not absorb their attention. Again, from time to time a law is passed and they are forced to deal with it whether or not it suits them. People seem to have the most need for governmental intervention in the suburbs and in quiet towns. Following decades of targeted marketing by corporations, the media, and news outlets, the collective ideals of the *middle class* have come to represent the norm and it is this norm, as it were, that will be exposed by this project. Just as this project stands in opposition to the great importance given to politics, so, too, it will we stand in opposition to the concerns of the middle class living in suburbia and similar kinds of towns."

Adams was startled by the shock of adrenaline he felt at the moment. He was jarred by how convincing Kepstein was and by the thought of creating social change. He felt, though, that he was too sensible to express those feelings. Instead, he matter-of-factly asked, "Why do you want to do this, Bill?"

"Frankly, General, I've made some bad decisions throughout the course of my life. I really never strived to become successful. Rather, it was a life that I was born into, and some of the responsibilities that have come along with this life have kept me awake at night. I've done nothing to further the good of mankind, and I'd like to change my life to one in which I am happy. I want to give something to the world to make up for my, so-far, insignificant past."

"I can understand that," Adams offered. "One of the films I've worked on in the past had a similar undertone, albeit a very different goal. It was the story of a well-known oil family in Saudi Arabia and the disillusionment experienced by two sons in one of those families. I also fully understand your desire to leave a lasting impression on society, one for the good. That is a goal I share with you, Bill."

"I'm glad, then, that we come to the table with a similar understanding," Kepstein said, smiling. "Are there any more questions, General, you need me to answer before everyone gets a chance to tell me how they feel about the project?"

"I'm interested in partnering with you, Bill. I think it's going to be a difficult film to shoot, but if it's done right, it's going to be very successful. And to be honest, if a man comes to me and tells me he wants to make a movie that will change the world AND money is not an option . . . it catches my interest." Adams winked at Kepstein. "I'm taking your word that finances are not an issue. My only concern is that, as I have said, a lot of politics goes into these things, and once the project is made public, the public has control over it. I mean, they will label it, categorize it, group it with similar films, and so forth, whether or not you agree. They will attack the people involved with the film personally, and likely search for details about you and your families. It can get very, very ugly. If anyone at this table has anything — anything at all — to hide, they need to come forward with that information now."

Kepstein took this statement to refer to him and he shook his head "no." Jack mentioned his payoff from the police, but said that if the time were right he'd be OK with allowing the deed to come to light.

"Great," Adams concluded, leaning back in the booth. "With that out of the way, and before we start signing papers, I have about twelve dedicated members of a team I like to use for this type of film. I also have a group of women in Europe who are always willing to assist in a project if it matches their philosophical viewpoint. Perhaps these are matters we can discuss over the phone this week, Bill?"

"That sounds like a great plan. I've also thought about some folks who might be involved with the film. General, I want you to produce this movie. You know how to do it. You have the tools and the people. Lenny, I'd like you to draft the narrative for the screenplay and be responsible for directing the majority of the film. Jack, I'd like you to be the main character. I'm comfortable that you'll be able to work in very unfamiliar settings with people you wouldn't normally interact with and I believe you'll handle it flawlessly. That will be the heart of the film and also a significant part of what will make the film difficult. With my connections, I can get us invited to some very unique gatherings, but it will take your charm and candor, Jack, to convince people to let their guards down. We will need you to get them to say what they're really thinking. That won't be easy, as I know you're not an actor. Perhaps your friend Milo would also be interested in working on this project? Your long history together and rapport could be most helpful."

"I'm sure Milo would be very interested, Bill. I think this could be a very exciting experience for all of us, but also, as General has said, if it's done right, it could be monumental."

"Agreed!" Lenny said, raising his glass and making a toast to one man's dream becoming a shared vision, a vision they could understand, but still had to bring into being.

Chapter Eleven

After the dinner at Kimpo, Jack, Lenny, and Kepstein continued their evening at a small tavern down the street. They were apprehensive, excited, joyous, nervous, confused, drunk, and happy. "So, this is going to happen?" Lenny asked, still a bit shell-shocked.

"This is happening, Lenny." Kepstein said. "Normally, I'd stay out into the wee hours of the morning celebrating, but tonight I think we need to get some rest."

"Why's that?" Jack asked, sounding a bit more disappointed than he had meant to.

"Because tomorrow morning I have to go home and explain it all to my wife."

* * *

After a few hours of driving through different boroughs and neighborhoods of New York City, Jack and Kepstein began their drive south. During the trip, Jack glanced absentmindedly out the window in between naps as Kepstein occasionally glanced at him with pensive curiosity. After Kepstein dropped Jack off at his apartment, he hurried home to see his wife. Although she hadn't objected to his trip to New York, assuming it was business, he still wasn't sure what to expect upon returning. He parked the car in the garage and entered the back door, hoisting his suitcase over the threshold while closing the door behind him.

"Rebecca," Kepstein shouted. "Where are you? Come here, please. I've got a lot of things to tell you. I have so much to explain."

Rebecca was sitting in the living room, leafing through a magazine. She looked up, startled, as her husband entered the room. She hadn't seen such excitement from him in years. Kepstein's eyes looked somehow different to her. In fact, *he* looked different. The sun was still shining, but an early spring dusk was filling the house with subdued shadows.

"I've been thinking about a lot of things lately and I've realized that so much has to change, so many things about the way I live and the way we live and how we communicate with each other — especially the silence! We have got to change some things, Rebecca."

Rebecca couldn't help but notice that her husband was speaking to her as a man speaks to his wife, not as someone who might be greeting a stranger on the sidewalk. As he looked into her eyes, she stared ahead, looking through him, not meeting his desire for contact. She felt aloof, tired and suspicious of his words, thinking that now was just another of those fleeting moments when he feigned concern for her.

"What are you talking about?" she asked caustically, pretending to continue reading her magazine.

"Rebecca," he insisted, "I met a fellow named Jack a few weeks ago at Betriebsnacht, where we got into a good discussion. I've met him a few times, and I spent this weekend with him and some of his colleagues in the film industry in New York City."

113

Kepstein had meant to approach the subject more slowly, but the moment got ahead of him. He stood near his wife and waited to see how she'd respond to what he had just said. She got up from her seat and indicated with one finger her desire that he follow her into the kitchen.

"Bill, please settle down. You seem very excited," Rebecca remarked casually. It was far too early for him to be drunk, she thought, but she'd seen worse.

"I don't need to settle down. In fact, Rebecca, I've settled for far too long. And, no, in case you're wondering, my excitement isn't coming from anything I've had to drink. I'm excited for once with life. I'm excited about the little things we see and do every day, but don't appreciate. I'm excited about the world, you and me and us and them." As he spoke, Kepstein raised and lowered his arms in an almost spasmodic manner, like a bird desperately trying to fly.

"You foolish fuck," Rebecca shouted. She rose from the table and looked out of the window, aware that he was following her closely with his eyes, then sat down on a barstool at the kitchen island. "Do you think it is OK to take a vacation — with whom, and based on what the fuck sort of premise, I have no idea — after all I've been through?"

Kepstein stared out the same window, his mind reeling. He knew Rebecca was right, but he also knew that what he was saying was difficult for her to understand, but he decided to push on.

"I've finally realized, Rebecca, that everything I'd always thought and felt, but never have really expressed, are true. I know that I've made many misguided, wrong turns over the years, but that doesn't mean I still have to live in some prescribed way. I still have time to be who I really am and do whatever it is I feel strongly I want to do. Now's the time, Rebecca, now's the time we tried to make some changes."

He grabbed his wife's hand. "You have to listen . . . you — you have to listen to me, Rebecca. I mean, I know this sounds a little crazy, but —"

"A little crazy, Bill?" Rebecca yanked her hand free. "You come home after a weekend away. I assume you're on business, and yet here you are telling me, 'You're excited about life for once,'" she yelled, making quotation marks with her fingers, "and meeting people in the film industry. And you're trying to explain how you've decided to change your life? What the fuck is going on here?"

"These guys I met, Rebecca —"

"And who exactly are these people, Bill?" she blasted, cutting him short. "I want to know a little more about this Jack guy. I mean, is there really even a Jack or is it some pretty barmaid downtown, or did you get a new secretary who wanted to see Broadway with her big shot boss?"

"I don't want to stir up any sort of argument right now — just the opposite really — you just need to hear me out . . ." Kepstein said, feeling a sense of deflation and as if a lifetime of bad behavior and bad decisions had caught up with him. "You see, I need to explain myself to you. You obviously know everything about me, I mean, but you, see I . . . No, Jack is a real person, and I want to tell you more about him and the group he's a part of."

"Well, if these are all real people, why haven't you told me anything about them before you left town?" she sneered. "This is nonsense!"

"That's a good question, but I assure you there is nothing underhanded going on. Listen, Rebecca, Jack isn't at all what you might imagine him to be. I mean, for one thing, he's younger than me, and a few years younger than you, actually. And believe it or not, he's got nothing to do with the bank. It's more of a social thing really . . . Would you like something to drink? Coffee maybe? I need a glass of water."

"Yes, I would like some coffee."

Rebecca turned on the kitchen lights and grabbed the coffee jar from the pantry. As she did so, she looked back over her shoulder. "You can start explaining now."

Kepstein placed his forearms on the countertop and sat at an island barstool. "What I was saying is, this Jack fellow is a bit younger than me. That's not the most pertinent piece of information, but he is a bit of a fresh air, you know, different from all those stagnant people I work with every day. Jack is in his late twenties, and he has two friends I've met, Milo and Lenny, around the same age."

"Jack, Milo, and . . . who was the last one?"

"Lenny."

"That's right, Lenny. Charming. So, you met these guys, a handful of college kids? What did you guys do, take shots at bars reliving the old

116

days at Columbia? Did you drink into the morning, play Euchre and tell dirty stories? This is bullshit."

"I know it doesn't sound like me, and that's what is so great about it. These aren't the kind of people I usually spend time with, as you're very well aware. And I can see what you are thinking, but I assure you I am not trying to relive my old college days."

"Well, OK . . . What *did* you guys do then?"

Kepstein laughed, even though he knew this wasn't the right time. "I thought you'd never ask!" Sitting back in his chair, he took a drink of water. "The first time we met we didn't do anything special, we just talked. We talked about a lot of things, in fact, some big, some small, the past, the future, the present. It was just really good conversation. It reminded me of the times I used to meet with that old professor of mine, Dr. O'Connell. Do you remember him? John O'Connell?"

"Yes, I remember him, now that you mention it."

"Well, I used to meet him for the same reason I enjoyed this group of guys. You know me, though, I've always liked to talk to people, all sorts of people. You've known that ever since we first met. I can remember you pestering me about it when we went out on dates." Kepstein placed his hand over his mouth and said, mocking his wife, "'Bill, what are you doing talking to the waiter? . . . Why are you so interested in talking to the waiter?' you would say to me at dinner."

Rebecca cracked a smile as Kepstein continued, "But, no, really, I met this Jack fellow after a long day of work. I stopped downtown for a beer and played a few old jazz favorites on the jukebox and, being a jazz enthusiast too, he praised one of my selections and we began making small talk. I realized what an intriguing young man he was, and as we continued to talk about music, I wanted to hear more about him and so I invited him and his friend, Lenny, to Betriebsnacht."

Rebecca sneered at the name of the afterhours club. She was on the brink of rage. "What night was it when you met Jack after work?"

Kepstein's face reddened. He knew that he'd been trapped and that there was no escape. "It was a Friday night a few weeks ago."

"Friday night — the same Friday night we buried my father and you didn't come home?"

"Yes." He took a drink of water, wishing it was something stronger.

"That's nice," Rebecca said, looking intently into Kepstein's face. "You know, you disgust me on so many levels. And yet you think it's all OK. You have your weekend getaways, make new friends, and make some jokes. It's disturbing, really."

"Let's not do this right now, Rebecca. I know your father passed, and I want to . . ." The hostility that was their marriage cluttered his thoughts and the moment's hesitation was enough to make it apparent to both of them. "But I want to be here for you."

"And I'd prefer not to be let down again, Bill. Please, go take a shower, finish your little glass of water, and get yourself together."

Kepstein slowly rose from his seat and began walking upstairs. He felt defeated as he climbed the stairs, continuing his slow pace.

Rebecca and her husband spent the rest of the day on separate floors of the house, Kepstein doing some work in his home office. As the sun was setting, he leaned back in his desk chair, laced his fingers behind his head, and thought about the fact that while he wanted to fix things with his wife, he knew that it was going to be neither easy nor immediate. He believed, though, that there was one way to speed the process up, but it would be a gamble. He walked downstairs to find Rebecca in the living room, idly clicking through TV channels.

"Look, I'm sorry if I've startled you," Kepstein said as he approached his wife. "I didn't mean to. It's just . . . it's just that there really is a lot I want to change, and so many things I want to tell you all at once, you know?"

"I know, I can tell you do. Bill, I am truly flattered by your urgency, but we both know, don't we, that this life we are leading is not what either of us wanted. Our life together depresses me, but I don't think a midlife crisis is the best solution to our problems."

Kepstein bit his tongue. He knew quite well that a fight was coming and that Rebecca wanted to get in a few more jabs, rather that talk to him honestly and openly. But he answered her, nonetheless, "I can't tell you how glad I am that you are interested in hearing me out. I know I can get a bit carried away with things."

The sun was gone by this time. The electric hum in the house reminded both of them that a long time ago they had decided to get married and that, for better or for worse, they were stuck with each together.

"I have an idea, if you'll just promise to at least consider it," Kepstein spoke again.

"I'm not promising you anything," Rebecca answered, staring at the television set.

The rift of emotion and understanding between them was palpable to both of them and as wide as the large living room in which they sat, Rebecca on the couch and Kepstein on the other side of the room, sitting on the edge of a recliner.

"I'm going to make a big change in my life, Rebecca, and I want you to be a part of it."

"You've said the same thing many times, since I've known you. Bill," she snapped coldly. "I'm afraid my answer is no thank you."

Kepstein continued speaking nonetheless. "I met with two screenwriters and one film producer yesterday, and I am thinking rather seriously about working on a movie."

She dropped the TV remote control on the glass coffee table. "You, making a movie?"

"Yes. You know how much I enjoy film and cinema. I've never done anything unique, and I obviously have no lack of funds."

"You're serious?" she asked.

"Yes, by all means I am serious. My life is a joke. You know this," he lowered his voice and muttered, "and your father certainly knew it."

"I thought I told you never to bring his name into conversation again," she said quickly and sternly.

"I've been thinking about that letter he sent me a few weeks ago. In that letter, he called me a coward. He's right, Rebecca. I need to do something meaningful for once, and I want you to be a part of it. I mean it." He searched her face for some reaction. Finding none, he continued, "I'd like you to at least meet Jack and Milo. Perhaps one night this week we can have dinner, or go for drinks or something."

Rebecca paused her channel searching, but still stared straight ahead. "No thanks"

"Please?" Kepstein asked meekly.

Rebecca let out a long and labored sigh. "Not if my life depended on it, Bill. I'll talk to you, alright, but it's as if you're not really there at all. Go ahead for all I care. Have your midlife crisis, hang out with your young friends, take trips on weekends to party and fuck, or gamble or whatever the hell you do. You can —," she paused, "*make your movie*. But, *please*, leave me the hell out of it. In fact, maybe you should go see a psychiatrist before you spend your money and make a fool out of yourself. Then, when you get yourself figured out, maybe then we can talk."

Chapter Twelve

While Kepstein felt that he was gaining ground in terms of his movie project, he still felt stalemated at home. Despite the latter, though, he felt freer than he had in a long time. Day by day any resistance to following a different life path began to subside, and he felt a sense of defiance in the face of his past. He refused to let the past control his future any longer. All the same, he was in finance, and the one comment that Rebecca made that stayed with him was her concern about his wasting all of their money, not in the sense that they had any chance of spending all of their estate's vast holdings, but whether or not his pursuit of his ideals was a good investment in terms of either his time or their capital.

Kepstein agreed with Rebecca. He knew nothing about the film industry. But he was the kind of man who approached the project the way he would any other investment, trying to learn as much as he could about it in as short a period of time as possible.

* * *

Kepstein walked into his office early on a Monday morning. It had been two weeks since he'd dropped the bomb on Rebecca by telling her of his desire to make a movie and do something more rewarding with his life than running a bank. During that time, she had expressed only minimal interest in continuing their initial discussion, but she was, nonetheless, aware that her husband's work schedule had changed. Since the time he told her of his desire, he was leaving earlier for work and getting home on time.

This morning, Kepstein was feeling jubilant as he looked down at the city, a city bursting with green and blue in an Atlantic mid-June morning. Like someone might feel after exercising on a routine basis as a result of a New Year's resolution, he was full of energy, wanting to maintain his momentum.

"Lenny, how do you do?" Kepstein asked, calling Lenny a few minutes before lunch.

"Hi, Bill, I'm doing well, thank you. How about yourself?"

"Good, Lenny. I know I asked you to consider writing some of the plot and settings for the proposed film when we met with Mr. Adams. And I know I haven't sent to you any form of payment. I understand it's not appropriate to ask someone to work for free, but I want to assure you that you'll definitely be compensated."

"Sure, sure," Lenny said, wanting to put Kepstein at ease.

"At this time, Lenny, what I am trying to do is understand what this project will entail, from a resources standpoint, you know."

"Yes, of course I understand that — it's a huge undertaking you're considering here." Lenny thought about projects he'd worked on in the past and how sources of funding had been derailed in one situation or another. "How did your wife take your news, if I might ask?"

"To be honest with you, she assumes that I'm having a midlife crisis. Hell, even I wonder that myself from time to time."

"Meh," Lenny muttered, "it doesn't matter what term or label you give to what men do with their lives, it's their way of doing things, the descriptors don't have any real importance."

"How do you mean?"

"Like if I can't find any work, and start taking on two-bit commercials and providing video service for online advertisements, people will say I am, quote-unquote, desperate."

"Mm-hmm."

"But what difference does the word 'desperate' mean to me? Does it change what I do? No. Is it necessary to do these kinds of things so I can pay my bills and enrich my knowledge and experience base? Yes. So, what do I care."

"Good points, Lenny . . . So, are you feeling desperate enough to take on this *crazy project*?" Kepstein laughed.

"No, no. I would describe this one more as exciting and promising," Lenny said, returning the light-hearted banter. "And those are words I don't mind using!"

Lenny went on to explain some of his thoughts about the film. He'd started to draft out simple plots and courses for the film to take. He started with a draft of an opening and a close, with loose direction in between as he assumed Kepstein had his own ideas about what to put in the middle and, indeed, he was correct, as Kepstein had been keeping track of his thoughts for a number of years, not months. In the depths of his memory, Kepstein had been cataloguing bits and parts of the world around him he'd taken issue with. Now he was finding a practical way of disseminating those thoughts.

* * *

Over the next few weeks, the project began in earnest. Kepstein and Jack spoke with each other on a regular basis, then relayed a distilled version of their conversations to Lenny, who, in turn, was taking their ideas and creating different scenarios that were to be the heart of the film. Jack began to involve Milo more and more in the project, further reviewing his discussions with Kepstein and Lenny with Milo and asking him for his feedback and his ideas.

Because Jack and Lenny were, essentially, unemployed, they acted as intermediaries between Kepstein and General Adams. Lenny's role was to take Jack and Kepstein's ideas and continue to turn them into a screenplay that could be produced by Adams.

One afternoon, seated at a small, round table overlooking 44th St. and enjoying coffee, Lenny and Adams were sorting through the plots that Lenny had been developing for the screenplay. Reviewing the notes, Adams exclaimed, "Lenny, this city is filled with relics of the past, ancient artisans of the craft, and you are a breath of fresh air, my friend!"

"You're a flatterer, General," Lenny replied, beaming. "The draft still needs a lot of work and I'm sort of going at it blindly, you know, flying by the seat of my pants as it were."

"Well you're flying high and in the right direction, Lenny. This is good stuff. Take this for example," he said, pointing to a headline on page 108, "Tennessee Valley Authority and Balkans Oil Pipeline. Can you imagine the cinematography of this scene! Shooting panoramic views of open lands before and after the dams, or before and after the pipelines. This is going to be monumental, Lenny. I'm not saying the US water distribution plan is the best model in the world, but the chance to discuss local subsidies and stories of successes or failures with the locals and then to even suggest a comparison with a South European oil pipeline is fascinating. We could make a movie on that basis alone, but to think! It will be just one small chapter in this beautiful story."

* * *

"Hi, Rebecca." Kepstein was changing out of his slacks and into his pajamas as his wife walked into the bedroom. "How has your day been?"

She walked past him into the bathroom without replying. Turning on a faucet, she looked back, appearing to Kepstein to have a coquettish look on her face. "It was nice, actually. Elsa came by to gather the laundry and we decided to go out for lunch to Simon's. It was nice to get out of the house."

"That does sound nice. How is Elsa these days?"

"She's good. Her son, Marco, is being picked for a soccer scholarship in Connecticut. We had a margarita to celebrate."

"A margarita?" Kepstein exclaimed.

Rebecca smirked at the surprise in his voice as she turned off the water. She walked back into the bedroom. "Yes, a margarita. You're not the only one that gets to have fun during the day." In fact, she had a total of three margaritas that afternoon and was fairly drunk as she moved towards the bed, thrusting her breasts out as she pulled her shirt over her head. "Speaking of which, how are things going with your little playmates in the film business?"

Watching Rebecca, Kepstein felt himself becoming aroused. At the same time, though, sensing an opportunity to plead his case, he ignored her sarcasm and told her, "Well, things are going well with my *little playmates*, if you must know. In fact, Lenny has made real strides in getting a manuscript together for a screenplay. I've been working with him and Jack."

"Wow, you're really serious about this, aren't you?" she asked, turning on the lamp on the bed stand and talking over her shoulder.

"I am. I need to do something, and I'm happy with the progress so far. I've been working with a director slash producer in New York. He's got over twenty-five years of experience in the business, and right now we're working out feasibility studies. It looks like the project's completely doable, aside from my binding responsibilities here."

"Here at home?" she asked, half-concerned and half-joking. Earlier that day, she had received advice from Elsa to confront any problems in her marriage with the use of seduction. At this moment, Rebecca was trying Elsa's suggestion, but she realized that it had been too long since seduction played any part in her marriage and she felt herself holding back.

"No silly, at the bank. People — investors — take everything I do so seriously. Any change on my part puts the bank, and its profitability, in jeopardy."

"Do you think the project is worth it?"

"I do, yes." Kepstein turned on the lamp on his side of the king size bed. He took out the newspaper that he hadn't read that day and settled under the sheets.

"Rebecca, I don't know what will come of all this, but I've already felt that I've begun to change. I just don't give a shit anymore what others think and I'm going to do what I need to do for myself, but in a responsible, and systematic way. And I'll say it again — I understand what things are like, here, with us. Of course I'm aware of that. Just as I am beginning to sense most of the problems in the world, I know, too, that the problems between us are due to gaps in communication. What we need to do is communicate better."

"That is what the marriage counselor said five years ago, Bill, right before you stormed out of the room." Rebecca pulled the sheets over her shoulder, turned her back to him, and turned out the light, leaving Kepstein with his thoughts.

129

* * *

That same weekend, on a different side of the city, Milo and Jack were enjoying Sunday brunch at Mel's on 7th. It was a ritual they'd kept alive as often as possible for nearly half a decade. It was a way for them to maintain at least one sense of normalcy and constancy as things changed around them. They found Mel's to be a relaxing setting where they could catch up on what was happening in their lives, sip mimosas at noon, and discuss different philosophies or books they'd been reading. Jack had his free time and Milo his inviolate principles of self-improvement; both were always reading. That day, the sky was grey and the two friends felt as if a state of melancholy, the seemingly preferred state on a Baltimore June day when the summer was heating up, was being challenged.

"Jack, do you remember when you got in trouble a few years ago? When you had to go to those classes and the AA meetings for a few months?"

"Of course I remember that — what a strange question. Why do you ask?"

"I got around to thinking about something. As you know, I went to a few of those meetings in my wilder days as well." Milo looked at Jack as only a best friend could. "I was thinking about this movie project. It's preposterous, really, but I'm not the type to put off something exciting, let alone crazy. I can't stop thinking about the ideas behind the movie, and it's not difficult, for we all try to communicate, don't we?"

"Yes, we do, old friend! Have you gone off track already?" Jack chuckled, taking a sip of his beverage and looking at Milo inquisitively.

"Piss off, Jack. Ass," Milo joked, grinning. "Like I was saying, talking with you and Lenny, these ideas are circulating in my head, and the more all of us talk and think about them, the more I think about different experiences I've had that have to do with these ideas. For example, I was thinking about those AA meetings. I mean, people really get personal at those meetings and dive into some very deep shit, with total strangers. I was thinking about how and why that kind of thing might work if it were done distantly — you know, over the web for example."

"What's the point of that? The benefit of those meetings is in getting to know people in your area so that you can feel supported and, not to be trivial, but a lot of the guys I've met at those meetings might not be so computer savvy anyhow."

"Bingo!" Milo exclaimed, so loudly that a group of pigeons flew from the sidewalk. "That's where it gets interesting, buddy. I came to the same conclusion and then I started thinking, why not create that sort of platform for people who *do* use web conferencing, but who also want the real-life benefits of having neighbors?"

"What do you mean by the 'benefit of neighbors'?" Jack asked, holding his fingers up in quotations.

"Well, typically one of several things, I'd imagine," Milo answered quickly. "Support, love, or finance. Just think what it could mean if somehow that type of platform was available for people who wanted to talk to

131

strangers about serious matters that were outside of their respective professions or classrooms. For example, what if people wanted to discuss a French film with real Frenchmen, or if real Frenchmen wanted to talk about rock 'n roll with American musicians?"

"That's interesting, Milo. Would you want the conversation, though, to be open or closed? I mean public or private? Like chat rooms, you know. They've been around since we were kids. I know you remember those days when the Internet first came out."

Milo laughed hysterically. "Yes, I remember chat rooms, but I hadn't thought about what you just said — the open or closed nature."

"Think of a private, virtual meeting place for intellectuals, Milo! A place that was invitation only and where you had to possess certain qualities in order to be accepted into it. Men and women from around all the globe would be tied together by the simple pursuit of knowledge."

"Crazy, but I love it! Just imagine . . ." Milo looked contemplatively over the steaming manholes and across the empty city street, then back towards Jack. "The only requirement for entry would be the desire to use your mind and talents for a purpose other than your weekly paycheck. That requirement alone would bring about some rather exciting discussions — think of it — architects talking with poets about how to create emotional responses for a public park being funded by a philanthropist, or philanthropists asking Syrian refugees how someone in the 21st century should spend their billions. Ideas could spread quickly, Jack, very quickly indeed!"

"Milo!" Jack exclaimed, jumping up from his chair, its legs making a piercing shriek on the concrete. "I think I get what he's trying to do! I mean I think I get whatever Kepstein's goal or aim is!"

Milo waited silently as long as he could, then placed both hands open-palmed on either side of the table and sat on the edge of his seat in genuine anticipation. "What is it then, man, c'mon already!"

"What makes those AA meetings work? Is it making sure that homeless alcoholics only meet with homeless alcoholics, or wealthy repentant businessmen only talk about their drinking issues with other wealthy repentant businessmen? No, it's not. You never know who might show up at a meeting. Perhaps it's the businessman hearing from the homeless drunkard, realizing for the first time the direction his life is headed, or perhaps the homeless man sees that he still has a chance of salvation and can end up like the successful businessman with the twenty-year token. Or perhaps it's neither of these, but the simple realization that in the end we're all the same and we all have our struggles and strife. It's the basic realization of shared existence that keeps people going." Jack was pacing back and forth in figure eights in front of the table, his hands in his pockets and his eyes darted directly towards the ground as if he were searching for something missing.

"There's no animosity in these meetings. Instead, people leave them feeling cleansed and generally aware of what's going on within them and around them. Imagine if we enabled that kind of interaction among people! Say we put a camera in a waiting room at St. Jude's Children's Hospital and allowed moms in America to talk to moms in North Korea who also have children with terminal cancer. Let people talk about how they love their boys and girls, instead of talking about treatments and governments. Let people who are fighting for a higher minimum wage speak with those who make less than one dollar a day. Just consider what that might mean in terms of people becoming more aware of, and empathic with, each other."

"Wow," Milo said, feeling things click for the first time. He was staring at the table between them, finishing his cup of coffee and then looking up again at his friend. "We're discussing fascinating — what is the word? Concepts. But a concept is a difficult thing to put on film, my friend. You know this. While the concept we're discussing is important, everything we've ever discussed has been important, but this is the first time we actually have access to someone who can help us materialize our thoughts into something real. But the question still is, how can we take these thoughts and put them into a film?"

"Maybe we're looking at this the wrong way, Milo," Jack replied, exhaling deeply and sitting back down. "Maybe what we are talking about is already taking place throughout the world, but in small groups. What if the real trick is to uncover those groups and show them on film, and in some way suggest that this shows that there is a potential for this kind of dialogue throughout the world?"

* * *

Lenny now began to play another role in the making of the film. He was a major resource for tracking down the kinds of groups and discussions that Jack and Milo had talked about and he would review and comment on ideas sent to him from Baltimore. For example, in thinking over Milo's idea

134

for intellectual video-chat services, he responded, "Of course you must know about the renaissance poets of NYU's Viral Virtual Village. They do this type of thing all the time, bouncing emails and conversations back and forth throughout Europe to anyone who will listen to them. I know a guy who helped start the organization . . ." Then he'd connect Milo and Jack with his contact at the Virtual Village, resulting in the development of a scene that could be part of the film before finally taking it to Kepstein for review. Then, once he had gathered together everyone's thoughts and translated them into scenes for the movie, he would present them to General Adams, who, in turn, would develop a concrete plan for shooting the scenes. Kepstein kept in close contact with both Lenny and General Adams during the process, his enthusiasm growing in proportion to the budget. Any hesitations he had felt from a financial point disappeared as the project's scope grew and concepts became reality.

Chapter Thirteen

While modern technology has made communication more convenient, some matters require direct human interaction. Despite the availability of telephones and email, businessmen and businesswomen still fly around the world to make a deal. Kepstein understood this and was returning to Baltimore after a meeting in New York. He'd been drinking with General Adams and a handful of investors at an upper west side condominium where there was a catered lunch and lively discussion.

Rebecca was aware of this trip, going so far as to wish him good luck as he left the house that morning. While it wasn't an outpouring of emotion, but rather a mumbled expression of goodwill, the gesture meant a great deal to him, and he thought about it all the way home.

While Kepstein was away in New York, Rebecca spent the day shopping with Elsa. As they enjoyed lunch and drinks that afternoon, Elsa shared her thoughts about the Kepstein's marriage with Rebecca. In particular, she said that she believed that the reason that Rebecca was angry with her husband was because he wasn't doing anything for her.

"He does everything for me," Rebecca had answered. "I don't work, you know that."

"This same thing has been going on since the beginning of time," Elsa replied. "You lost the spark in your marriage and it's been cold between the two of you for some time. You may read books, watch TV, or listen to songs together, Rebecca, but that's not enough. There are other things that keep a man and a woman together . . . I call them Elsa's three S's: safety, stability, and sex. You have the first two, but you are missing the third. So is Bill."

Rebecca blushed, wondering whether or not what Elsa was saying was true. Then she asked herself if she and her husband were still attracted to each other. She hadn't considered him in a sexual way for some time, as any other ways of feeling were clouded with the familiar animosity she felt towards him. With his recent pleading for understanding from her, however, she found herself, even if a bit reluctantly, feeling turned on by what she took to be a change in a usually cold and pompous man. In some sense, what she saw as his new-found humbleness made him seem more approachable and attainable. But she questioned whether or not she was still attractive to him, realizing that this thought had not occurred to her for a long time.

Hearing Rebecca talk aloud about her concerns, Elsa had said, "He's been watching you, Rebecca, I'm telling you. I've known you both for a long time now and I know that look. He's been watching you when he comes home. You need to make him need you — not want, but *need* you."

* * *

Rebecca heard her husband pulling into the driveway. Elsa's incessantly friendly banter and several glasses of wine that afternoon had left Rebecca feeling tipsy. She had started chili in the slow cooker immediately after he had left for the meeting, using Elsa's secret recipe. It was Kepstein's favorite dish and she was excited to surprise him. She opened the backdoor when she heard him fumble with his keys. "Here, let

137

me help you with your briefcase," she said, reaching for it and catching his eye.

"No, no thank you, I've got it," Kepstein said, smiling, and it was obvious to him that his wife was in high spirits.

Although it was a recent and abrupt development, it seemed to Rebecca her husband was changing in some way. As Kepstein approached her in the kitchen, he was amazed by her mood. She returned to her cooking, looking beautiful and beaming to him as she stood with one hand on a ladle pretending to be surprised that he had come home right in the middle of her cooking. She was surprised how confident she had felt that he would arrive home on time and not spend the weekend away from her doing something reckless. As Kepstein removed his jacket, he was aware that the house smelled amazing. The windows were open and the fireplace was crackling. Although it was summer, he felt the charming scent of oak hanging in the air. The sounds of Slim Harpo were coming from the Bose stereo tucked under the kitchen cabinet, Rebecca tapping her foot to the blues rhythm.

"How did your meeting go?" she asked, bending over so she could pick up his briefcase. "Did it go well?"

Rebecca was wearing an old college sweatshirt, the front of which had been torn slightly so that when she bent over Kepstein could not help but notice her breasts, free and unconstrained by a bra, a liberty she allowed herself at home that he'd always loved. And as if that weren't enough to make him happy after his long drive, she was wearing a pair of shorts that exposed the ends of her butt. He felt his blood warm as he realized she was

138

enticing him with her body and her kindness, seducing him, as it were, with food, fragrance, and lust.

He moved closer. "Yes, it is very good — I mean, yes, the meeting went very good. Well, it went well."

"That's great news," Rebecca said with a sly charity, standing up and taking his briefcase to the hallway closet. *Elsa was correct,* she thought, *I can control him.*

"Yes, it was great news. I think we have lots to talk about, and is that chili I smell?" He took a long, overdramatic inhalation, then returned his gaze to Rebecca. "It smells amazing . . . and you look great in those shorts!"

"Oh, Bill, give it a rest."

"I mean it! To hell with how the meeting went, you're so sexy in those shorts and that cutoff."

"Yes, it is chili," Rebecca said, winking. "But truly, I'm happy to hear that the meeting went well. It was with the producer, right?"

"Yes, a fellow named Mr. Adams. I met with a few investors who'd worked with him in the past. We signed documents of privacy, and I know this will sound crazy, but we had to meet in darkness — lights were off and the blinds were drawn the entire time!"

"Pardon me?"

"Yes, I knew some of them and they'd certainly known me, so the reason for the darkness was to maintain privacy. I know it all sounds bizarre, but I have to make sure everything is legitimate."

"I see."

"Come, let's sit on the porch for a moment, can we." He took a bottle of white wine from the cooler and two glasses from the cupboard.

Rebecca sat on the swing, wondering how far her husband was going to take this midlife crisis. She wanted to have another glass of wine, but knew she could miss something important her husband might be saying to her.

"Before you tell me about your meeting," Rebecca said, "let's start from the beginning. Who is this friend of yours again, Jack?"

Kepstein was preparing to explain the life of loafing that Jack had adopted when he realized his wife's likely reaction, so he decided to skirt around the subject, much like Jack had done the night of their first meeting.

"Jack writes for a few local papers as well as the *Baltimore Sun* and he's working on a script for Lenny right now. Lenny works in New York in the film business. Then there's their mutual friend, Milo, who is the kind of guy that's worked about fifty different jobs. Right now he's an electrician, working on a handful of high rises downtown.

"You know me, Rebecca. You've heard my bellyaching for years, and you know that ever since I was a kid I've wanted to do something different. I've been shuffled into this whole banking business out of respect for my father, God bless him, but things are different now, and I'm starting to think that maybe I should spend a little more time pleasing myself instead of everyone else."

Rebecca looked into her husband's eyes with compassion and gently set her glass on the table. "I have to admit this is the most I've heard about anything other than work in a long time. I don't know how to describe it, other than to say it does my heart good to see you so honestly excited about something. Bill, listen. I love you, you know that I do, and I want you to be as happy as you can possibly be."

As Rebecca spoke, it was becoming obvious to her that her husband wanted to recapture what little bit of youth he had left, and it was clear, she thought, that this was the underlying reason for his newly-found friends twenty years his junior. She believed he was going through a stage every man goes through and decided to help him through the changes. She reasoned that his pleasure in spending time with a younger crowd was due to a lack of companionship during his youth and that his desire to do something drastic and new was a way to escape a reality that felt brutal to him. And, like any man his age, he would attempt to escape that reality by behaving irrationally, spontaneously, and childishly.

"How about we go out tomorrow night," she said, "and you can tell me all about it? We'll be able to discuss everything over dinner, and maybe a few cocktails afterwards if you'd like. That way we could have a better talk, and I could probably understand everything you're telling me much more easily. Right now, I think you need to rest. You look haggard."

With a gentle nod, Kepstein agreed, pleased by the suggestion, but also surprised by her rationality. He placed his half-empty glass on the ground, looked into his wife's eyes, noticing also that she was biting her lip.

"You know I'll be behind you, whatever it is that you're going to do," Rebecca said.

"You know what I'd like, Rebecca? I'd like you to meet everyone I've been talking about. I can see if Jack and the others can make it Friday night. We could go for drinks."

"I'd love that," she agreed, surprisingly comfortable with the idea.

"Great! And there's one last thing I have to mention, while I've caught you in a 'yes' mood," he answered, winking. "There's also been some discussion about my needing to relocate to New York City."

Rebecca picked up her glass of wine, drained it, then refilled her glass. She took another sip, then turned to face Kepstein. "How far are you going to take this?"

"As far as it has to go, Rebecca. I want — no I need — for you to be a part of this." He took her hands. "I cannot do this alone."

"Bill, I can't do this. I don't know what's gotten into you." She had reached her limit. Her husband's assumption that he could off-handedly bring up relocating their home vexed her. She became quiet and stared straight ahead.

Kepstein and Rebecca sat silently together for some time. Then Kepstein spoke. "Please, Rebecca, just meet these guys and at least consider the idea. If you can't be part of this, I'll call the whole thing off. You and our marriage mean more to me than anything. I want both our marriage and my sense of what is really important to me to improve at the same time, and I think that will happen because of my being involved in this project. Please." He looked into her eyes, desperately attempting to convey to her all the sincerity and passion he felt at that moment.

* * *

When she thought about it later, Rebecca felt strangely excited by the idea of a night out with her husband and his friends. She'd been surprised to learn how much time and energy Kepstein had put into his project so far. And she realized that what she had labeled as a simple midlife crisis was actually her husband's battle cry against his worst adversary — himself. She remembered the tension in his voice as he spoke to her about his project and seeing his passion stirred a feeling of lust in her that she hadn't known for years.

When Kepstein came home early from work on the day of the night out, Rebecca approached him in the kitchen. "There is something I need to get off my chest, Bill."

"What's that, Rebecca?"

"I'm awfully nervous about tonight."

"What could you possibly be nervous about?" he asked softly, putting his hand on her shoulder.

She stared out the living room window. "I believe I know why you enjoy spending time with these men. Although you haven't mentioned it outright, I imagine they're eccentrics or intellectual types or something. In some way, I assume that it's your peculiar love for these bizarre topics and conversation that keeps you interested."

Kepstein started to speak, but his wife continued before he had a chance.

"And further, I feel like you might be feeling compelled to do this because you can't have these types of conversations with me. While some men run off with younger women, for God knows what reason, my husband spends time in conversations with eccentric men."

Kepstein was stunned by his wife's comments. "Well, Rebecca, I've never wanted a wife that could talk about the many things I like to talk about — in fact, it would be weird if you did. All I've ever wanted is for you to have an openness to learning and understanding what I find so interesting."

"I know that, Bill . . ." she replied, her lip quivering, "but you've never really given me the chance. And I've always felt that you cut me short when I tried to understand things."

Kepstein didn't have the heart to admit that his wife was right. He embraced her, offering unspoken apologies for his actions of the past years. Rebecca's warm embrace told him, in turn, that their differences could make them stronger and shouldn't have to separate them. In that moment, they shared a mutual acceptance of each other.

"Well, you look beautiful," Kepstein said as they ended their embrace. "You are my darling wife and it is going to be a spectacular evening. I can feel it! I can't wait to see the new dress you bought."

"Well, today is your lucky day," Rebecca replied, making a small curtsey. "You will be the very first to see it."

"I'm excited . . . and I feel very lucky." he said, eyeing his wife's body.

"Do you now?" she answered with a flirtatious grin, bumping her hips into his and biting her lips seductively. "I suppose we probably should think about getting ready. What time did you say we need to meet the others?"

"We'll meet at Betriebsnacht between eight and eight-thirty. We still have plenty of time. It's only a little after six now."

"A little after six! You know how I am about getting ready!"

"Oh yes, believe me I know. We'll be lucky to get there by midnight," he joked. "I suppose we could probably save a good bit of time by showering together or — or better yet, by taking a bath?"

"You've always been a smart man when it comes to timing. You pick out what to wear this evening and I'll start running some warm bath water." She grabbed his crotch and turned to go upstairs. He hadn't been kissed or touched by his wife in that way for nearly two years. A deluge of pleasure coursed through his body as he recalled their lost fondness and togetherness and Rebecca's remarkable sexual prowess.

Kepstein was now drunk with lust. He gazed into the bedroom mirror, trying to decide which shirt to wear with what pants. He was mesmerized by the reflection of his wife, undressing in the bathroom doorway. She caught him looking at her and began to undress more slowly, taking each article of clothing off a little more seductively as she went along, arm by shimmering arm, leg by lustrous leg. When she only had her panties on, Kepstein hastily ripped off his shirt, pants, and socks. At the bathroom doorway, he was met with the sight of his naked wife Rebecca bending over the tub.

"I'm so wet, Bill," she said as she rubbed herself between the legs. He rushed towards her and they passionately embraced. Rebecca spun around and her husband set her body on the edge of the tub, then dropped to his knees. She wrapped her legs around his shoulders, arching her back and letting herself go.

Kepstein's tongue experienced a taste that he realized he'd been missing for far too long. Rebecca felt a sensation she'd thought might be gone forever and she came again and again. She then returned the favor by taking him into her mouth and her body. She was in the tub of hot water, her husband hovering above her. As she enjoyed every inch of him, she stared intently into his eyes. He experienced this gesture as one of submission, one that he had earned by respecting her, and felt himself release inside her.

146

But their passion for each other was not over at that point. Feeling more desirous of her husband than she had in God knew how long, she stood up in the tub, turned around, and asked him for more as they enjoyed acting out fantasies and experiencing pleasures that they hadn't shared for years.

As their passion spent itself, Rebecca noticed her wrinkled fingers and realized how long they'd been playing in the water. "Bill, I think we may have lost track of time," she said, her cheeks glowing as she stepped out of the tub and wrapped a towel around her head.

"You might be right, but if that's how we lose track of time, who needs it anyway?"

"Oh, I agree. I just don't want to be late the first time I meet new people — your new friends!"

"That's not a problem at all. I can assure you they're an understanding bunch, and very easily entertained. Besides, I wouldn't have traded a second of this for anything in the world. You are . . . amazing."

"You're not so bad yourself either, hotshot. I didn't know you were thirty years old again."

"Ha! I didn't either. You bring out the best in me, it seems. I feel like a million bucks."

"Well, good, I feel more like ten million. But you better stop pestering me and get dressed! I have a lot of work to do, you know. This face doesn't paint itself."

Kepstein made his way into the bedroom and tried a second time to pick out his wardrobe for the evening. As he floated about the room, he began whistling the classic John Coltrane piece, *Naima*, then played the album version, its opening horn conjuring up a sense of excitement as he recalled the night months ago when he'd first met Jack and Lenny.

Chapter Fourteen

Kepstein and Rebecca left the house at nine-thirty, stepping gracefully into the summer night air under an array of luminous stars. They looked like stars themselves and were dressed to kill, as any well-to-do American couple might be on a Friday or Saturday evening in the Northeast summer. They were curiously infatuated with one another, feeling as if years had melted away. Rebecca drifted behind her husband as he opened every door for her with chivalrous embellishment. As the car started, Rebecca grabbed Kepstein between the legs to let him know that he was still the powerful man whom she'd always adored. In return, he kissed her to let her know she was still the object of his admiration.

On their way home from the evening with Jack and Milo, Rebecca realized that although her husband was not crazy, she believed that he was trending in that direction. She saw that his new friends had become his de facto business partners in a project that would most likely throw their lives into a state of complete chaos. She accepted all of this, though, with unquestioned benevolence, for she did not care what her husband did as long as he continued to behave the way he had for the past couple of weeks, and especially that evening in the bathroom.

Lying in bed in the dark, Rebecca turned toward her husband. "I guess I didn't realize how serious you were about this movie business. How much does something like that cost? How hard is it to do? Is it really possible?"

"It is something big, Rebecca. To be honest, though, spending the money and putting in all the time and effort is not much of a decision for me — I've already decided this has to be done. I can't go on with my life as it is right now. Working at the bank is not fulfilling for me and I'm convinced that I can use my resources for a greater good. After meeting with Mr. Adams, I realized not only that the project's feasible, but also that my ideas might have great appeal to a broad viewer base."

"That's important, Bill," Rebecca said softly, rubbing the hair from Kepstein's forehead. "You need to have a great deal of public interest if you want to make a hit at the box office, I suppose?"

Kepstein laughed. "Oh, I don't know about the box office. Everything about this is new to me. I think it could also be a great change for both of us . . . There are a few issues that trouble me, though, Rebecca. The producer, Mr. Adams, mentioned that there would probably be some form of repercussions as a result of carrying out this kind of project. When the word gets out that an old banker turns social-scientist-film-producer, people are most likely going to start searching for details about our lives, looking at our family histories and anything we've done in the past, looking for things that we're not proud of."

"What are you going to do about that?" she asked. "The backlash of that information becoming public could lead to serious consequences. Lawsuits, imprisonment, or . . . worse."

"Adams made one thing very clear. For this film to succeed, it's going to have to be done within a pretty strict atmosphere of secrecy, and due to the high-profile nature of the bank, I'm going to have to distance myself from Fidelity Sworn. There's no other way. That's why the project will be headquartered in New York City."

Confused, stunned, and overwhelmed by her emotions and this new information, Rebecca said nothing.

"What do you think, Rebecca?" Kepstein asked gently.

"Rebecca," he repeated. "I honestly can't do this without you. If you have any reservations, say so and I'll put an end to all of this."

"I don't know. It's scary to think about, but at the same time, this is our life."

"I can't stay here if I am working on this film, and I can't stay at the bank. There is only one option —"

"We have to leave," Rebecca said, softly finishing his sentence.

"I think so," Kepstein agreed. After a moment's pause, he continued, "I have thought about who might substitute for me in my duties at the bank and have created a short list of possibilities. I think Kenneth Blackstone would be the one most likely to take my place."

"He's a smart man, and probably your closest ally at the bank — good choice, I'd say, from what I know of him." She was drifting into much needed sleep.

"Right. He's loyal, smart, and knows how to keep quiet if it's to his benefit."

"You're serious, aren't you, Bill? I have to admit, I think the idea of moving to New York is very exciting, but what about our house and our life here?"

Kepstein answered all of Rebecca's questions as they drifted into their dreams: they had no friends and family to speak of in Baltimore and what they had to gain would be personal, spiritual, and self-fulfilling, while any losses they experienced would only be of a monetary nature.

Rebecca slept deeply and awoke the next morning with the realization that a tremendous change in their lives was underway. Her husband had experienced a metamorphosis over the past month and what Rebecca had assumed was just a midlife crisis was starting to take on the proportions of a sea change that would alter their lives, a change that took on a new meaning for her when Kepstein started talking about leaving the bank. That had never been discussed before and introduced a new level of seriousness to his actions. As far as she was concerned, leaving the bank had always been a non-option, never to be thought of until he retired.

* * *

Kepstein contacted Adams and Lenny often in the days that followed in order to formalize how they would work together on the project, and with each passing day and his frequent calls to New York, he fell more in love with its reasons for coming into being. Like an entrepreneur with a sure-fire business plan, he was convinced that the project was pure brilliance.

Kepstein had a lot to think about and his diligence regarding his work at the bank suffered. He knew he would miss working at the bank, but he also knew that it was time to let go.

"Kenneth," he said one morning, speaking into his intercom, "I'd like you to come up to my office if you've got a minute."

"I'll be right up, Bill."

In a few minutes, Kenneth knocked on Kepstein's door.

"It's open. Come in, please." Kepstein greeted Kenneth in the center of the room and motioned for him to take a seat on the couch near the window. "Kenneth, I've got a lot to tell you in the next few minutes, so it'd be good for us to have a scotch while we get down to business."

"OK," Kenneth said, trying to appear casual, but feeling the lump in his throat.

"I've been running this bank ever since I graduated college, Kenneth. It's been a fine time, but now it's my turn to enjoy the fruits of my labor. Rebecca and I have been talking about taking a vacation — a long vacation. Of course, I can't just leave the bank unattended, so I'm going to leave it under your care, Kenneth, as the CEO. We don't know how long we will be gone, but during that time I will be meeting with financial interests from around the world."

"Financial interests from around the world?" Kenneth asked.

"Yes. We're living in a global economy and I'd like to better understand how it works on more of a regional, micro level . . . What do you say?"

"It's certainly unconventional, Bill, but — "

"No, Kenneth. What do you say about transitioning to CEO?" Kepstein said with a congenial finality.

"It'd be the best news I've ever heard," Kenneth answered as he grinned uncontrollably.

"Good. It's a deal then," Kepstein said, shaking his old friend's hand. "I know you can be diplomatic when necessary, and that's how this situation needs to be handled. A lot of people are going to ask a lot of questions after I make the announcement and you will have to answer their questions without saying anything specific. I am going to purposefully keep you in the dark as to my whereabouts. I need peace and quiet, Ken. You understand, don't you?"

"Whatever you say, boss — you tell me what you need me to do and I will do it. End of story. So, when do you plan to make this announcement?"

"Next Monday. A few of our most important contacts and clients will come to the bank, so we'll need to prep them until then. Please keep this between you and your wife for now, and get some rest with your family this weekend. Come Monday, it's going to be a wild ride for you . . . at least for a while."

Kenneth stuck to his end of the bargain, but with contracts being signed, and terms of employment being adjusted, rumors leaked out. Kepstein's meeting with him had been on Tuesday. By Thursday, the news of his planned disappearing act had spread through the bank and across the regional financial industry like a tidal wave. Overnight, the bank lost numerous accounts and hundreds of thousands of dollars in investments. What had not been expected, though, was that the bank also gained new accounts at the same rate, if not faster. Such a stir of curiosity had been created that everyone in the Northeast financial sector spoke of it and wondered what Kepstein could possibly be planning, the rumors building up to the point of alarm, as if no one cared any longer if there were some form of conspiracy or who the conspirators were, just that something unknown and questioning was taking place.

* * *

It was a rainy afternoon on the first of July when ten associates whom Kepstein had known for decades and whom he considered to be friends walked past Jolene's desk, each one hoping to read something in her eyes that could give them a reason for being called in to the snap meeting. They entered the conference room adjacent to Kepstein's office and sat down at a conference table, wishing they could eat the food that had been catered in for the gathering and that looked delicious, but they felt too nervous to do so. Instead, they cursed their empty, churning stomachs, drank hot coffee, and listened to Kepstein's words with attentiveness.

"You are my closest and most valuable relationships in the financial community," Kepstein began, "and that is why I have asked you to come here today. As you know, it's been a rough few years for our industry as a whole, and likely the good days will still be behind us for some time to come. Yet I am sure that many of you understand the nature of change that is affecting our industry, and I have, as I am sure many of you have, determined that certain steps must be taken to avert loss . . ."

Kepstein paused and looked into what he saw as ten stone cold faces.

"I will not hide anything from you," he continued, "and will be clear about my intentions. Within the next two weeks, I will be taking a leave of office. I will be embarking on a tour of the world unmatched even by the diplomats of our White House. I believe that the financial trust of the world that has been held so carefully in our hands for the last century will be changing hands and will soon be held by various governments around the globe. This planet's inhabitants believe, blindly or not, that this is the best course of action. There will be no stopping public opinion, so my desire is not to stop it, but rather to be in a position to influence it with all my might. It is an, 'If you can't beat 'em, join 'em' way of doing business and while I don't like it, I understand it, and I do not want to be left holding an empty bag when the current way of doing business fails. I have meetings planned with governmental heads of state, as well as corporate heads of finance, throughout the world. I'm unable to divulge any of the names of the people or the places that I plan to visit, but I assure you that my labor will not be fruitless. There are things that need to be discussed and certain, sensitive topics that need to be explained properly if we are to maintain our status in the financial world. Your money — your investments — in my bank will multiply, I assure you. Because of my father and his father, I am able to maintain certain connections, and it is through those connections that I am able to assure you of this . . . That is all. I thank you for coming and I look forward to watching your investments continue to be profitable."

Although what Kepstein had told them wasn't necessarily what they had expected, the meeting attendees agreed that Kepstein's knowledge was superior to theirs and that his decision and opinions should not be questioned. If he said it was necessary to travel across the world for however long — he provided no time frame — then that was what was necessary and there was no space for questions or disagreements.

As Kepstein had expected, after leaving the meeting the men quickly reached for their phones and began to schedule calls and request emails be sent to the appropriate people. Throughout that afternoon, word spread rapidly and the ticker on the stock exchange fluctuated spasmodically as Wall Street hesitated with each new train of information along the phone tree. By the end of the day, Fidelity Sworn bank stock had finished higher than at any other time in its one hundred-and-twenty-year history.

Chapter Fifteen

Kepstein closed on an apartment in New York City the day after his meeting with the banking establishment. According to his unofficial timeline, production on the film was set to begin August first. At this point, the film was scarcely more than a dream to him, but he knew that timelines were as necessary as contracts, accounting, and legal protection.

Kepstein relished the opportunity the project presented for camaraderie and he invited Jack and Milo to relocate. Because they were excited to work on the project, they agreed with little reservation. Lenny helped to find and set up the home base for their production, a nine-bedroom brownstone hidden off Lowry Street, near the train tracks in Brooklyn. Kepstein knew this move wasn't going to be easy for either Rebecca, Jack, or Milo and he felt responsible for their uprooting.

As Kepstein and Rebecca careened down the street in their Mercedes, Lenny, Jack, and Milo were inside the house, pushing heavy brooms across the dusty, wooden floors. The afternoon sun beat through the blinds like time past, and they felt like kids again, drinking beers with their shirts off, pant legs rolled up, sweating in the breezeless New York townhouse.

"This is fucking awesome," Milo said to Lenny, tossing him a bottle of beer.

"Yes, it certainly is — hey do you hear that? Someone's pulling up."

Jack was leaning in the doorway against a broom stick like a foggy character in a Ferlinghetti poem. "It's the Kepsteins!" he exclaimed, loudly enough for those in the house and the newcomers approaching the house to hear.

"For he's a jolly good fellow, for he's a jolly good fellow," Lenny was singing, his arm around Milo, as they came to the door to meet the Kepsteins.

"Howdy, fellas," Kepstein said with a gracious smile. "How'd you get in here? Did they drop off the keys already?"

"Indeed they did," Jack said. "A rep for the previous owners came by and showed Milo where the electric boxes were and all that important shit. He got the lights up and running a half hour ago. Now we just need fans!"

Rebecca was a bit shaken by all that had happened over the past two days, but was happy to see so many smiling faces. She'd always wanted to live in the City and was excited by this bizarre turn of events in her life.

"Milo, it's great to see you again," she said, stepping away from Jack and her husband who were conversing near the doorway, "and this must be Lenny?"

"Likewise, Rebecca! Yes, this is Lenny," Milo said, introducing Rebecca and Lenny to each other. "I forgot you two have not yet met in person."

"Yes, but I've heard so many great things!" Lenny embraced Rebecca with a congenial hug. "It's so good to finally meet you, Rebecca. How was the drive in?"

"It was good, a bit of traffic, which I suppose is expected — it looks like you guys have been busy."

"Yes, cleaning things, but it has been a fun day drinking beer and listening to tunes on the radio," Milo said, sweeping his hand around the room behind him. "This place is beautiful!"

"I know. It's magnificent, Lenny. You did a great job finding it," Rebecca said, beginning to look suddenly concerned. "So, you just quit your jobs and moved up here this week? Was that hard to do?"

"Well, not really to be honest with you," Milo said. "As I was telling the fellas here just a bit ago, the only reason I work is basically to pay for my home and my food. And as you guys have been so generous to offer both for all of us working on the project, I'm very content."

"It's the least Bill could do," Rebecca said softly. "He's well aware of how difficult it is to relocate and needs to make sure everyone knows how much he appreciates it. I know this is all new for you guys, but it's new for him and me too. He truly appreciates all that you're doing. And I do too."

Milo was more appreciative of the Kepstein's generosity than they could have ever imagined and he vowed to himself to make sure their investment was a good one.

Everyone took turns walking through the house, picking out their rooms and commenting on the plans for décor.

"And here is where the minibar will go," Kepstein said, laughing as Jack and Milo carried in a carful of beer and wine for the unofficial house warming party.

"It's as good a spot as any," Jack agreed merrily, setting down the heavy boxes. It was the perfect recipe for a fun, laid back evening in which to christen their new home, a joyous day that they knew would be the first of many.

* * *

At nine o'clock sharp the following morning, the doorbell rang. The doorbell's pulsing screech had the effect of causing Kepstein to slide his pen across his paper, Rebecca to drop the plate she was putting into the pantry, and Milo to fall off his ladder while wiring a light fixture. General Adam's voice came over the intercom.

"Gooooooood morning, friends," he boomed through the speaker. "It's General and the troops!"

Kepstein opened the door and shook his hand. "General Adams, how good it is to see you — and these are the — "

"Yes, yes, I said 'troops.' I know I told you it was in no way a military reference, my name that is, but it does lend itself to humor, does it not?"

Rebecca came up behind her husband. She was barefoot and wearing a sundress. Stepping around her husband, she opened the door. "Move it, Bill. Let them inside already, would you!" She extended her hand and introduced herself to General Adams. "Hi, my name is Rebecca. It's a pleasure to meet you."

"Hello!" Adams boomed again, his arms uplifted as he greeted her, Kepstein, Jack, Milo, and Lenny. He gave Rebecca an especially generous and warm hug and vigorously shook each man's hand. Everyone was moving towards the dining room, which at this point consisted of a few box fans, a few old card tables, and lots of chairs. A small refrigerator hummed quietly in the corner and a radio on the paint shelf of a folding ladder broadcast some scratchy sounding jazz.

"This is the enigmatic bunch I was telling you all about," General said as he turned back towards the people behind him who were entering the room, "the genius, ambitious, and otherwise crazy banking mogul and the gang!"

"Please, just call me Bill," Kepstein said off-handedly.

Adams's crew could not believe that the room they were standing in appeared so shoddy to them. Adams had promised them that they'd be meeting a man with so much wealth that he planned not only to fund the entire project on a whim, but also that he had decided to buy a house in New York and relocate there with his wife — again on a whim. Instead, they found themselves sitting on dusty chairs in a stifling hot, dirty dining room with barely any furniture.

162

"Ok, Bill. As you can see, I went ahead and invited some of my colleagues to join us today, as I am sure Lenny has explained to you. This business involves a lot of players if it is to be done right . . . and as I'm sure you want to do it right, I felt it best to have a key team on board for the first day of discussion so we can determine what we can and can't do."

Before the discussion began, Jack asked the question that was on everyone's mind, "What do you all want to drink?"

"Fantastic question," Kepstein declared. He walked past Jack towards the kitchen as Rebecca rolled her eyes and continued looking at the people assembled in the room. She was in the same boat as the rest of the group, unsure of why she was there and what would happen.

Kepstein brought a few bottles of wine into the living room. He passed a wine opener and the bottles to Jack, then began the meeting. "The topic of expenses has been covered in a previous meeting with Jack, Lenny, General Adams, and me. I will be handling that part of the project. We'll be using this house as our home base. The house has two large open spaces, one towards the back of the house, adjacent to the dining room, and another on the second floor. There are a total of eight bedrooms and I'd like to open those up to anyone who finds they're spending enough time working on the project so that it makes sense for them to take up residency here, either temporary or permanent."

Everyone in the room was surprised by what Kepstein had just said and he saw smiles on their faces. After they made a congenial toast, he summarized his thoughts about the project, the same thoughts he had presented to Adams in their first meeting. Then, as he knew that Adams had relayed much of this information to his crew beforehand, he began talking about specific scenarios for the film as members of the crew, including Jack, Lenny, and Milo took notes.

Over the next five or so hours there was much discussion of possible parties to attend, possible scenarios to review, possible people to invite, possible disguises, and other possibilities that had to be considered. Ideas for the plot and the setting came from a list that Kepstein had developed. Like a great dam opening in the spring, ideas spilled from his mind. His imagination was like a racing current that swept everyone into it, dragging them along. He spoke feverishly, Adams and his crew correcting him on certain points and expanding on others as they wrote down everything Kepstein said in their notebooks and scribbled storylines, plots, and themes.

At one point, Kepstein stood on a chair, stating loudly, "I am sure all of you are familiar with the health care dilemma occupying the news as of late, and NO, I DO NOT wish to discuss everyone's opinions right now, but hear me out." He looked around the room derisively, waving his arms like an umpire signaling "silence!"

"We gain entry to the National Association of Health Insurers to be held in Louisiana this year, or better yet, the American Medical Association Healthcare benefit dinner. We make it possible for Jack and Milo, or Jack, Milo, and a few members from your crew, General, to gain entrance to the event, pay for their tickets, get them a grand table at which they pretend to be something like, let's say, low level executives for some insurance agency. After many drinks have been poured throughout the evening and everyone is getting loose, we then create situations in which they are able to discuss policy with other people at the dinner. They would have a list of questions to ask them, the same list that we would ask the men and women on the other side of the power spectrum — let's say, for example, those living in Birmingham, Alabama's project housing blocks. If we are able to put forth a question that elicits the same response in both groups about their needs and wants from healthcare, then we will start to have something to work with, you see . . ."

The room became quiet and Kepstein continued, "For example, we ask the people at the dinner how they feel about creating numerous inner-city clinics to be utilized only by the poor in their respective communities as opposed to, say, the Medicaid program. If they reply with a unanimous 'no,' which is highly likely, then we prod them further by asking, 'What if the clinics were run by the people in the communities?' To which they would most likely reply, 'Co-ops don't work!' We would then go on and on with our questions and comments until we have demonstrated the absence of a dialogue between the state, the schools, and the poor citizens who want to help their communities. That is when we offer a solution. For example, paid tuition for nursing schools in those communities, with repayment for the tuition in the form of the nurses staying in their community clinics for five years or so. Then we would say to single mothers of those children in these communities, 'What if there were a deal where your kids could go through a college program and have their tuition paid for if, and only if, they sign a five-year contract to work as a well-paid nurse, here, in your local community?'

"You see, it would be just that simple to demonstrate that the same concept can come from opposite ends of the spectrum. Our goal would be to get those on the supposedly opposite sides to agree to the exact same premise, thus showing what could happen if people spoke to one another freely and not through the monolithic mess of government and business. We could truly drive this idea home if we were to take something like this healthcare issue, for example, and then describe in detail how long any type of action would take if it were to go through government channels, making this governmental route seem all the more ridiculous because both sides will be shown already agreeing to the same proposal.

"This same process could be applied to many other issues. For example, the common nuisances that we deal with every day, such as laws mandating permits to burn leaves in your backyard or hold a neighborhood block party, or the laws making it illegal to put quarters in other people's parking meters. The list goes on and on, the situations are numerous, and in each case no one actually wants those laws. They're just relics of bad, unintelligible and overly *sophisticated* governance, and we're stuck with them."

"Excuse me, Bill," Adams interrupted, "but I can't understand how we'll be able to convince these people to say what we want them to . . . or, for that matter, how we'll be able to get it down on film so that it is compelling enough for people to make the leap from watching to feeling."

"We will need to shoot a whole lot of film . . ." Kepstein replied, "a very, very great deal of film."

Jack was leaning against the kitchen doorframe, one hand nervously clicking a pen, the other holding a highball glass of ice-cold whisky. He was absorbing everything Kepstein had said and was trying to

166

determine how he would fit into each scene and how he would manage to get the intended results. While he thought the task was monumental, he was able, though, to see himself discussing the healthcare issue with the governor of Nebraska, rubbing his hands together as he spoke to the governor of how his insurance company could save millions for the state. He could just as easily imagine himself in a Birmingham ghetto, speaking at a community planning meeting, the heat from the streets invading the room and the debate. He was picturing capturing two people on tape speaking about the need for quantifiable preventative health care and he began to realize that if he acted sincerely and asked the right questions, both persons would not only have the same opinions, but their passion for the topic would share the same degree of intensity.

"I think I know exactly how we could do it," Jack said abruptly. "We will definitely have to shoot a great deal of film, and it will sometimes be necessary to take the dialogue out of context, but it will be extremely important to stay true to the message. I was just thinking, for example, about how things would pan out at a big political dinner. I can picture asking questions and being met with blank stares or total avoidance. Then I realized that if we do our homework, we can cut everyone down to size by knowing exactly what to say, what to ask, what to do, etc. . . . I mean, if this whole project revolves around communication — as it does — then it is our duty as creators of this film to ensure that we use our communication skills to extract the most poignant discussion and footage possible. Since the primary content of the film would be dialogue, I feel that our primary concern in our preparations should be carefully preparing the dialogue so that we have scripts for every possible question we might ask and every possible response we might encounter."

"Jack's right," Kepstein agreed. "Like a well-written persuasive essay, the most important thing for us to do is to put ourselves in the shoes of the person who is being interviewed and anticipate anything they might say. This will allow us to coax the conversation in the direction we want it to go."

At this point, Adams spoke up. "There is one thing I think we all need to consider before we go much further. When we're talking about recording people saying things and they don't know they're being recorded, and we're talking about *coaxing* conversations in certain directions, there's a tremendous number of legal ramifications to consider. You especially have to understand the laws that apply to recording politicians or businessmen. If they are rubbed the wrong way, you will hear terms like 'espionage,' 'public danger,' or 'intellectual property theft,' words that can show up on paper and in a courtroom. I've seen this a number of times, and working on projects far more friendly to the establishment."

"Everyone," Kepstein said, "listen to what General is saying. We are going to have to be unified on this point. This is not going to be a friendly film. In fact, it's going to piss a lot of people off, cost others their jobs, and, if done correctly, it could change some aspects of society at large. I've spent the last twenty years behind the closed doors of finance. The truths that we'll uncover are hideous. I'm not a lawyer, of course, and I don't know any that deal with these matters. As we proceed, if we find legal council is necessary, we'll need to contact someone who understands the film industry and exactly what we're doing. Right now, we have to work in secrecy. It is extremely important and I will not allow any of our work to be made public until we have complete agreement on who wishes to be associated with the film and in what way. If the film causes trouble, I will do whatever I can to be the target of the trouble, both on paper and in person."

"It's not going to be that easy, Bill," Adams said. "How can the men and women working on this keep such a secret?"

"You're right. It's not going to be that easy, General. Everyone has to think about this and determine if they're able to proceed with working on the project. I urge all of you, if you're not able to continue being part of the project, to keep today's discussion private. This is my life's work and I've taken a tremendous risk to make it possible."

* * *

The days that followed the meeting were difficult. Kepstein and the crew were unsure what problems their production would run into or how they would handle them. Kepstein hadn't mentioned his timeline to the group, so when the production company met again the following Saturday night, the company was amazed to learn that in five weeks Jack, Milo, and Bruce, a member of Adams's team, were scheduled to attend a dinner symposium in Madrid and sit with Israel's senior commodities officials during the 23rd International Gas & Power Summit. They realized that they had less than a month to gather their equipment and be ready to start filming. Fortunately, Lenny had prepared most of the film's screenplay. Adams and his team had seen the manuscript, but they were not aware that Jack and Kepstein had already reviewed it and had begun making phone calls, acquiring phony documents, and rehearsing the movie's scenarios.

Adams felt confident that it would be OK to add a few more crew members who were on board with the film's goals and purpose, resulting in the project having a small band of thirteen dedicated workers, comprising the roles of writers, directors, and cameramen. Kepstein thought this small number was fine from a budgetary point of view. If it turned out to be necessary to increase the budget and utilize more people so that the film's scenes could be properly completed and edited, then that was a decision to be made further down the road, most likely once word had leaked out about what he was doing. Although he was a multimillionaire, he knew that the costs of attorneys, travel expenses, conference fees, and the crew's room and board would add up and he wanted to be prepared for that.

August 15 was the date of the Gas & Power Summit and the debut of the Coalition for Open Boarders Commodities Exchange. The head of this organization was to be played by Jack, a multimillionaire from Nebraska making his money in the titanium and oil fields of Russia through a firm passed down to him by his father. The Coalition was to consider itself lucky that it had been granted access to the European gala. They were to pretend to be extremely embarrassed that a mistake had been made that allowed them to share a table with the foremost central commodities regulator of Israel. As the evening continued, however, both parties would realize there was a great deal to learn from each other. They would discuss the free trade of petroleum and other non-renewable resources. While the hook for the conversation was entrenching strategic partnerships, the hidden agenda was in extracting a heartfelt omission from the Israeli man that supplies were running out.

The dinner conversations would be recorded and catalogued as one side of the thought process. Similar discussions would take place among refinery workers and oil riggers throughout the Asian continent and South Americas. The focus would be on the dependence on petroleum and the fear of its loss. With greed at stake on one end, and one's livelihood at the other, it was hoped that the viewer would understand not only the nature of the dilemma, but the similarities of the thoughts and desires of the people involved in the discussions.

The mission was going to be more difficult than anything Jack had attempted before and the stakes were high. Lenny developed false identities and backdoor escapes, just in case. In the Madrid situation, for example, he explained that should things get hairy or anyone realize they were full of shit and not actually part of the Coalition for Open Borders Commodities Exchange, they could simply stop acting at once and explain they were part of the Freedom for Gaza Coalition, activists trying to seek favor with the Prime Minister. If this were to fail or if the authorities were notified, then they were to explain that they were simply animal rights activists hoping to stop some unknown and unheard of atrocity being done at some chemicals plant in an undisclosed location in Israel.

Jack was going to the International Gas & Power Summit in Madrid, not only to expose investing, public-private agreements, and high-level corruption, but to begin to show the interrelated concerns of people at different ends of the socio-economic spectrum. He was going to take part in demonstrating the process of change, less than one month away.

Part Two

Chapter Sixteen

The day had come. With nothing more than their own thoughts and the clothes on their backs, Jack, Milo, and the rest of the Barcelona crew set out for the airport. Few words were available to guide them as they flew from La Guardia, offering each other shots of whiskey and salutes of good luck. Jack and Milo were scheduled to take one flight, while the rest of the crew were taking another.

The airplane left America drifting behind it like a wafer of salt dissolving into a sea of warm water and, as the plane rose in the sky, the clouds dropped past the windows, eroding the images that Jack and Milo had hoped to hold onto for a few minutes longer. The realization that they were on their way to Spain and the beginning of filming a movie that had only been discussed in theory unexpectedly generated a sense of worry in Jack and in Milo, a sense of freedom, thinking that this movie was his chance at success and he was going to take it.

When the first rays of sunlight entered the atmosphere, Jack and Milo awoke to find the plane hovering over the landmass that was Europe. They were well-rested from their nearly six-hour nap in the warmth of nighttime safety forty-thousand feet above sea level. Below them, Europe was awakening to a new day.

Jack ordered a round of vodka and orange juice, bolstering himself for the day ahead: first to the hotel, where he and Milo would register under fake names, then to the tailor to be fitted for the big event the following evening, then back to the hotel for rest and recuperation. The next day was spent resting and practicing for the evening's event. Then it was show time.

* * *

"Amzi Kader Bahn, this is Jack Shales. Jack, my good friend and colleague, Amzi — spokesman for CALEAN."

"Very good to meet you, Amzi, and thank you for allowing me the pleasure," Jack said as they took turns shaking hands.

"Please, Jack. Pleasure is embraced tightly by us on this rare occasion. How it is we have not met, I am unclear. Maor tells me that you speak not as an American, but rather as one man speaking to another man. I mean this in no offence."

"Of course, none taken. And I apologize again that I've not taken greater recourse to make acquaintances with you previously." Jack spoke confidently as the three men followed the red Berber carpet from the exit doors and towards a row of tables. "As I was discussing with Maor, there is a great deal troubling me in these times, and as we — all of us here tonight — have a great deal at stake, I think we should be talking to one another as men. There are times to leave details out and there are times to bathe in pleasantries. I do not believe dialogue is a place for either."

"As goes a line from Tagore," Maor beamed, throwing his arm behind Jack's shoulder. "Depth of friendship does not depend on length of acquaintance."

With this quote from a long-dead poet, given to him by a man on the opposite side of the world, Jack began to feel overwhelmed. He felt that he was shaking around the edges and that at any time his deception could be exposed.

"Please sit, gentlemen." Maor invited them with a wave of the hand, his cufflinks shining under the lights of the opulent ballroom. The tables were circular and could sit eight people comfortably. The formal dinner had ended and all but a few delegates and escorts were to be seen milling about, typically in groups of two or three, too absorbed in their own conversations to notice anything else.

"Has Maor explained to you many details of CALEAN, Jack?"

"No. I'm afraid I only know what I've heard this evening," Jack admitted sheepishly.

"Very well. It is an organization not yet popularized in the media, and that suits us just fine," Amzi said, grinning widely but seriously.

"It is not a secretive organization, Jack, but we have not yet found purpose in expanding membership or notoriety," Maor insisted. He was a diplomat and approached subjects under that guise, allowing only the noblest portion of truth to see light.

"The world needs oil, Jack. And she has a thirst that will only grow. As I like to say, 'We are not in the business of selling oil. We are in the business of selling oil — right now.' Do you understand?"

"I believe so, but if you could please explain further, I would be most appreciative."

"Of course. You are a to-the-point man and I will speak to you bluntly." Amzi laid his well-maintained hands palms up in front of him on the tabletop. "My country has some oil. Our neighbors have some oil. Our firm operates through many components of the petroleum supply chain domestically and throughout the Middle East. We interact with OPEC, the US, the EU, and so forth to provide two key functions: to speculate on oil futures and to allow our clients the ability to foresee change. The world is not going to run out of oil any time soon, Jack, but what supply we have now will come under increased scrutiny. We expect the recent uprisings in the Middle East to have heavy influences upon the instability of the availability of oil. The focus will no longer be on finding new sources or controlling the current supply, but rather in maintaining security."

Amzi's nostrils flared. He was excited and it was hard for Jack not to feel the same in the presence of such zeal. "Think of the consequences as the supply continues to be affected: terrorism here, nationalization there, and soon speculation means nothing and governments feel the need to remove the middle man — us, my friends. The prices will fluctuate with the regime changes, natural disasters will be impossible to rebound from, and so

175

forth. Our mission at CALEAN is not to get out of the oil business, of course, and not to minimize our importance, but rather to increase our presence. We feel there will be enough instability in the Middle East for us to operate on many small scales."

"Isn't this going to hurt your business, Amzi?" Jack asked, interjecting for the first time. "I don't mean to speak out of turn here, but as a man in the business of controlling the supply, I would do what I could to prevent an expansion of the supply chain. I know there are numerous bidders who wish to distribute my titanium, for example, but all it will do is drive prices down, which is not desirable."

"I'm afraid these changes are not desirable, Jack, but they are unavoidable in my industry. We feel the central control of oil has reached its pinnacle. As these freshman governments determine what to do with their primary source of income — think Libya, for example — rogue greed will be our number one asset. We will simply provide direct-to-seller distribution of energy and we can do this for many of the historical utilities."

"You plan to operate in other areas as well?" Jack asked, feigning the indignation of a man with a lot at stake.

"Your titanium is safe my, friend," Maor insisted, grinning once again with diplomatic preening as he put a warm hand on Jack's.

"Yes, Jack. Consider for a moment the scalability of this system. We provide an avenue for small scale distribution, let's say ranging in size from an industrialized city of one hundred thousand people to a small air-shipping contingent of perhaps ten planes, and let's say further that we can guarantee a set price for gasoline of one-years' worth. We deliver it directly from the source, on a smaller scale, and a slightly higher price than the market asks — but we ensure it's a secure source. The price is guaranteed for one year, allowing a small group the security it desires and it allows us the flexibility to keep on the pulse of emerging technologies. We would not require top-down restructuring. Ergo we are in the business of selling oil — right now."

"Tomorrow it could be —"

"Exactly. There is no need to put all your eggs in one bag," Maor said with great pride in his use of English idioms.

Amzi's nostrils were flaring again. It was not enthusiasm driving him this time, but rather laughter. "It is eggs in one basket, Maor!"

The three men laughed like old friends. In fact, they held a stronger bond than childhood pals in that they were businessmen furthering their fortunes. Maor and Amzi were not divulging information for the sake of conversation, but rather to further their interests among Jack's Russian connections. His titanium was a great resource, but the real advantage to them was his knowledge of short-selling petroleum. In this regard, the paucity of information regarding his background came to be a great blessing as these men did not wish to speak with the establishment, but with their greatest asset — the ambitiously greedy.

The conversation continued into the late evening, when the three men were joined by Milo, who was introduced by Jack as his associate. Fortunately for the interviewers, and again, unfortunately for Maor and

Amzi, neither held strictly to their religious precepts so that a sprinkling of liquor allowed for conversational lubrication.

As midnight approached, Milo interrupted the conversation. "It's nearly Barcelona midnight, my friends, can we not agree to celebrate the moment? You have the rest of the year to discuss how you'll grow our businesses together. Can we not save tonight to discuss how we will grow our relationship — our growing friendship?"

"Milo is right. We have made it past the first date. We've been invited upstairs, now let's take the time to enjoy the walk home. Let's hold hands a little bit," Jack joked, a joke only Maor was able to understand. Maor had done some undergraduate studies in Massachusetts and had spent enough time in the States to understand crude humor.

The evening with the Israelis continued until three or so. Much was learned and gained. It was the first tangible evidence that Jack, Milo, and the rest of the production cast were creating something new and unique, and while it may have been beginner's luck, they felt themselves fortunate to have avoided any major conflicts. In fact, not only were their primary objectives met, but also their secondary objectives, as Jack and Milo were able to bring the men back to the hotel where the ubiquitous cameras recorded them from more than one angle.

* * *

Waking early the next morning, Jack, Milo, and the film crew who had been responsible for all the technical requirements for filming and recording the interactions with the Israelis gathered their equipment and documents and made quick haste for the airport.

It wasn't until everyone was back on US soil that the overwhelming sense of anxiety that any of them had felt could be relieved. They were eager to see Bill Kepstein, perhaps because of the security that a sense of wealth brings, or maybe it was the way a team puts their trust in the coach when times get rough. They believed that Kepstein would see their work and his approval would help them regain their sense of balance.

"It is true," Kepstein said solemnly as he looked at their faces and saw what he thought were expressions of guilt, "to create a new city, some old buildings must fall. But we are not trying to create a new city. We are trying to illustrate a new way of behaving and thinking . . . and God only knows what that means."

After a few celebratory cocktails, the production crew convened in the projection room to watch the tapes that had been made of the event. They sat in silence, their jaws hanging as they witnessed Jack and Milo's work. As the reels of film spun before them, each knew that Jack was the right choice for the job, as he had been able to procure, nearly verbatim, the words he had hoped the businessman would utter.

There were nearly four hours of usable footage. After watching about forty-five minutes of footage, the viewers felt sure that they wanted the film to be a success and a torrent of discussion erupted so strongly that Kepstein had to stop the video and intervene.

179

"Rest easy, my friends. We can easily see that the crew has surpassed everyone's expectations. These guys prepared for this job relentlessly. Now let's enjoy it."

"I'm not completely sure I'm comfortable with this material," a production cast member named Ellie said at the first break in the clamor. "When I signed up for this, I heard about juxtaposing various thoughts and ways of life, and telling the story of a common human bond, the fabric of communication. I hope all of our efforts are not exactly like this one."

"What is it you feel most negatively about, Ellie?" Kepstein asked.

"I mean, the footage is amazing — you guys really nailed this one. But I'm a little nervous about exposing some of these people. Especially these guys operating out of Israel, discussing the oil trade! They could all be hanged at once should this film upset the wrong people. That'd be blood directly on our hands."

Others in the room nodded their heads in agreement. They knew Ellie was right, and knew the inevitable was coming — Kepstein's next words.

"Ellie, each of us will be touched by this footage in a different and unique way. I think it is necessary that we all watch this first round of film in its entirety. Let it sink in, let it reach you. Internalize the content and see how it might be applied to our greater mission. You've brought up a sound point, Ellie, and I think it will be reassuring for you to know that not all of the footage will be exactly like the film we're reviewing today. All the people we're interviewing and filming are not successful. They're not all wealthy or important. Some will be the opposite: poor, marginalized, and insignificant to the greater power structures of our world. You have to think of this as you watch the film, and each of us has to make the personal decision as to whether or not you feel the project is ethical and just."

"No, I do feel it is ethical and just," Ellie said, "It's just nerve-racking to see these men seal their own fate."

"Perhaps they're not, Ellie." Lenny interjected. "Bill, do you mind if I mention one of the concepts we're considering coupling with this footage from the International Gas & Power Summit dinner?"

"Please do, Lenny. That's a very good idea, and it will help us keep further questions in mind as we review the tapes."

Lenny stood, a notebook in one hand, his other hand in his pocket. He looked down at the pad of paper. "We will likely pair this footage from Barcelona with sentiments among the refinery workers and common citizens of Brazil. Both countries have promising energy reserves, great disparities of wealth, and, as we will see, very similar problems."

"Lenny is right," Kepstein added. "As you watch the work our friends have done on this first journey, imagine the scenes being juxtaposed with a small shanty town on the Brazilian coast. Imagine the setting of ultra-wealth in the Barcelona ballroom paired with disparity and disenfranchisement. Imagine both groups of people saying the exact same thing, and you can see this project take shape before your eyes."

Rebecca spoke up. "I have one question for those of you that have just returned from Barcelona, and I think it's something others might be curious of as well," she said, looking around the room and resting her eyes on her husband before continuing. "Were you concerned about the repercussions of maintaining a false identity at such an important event? I ask this because, as my husband has just mentioned, we each need to determine if we feel the project is just and ethical. In my case, I certainly do. However, I worry less about the ethics and more about the legality of our efforts."

"That is another point that is troubling me," Ellie interjected before anyone else could answer. "I can understand the moral merits of this project. But is this legal, what we are doing?"

"No, using false identities is not legal," Kepstein replied. "We'll need to limit the number of instances where that type of activity is required. To be completely transparent with you, there will likely be legal repercussions in the US, worse if any of us are caught abroad. With this in mind, General Adams and I have discussed a timeline to follow to limit our exposure. General, would you mind?"

"Of course. Yes, unfortunately from my past experiences on other productions, I can be certain that there will be legal consequences to this film's release. To avoid unnecessary risks, we've decided it will be best to proceed in the following manner: we'll be drafting an extremely aggressive timeline for gathering all the necessary footage. We will do this in six months, leaving an additional six months for editing, and then an additional six months for publicity. It's going to take a lot of dedication and a tremendous amount of time and energy to meet these goals, but I'm confident we can do it."

"Thank you, General." Kepstein said, hoping to close the discussion so they could continue reviewing the tapes. "The outcome of this project is in your hands. The potency of the footage and the interviews, and the creative subject matter you generate, will likely dictate the level of backlash we can expect. As we are working on the project together, we will collectively decide our fate, and to the very best of my abilities, I will take all legal responsibility for what may come. With that said, let's watch the tapes!"

Watching the footage helped the production crew get a sense of the essence of what had transpired at the Madrid dinner and consider how that essence could be reflected in the footage that was to be shot in Brazil. It became clear that, by comparing their particular setting to one found in a novel written by Hamid Krysvaini, a man Jack knew the Israelis would have recognized, Jack was able to dissolve four thousand miles of separation, making the men feel as if they were talking with childhood friends in the comfort of their mothers' kitchens. Watching the footage reinforced their desire to generate similar footage in Brazil. They wanted to show both the futility of central control and local control, and the benefits of Amzi's plan. A quote from Amzi served as a guide for the motive for the Brazil footage: "That's the nature of the problem. There are not rich and poor, lions and lambs, but rather we're all stuck here together. Each day we continue drinking from the Earth, the less there will be to drink — it's not magic. We will continue to be thirsty, but some of us will grow thirsty much sooner than

183

others. This is not magic, or politics, or something to scream about — it's just life."

At the end of the showing, Kepstein announced that the next production goal was to meet a few people in Brazil to discuss the oil trade there. In Brazil, they would not only find people willing to discuss their views of the oil trade, but people wanting — needing — what CALEAN could offer. Kepstein admitted that he would not have as many strings to pull on the trip to Brazil and he felt it best to send only Jack and Lenny. This was known to Lenny ahead of time, but startled Jack. He was tired, but still felt a sense of great joy in the assignment. Any of the men and women in the room would have felt the same.

Chapter Seventeen

The production crew found an oil town in Brazil where there was a flourishing population, as the locals had expected to find high-paying jobs, cheap oil, and thriving commerce at the port where the crude came in. Over several years, however, the workers found themselves basically enslaved, with few options for relocation. Instead of the oil creating wealth, the proceeds were funneled out of their town and into others' pockets. By the time the fuel was refined and shipped back to them for their own use, it was significantly more expensive than the average domestic price. The town was remote, so the cost of shipping was high, and the people didn't believe there was anything that could be done to change this. Noting the juxtaposition to, and hidden similarities with, Amzi's plan, Jack and Lenny set off for a few days of shooting.

"Tudo bem meus amigos," the tour guide said as Jack and Lenny were boarding the bus. There was a mist of sea salt on one side of the road and a busy row of nickel-and-dime stores on the other. The power lines stretched over their heads, creating an interwoven network of black rubber, metal barbs, and yellow warning ribbons.

"Oi Captain!" Jack yelled above the sound of the diesel engine, strongly gripping the driver's shoulder.

"I don't like the looks of this," Lenny said softly after about five minutes of driving. The bus had begun a downward descent into a favela where roughly ten thousand people lived at the bottom of a gritty, dirt road alongside the mountain, all of them directly or indirectly reliant on the nearby refineries for survival. Lenny had his handheld camera and Jack a simple notebook. They were under the guise of Amnesty International, posing as reporters seeking to gauge the current state of human rights in the village. It was not quite an exact replica of their exploits in Barcelona, but Lenny had felt confident that their brass-knuckle journalism would be well-received. Now, though, he was having second thoughts as the bus came to an abrupt stop in front of a make-shift domino hall.

"This is as far as I go, my friends. Boa sorte!" the driver yelled in a thick accent.

"Fuck me, this is not what I had expected," Jack blurted out, all of a sudden feeling embarrassed about his notebook and their general appearance. "I expected the area to be a little more built-up, I guess."

The power lines that raced above their heads earlier had disappeared, replaced by clothes lines and blue sky. The ground was close to the water and appeared to have been muddy since time immemorial. They were on Texas Street —of all names, thought Jack — and needed to walk about four blocks to find a man named Christian. Christian was their liaison to the world of oil and the people. He was supposedly a great advocate for the laborers and was pleased to hear of their visit.

As Jack and Lenny wended their way down Texas Street, an empty bottle of Coke was hurled by a young kid on a moped. Because the event took place so quickly, the boy's face was impossible to recognize. The glass shattered against a warehouse wall just above Jack's head, and after the glass had fallen to the ground, they heard the giggles and bellowing laughs

186

of those close enough on the street to see the two men jump. They were not kind laughs, the type uttered agreeably, but were laughs that indicated disdain, the ubiquitous get-the-hell-out-of-my-town laugh men can make.

After five minutes of walking and worrying, Jack and Lenny arrived at the address Christian had emailed Lenny several days earlier. It was not the address of a small house or an apartment, as they had expected, but rather what appeared to be the newest building in the neighborhood. The building was three stories tall, with a metallic face and dark windows on the second floor. There were no doors on the front, but a freshly paved street along the left side that led to the entrance. As they moved towards the rear of the building, they found a set of steps leading to a glass door with ENTRADA written above it. To the left of the steps was a bay of loading docks that were busy with trucks, forklifts, and men vying for position.

One of the workers approached them, flicking a cigarette towards the curb and smiling. "Greetings, my friends," he said, leaning forward to shake Lenny's hand, then Jack's.

Jack and Lenny introduced themselves and followed Christian through the door and towards the back of the warehouse where a makeshift encasing held a busy office with a desk littered with coffee cups, papers, folders, and overflowing ashtrays. This was where Christian lived when he wasn't at home.

"You have come a long way," Christian said as the men settled into folding metal chairs.

"It was a nice trip, but I thought we were meeting at your home. What is this place?" Lenny liked to cut to the chase and never knew if his voice was abrasive or not.

"You wanted to see how things work in our country, so I thought it would be best to take you on a tour of our operations," Christian explained. "This is Petroleo Brasileiro, Lenny. As you may know, Petroleo Brasileiro is the state-run agency that deals in our nation's oil affairs. We use the resources and expertise of outside firms to find and procure the oil, but our government has been gracious enough to prepare deals in which the people can reap some benefit. I've spent nearly two decades of my life creating what you see here."

"You are responsible for this operation?" Jack asked casually, opening his notebook as if to say, "May we begin now?"

At that cue, Lenny began fidgeting with his camera and waiting for the go-ahead.

"You gentleman would like to record our conversation?"

"Please, if it is OK with you. If not, that is OK too," Lenny replied uneasily.

"No, no, please. Anything we can do to further our cause is greatly appreciated and certainly desired. To answer your question, yes, as I was saying, I conceptualized this vision some twenty years ago. It was a different time then, but you knew something was in the air by all of the men in suits snooping around the shores."

Christian explained to Jack and Lenny that he was in charge of spearheading an operation to manage a certain portion of the oil and revenues that were produced from the region. The proceeds would then be divided among the surrounding states to satisfy local needs. The oil went into the gas tanks of government vehicles and was also partitioned in a controlled manner so that, hopefully, prices would be maintained at a set target.

"The truth is, anything you do with the government in Brazil — especially when you are talking about millions of dollars — is going to result in wide-spread corruption, insecurity, and eventual instability." Christian was leaning back in his seat as he spoke, stubbing out a cigarette. "Can you please turn the camera off for a moment, Lenny?"

Christian continued to describe the process of energy production, distribution, and consumption in Brazil. Jack and Lenny quickly observed that their guide was talking about the same things Maor and Amzi had mentioned weeks before. It was the same language — the same misguided hopes turned into greed and the same forlorn despair when those hoping for change have no voice. And it also became apparent to them that anything worth hearing from Christian could not be recorded on film. Against Lenny's better judgment, Jack decided to record everything that was said with a small cell phone microphone.

Christian kept his promise to introduce Jack and Lenny to local men and women, but strangely disproved of their contact with the employees at his shipping center. It was obvious to Jack and Lenny that there was foul play somewhere, but they also believed that Christian had a good heart — at least he had, they thought, at one point. The people revered Christian as a man who was doing what he could to save their livelihoods. They were like the men working in the diamond mines in Africa, but as the oil served no purpose unrefined and could not easily be placed into one's pocket, their situation was all the more desperate. Despite Christian's attempts to prevent it, Jack and Lenny were relieved to find that the local people were eager to talk with them and to be videotaped.

"We cannot find food to feed our children at times," a woman said, pleading into the camera. "There is food and there are jobs somewhere, but it is not here. Here we have enough oil for the whole world, but we do not have enough gasoline to drive to where the food and jobs are. It is not a mystery. It is life."

After four days of talking with the people and videotaping, the planned time in Brazil was over, and both men needed a few hours of rest before taking the cab to the airport. They were back in the safety of Rio and it was nearing seven o'clock when the phone rang in their hotel room.

"Oi," Jack said into the receiver.

"Jack, there is one more person I wanted you guys to meet before departing," Christian said calmly. "There is a group from the local university working on the future of Brazil and her position in the world economy. I apologize, as I know you are preparing to depart this evening, but one of the men from the program became so excited when I told him of your film that I could not prevent myself the introduction."

"Thank you, Christian, I will let Lenny know. What time?" Jack was excited and considered it one more successful connection to cap off an extremely productive week.

"Great! He will be there at roughly 7:30, if that gives you enough time. And between us, I think he is eager to become famous in America. Unfortunately, I know that he will not be able to be recorded on camera due to his unique position with the University, but I am confident he will be very receptive."

At 7:30, Jack was packed and Lenny was napping. Jack decided to take his gear and belongings to the lobby, while Lenny left his behind, intending to pack up after the brief meeting.

Their flight was at eleven PM and when Lenny noticed it was getting late, he left the meeting early to pack. When he returned to the room, he found all the drawers lay open, the mattresses strewn sideways. The TV was unplugged and the phone lines were cut. He discovered that everything was gone, including the majority of their footage and his passport.

Lenny immediately called for a taxi and sent Jack a text message: "bad guys. bail. meet me in alley behind hotel. cab waiting." Lenny rushed through the hotel room, frantically pulling off the bed linens, looking behind the bed board and under the bed in a desperate search for his documents. He checked every drawer in the bathroom and found nothing. His mind raced around the thought of returning home without documentation of his citizenship. Finally, as he lost all hope, he lay on the bed, breathed deeply, and attempted to retrace his steps that day. As he did so, he found his passport. It was stuck to the ceiling, open to his picture, a knife directly through the center of his face.

Meanwhile, the university student was pleading with Jack to stay for one more night so that he could introduce Jack and Lenny to the real brains behind Brazil's future. Jack sensed the eagerness in his voice and the malice in his eyes. He excused himself on the pretext of needing to use the bathroom, then darted out of the building. Racing to the airport and onto the airplane, the men knew true corruption for the first time in their lives. Christian had sold them out and ruined the chance for his interview to see the light of day. They felt betrayed and understood the stark reality of their exploits — that change is seldom sought by the established. At the airport, Lenny had to answer many questions about his passport. Due to their mission, however, they could not give the full story, but, with some fast-talking, they were able to board their plane and make their passage home.

When Jack and Lenny finally returned to the house in Brooklyn, their hazardous trip was well known to everyone in the house. Rebecca's motherly instincts kicked in and she pulled her husband aside. "How long can this go on, Bill, before we need to review the risks and benefits more seriously? The risks being death or the personal harm that Jack and Lenny came so close to yesterday."

"I understand your concern, but I'm not worried. I think things will work out."

Rebecca furrowed her brow. "I hope you're right — I couldn't handle the guilt if one of these men or women were hurt on our watch."

Chapter Eighteen

Over the next six months, filming continued. Locations and people were found and the dialogues were worked out. Scenarios were developed through the experiences the production crew gained by filming the world around them, including dialogue and social and emotional encounters. Through those experiences, the crew learned to look through the lenses of their eyes and cameras and into the windows around them, into the eyes of the people they saw. This helped them get a more accurate feel for the project.

During those months, virtually every continent was visited, and by the end of the third month, six hundred hours of film had been shot. All of the scenarios had as their goal the pairing of two similar ideologies with two seemingly opposite points of view, and the production company was surprised to discover that their preconceptions were borne out the majority of the time.

There was one pairing that seemed to represent the essence of their approach and the theme of the film. In the first scene, Lenny was with a group of seventh graders in a Chicago school. Their teacher explained to Lenny the reasons for her avoidance of small group activities, saying, "You know, you cannot allow them too much time together on their own. It's important to keep them together in one large group or you run the risk of cliques and unhealthy opinions."

"Do you allow them time to work together on small projects or discuss assignments in groups?" Lenny asked.

"That would be altogether detrimental," the teacher responded. "They're too young, Mr. Keibers. They don't know how to talk to one another yet — we have to gently guide them on how to do it properly."

In the second scene, Lenny was at a Russian retreat, discussing political science with a middle-level czar from the Institute for Central Supervising Authority, a Moscow think tank with far reaching powers inside and outside the Kremlin. The man being interviewed was so unaware of the true purpose of the interview that he invited Lenny for a private discussion over tea on the balcony of his lavish hillside villa. The railings were decorated in gold and the balcony overlooked a courtyard with hanging vines and marble facades and fountains that appeared to come from a time that was long gone and had no place in the modern world.

The man was describing to Lenny the change in thought that had occurred since the fall of the Soviet Union and the last of that society's mistakes. He said that the goal of Tsarist Russia was to keep people grouped together by class, job function, and geographical location. He explained how this stratification led to an uprising that became the Communist revolution and said that those who were smart enough knew that unification was the means to oppression, or 'governance' as he delicately described it. "What we now understand is that when men are stratified into different groups, they begin to think differently and that can be dangerous — talking amongst themselves that is — and what we have found more efficacious is to unite them towards a common goal, much as our southern neighbors in China have done. This will prevent them from looking too far beyond the green fields we have created for them."

When Jack reviewed the film, he realized that the powerful Russian could just as easily have been the seventh-grade teacher in Chicago. As he heard the last utterance about green fields spoken in thick broken English he recalled a trip he'd taken weeks before.

Jack pulled up a third reel of footage, finding himself under a pixelated sunset, standing toe to toe with a Venezuelan cocoa farmer. The man was explaining how he was able to enslave workers by systematically raising their rent and food costs, explaining that it was worth it to ensure the farmers appreciated the lush fields provided for them. Jack saw the same person, whether it was the Venezuelan drug lord, the seventh-grade teacher from Chicago, or the czar on three different continents and in three different roles, each subscribed to the same opinion, each believing that the only way to reach their goals was by autocratic rule, for if the people they depended on began to interact individually, then their goals would be threatened and, replaced by other goals set, instead, by the people they wanted to control.

* * *

Although the film was progressing and the production crew was focusing intensely on the scenarios and interviews, Kepstein began to feel a sense of unrest and a lack of ease. Being a financier, he kept up to speed with what was taking place in the financial sector by reading the usual news outlets, but he began to be troubled by the far-fetched blog posts or the short *Wall Street Journal* articles about his bank's financial ventures. Some of those ventures had done quite well in his absence, while others had lost a tremendous amount of money. He had the sense that a scapegoat was needed by those who had lost money and that he was the perfect target.

At first, there was the typical murmur of interest that arises when anyone does anything differently, but after Kepstein hadn't reported to the office or attended any board meetings in over half a year, concern and speculation grew in the financial community. The business community wanted to know whom he was talking to and the government wanted to make sure that everyone knew it wasn't them. This meant that the government needed to know where Kepstein was and what he was doing.

Because Kepstein felt responsible for every aspect of the project, he began to worry about the safety of those who'd been traveling as well as the safety of everyone in the Brooklyn house. For all everyone knew, their mass of footage could have been considered illegal under numerous laws — both real and made up. He worried that if anyone besides the production company knew what the project involved, the house could be raided and those living there would risk being injured, or worse.

Kepstein's concerns weren't just based on his fears. In September, a black Crown Victoria positioned itself across the street from the house for an entire week. Door-to-door solicitors approached the house daily, pressing their noses in the doorway once it opened and asking to be seated before they could be shooed away. The phone started ringing off the hook until it finally had to be disconnected. Then vaguely marked packages started showing up at the house with threats and accusations directed at Kepstein. He knew his cover was blown and that it was time to make some changes.

In order to eliminate any suspicion of illicit activity and quell what appeared to be surveillance, Kepstein decided to begin managing the project from abroad. While the next phase of production and editing would still primarily take place in Brooklyn, Kepstein would be involved in managing that process off-site. He was thinking ahead, as he knew that a nine-bedroom house filled with totally unrelated inhabitants who traveled the world on a constant basis, often under false identities, would continue to raise suspicion. He didn't want the project to become public knowledge, at least not yet, so he decided to set up his managing production base in a historic townhouse in Dublin, Ireland.

The night before their departure, the Kepsteins had a cup of coffee with Jack and asked him to join them in Dublin. While Kepstein and Jack understood that their direct input into the project over the next few months of editing would be limited, they nevertheless believed that they could still do a great deal from abroad. "I'd be delighted, honestly. I've always liked New York, but I'd be happy to get out of this house and the city for a little while," Jack admitted.

* * *

Their conversation continued on the following morning and into the next evening as the three sat together in the living room of their new home.

"Do you remember that jukebox they had at Betriebsnacht?" Kepstein said yawning as he leaned back in his chair, cracking his back against the grain. He took a drink from his glass and spun the brim, contemplatively watching the cubes spin in circles. There was a fireplace in the living room, burning quietly amidst the hum of central air-conditioning, and they were sitting at an old oak table which matched the home's interior.

Jack laughed, reminiscing, "How could anyone forget. We watched that Japanese rock festival. It was the loudest, most disorienting thing I have ever seen."

"Well I don't know if it was *that* bad, but all the same, the idea is interesting. The idea of on-demand live performances means there are thousands of cameras stationed all across the world just waiting for the next show to be broadcast. I thought about this today coming from the airport. There are surveillance cameras here and throughout most of Europe, generating a lot of footage, which is essentially wasted unless something worth recording happens." He allowed the concept to set in for a moment before he continued, "What if we could use these types of cameras for our own project?"

"I like the idea," Jack replied, "but we're having trouble editing and dealing with the shots we have now. I don't know if we could handle the load of twenty-four hours, continuous footage."

"I am thinking of this more philosophically," Kepstein explained. "For example, instead of having cameras stationed on the corners of a music hall and focusing on the stage, they could be in the hallways outside of the venue. People could discuss their thoughts with the rest of the world who had been watching remotely. Or, instead of cameras posted surreptitiously on the top of lamp posts as they are here in Dublin, they could be posted on city walls, or on the back of bus seats. A person sitting economy-class on a greyhound in Arkansas could chat with a person riding first-class on the

198

Tokyo light rail, and all at random—the feeds could cycle randomly. It would remove the necessity and hierarchy of how we meet and speak with one another."

He began thinking of the project's aspirations differently and envisioned cameras on automobiles, on the lower levels of skyscrapers, and outside of cathedrals; in the bathrooms of soccer ball factories, the hallways of executive suites, and in the locker rooms of military training quarters. Everywhere. In the weeks following their move, Kepstein finally had a chance to focus his energy on strategic concepts. He saw the downstream effects of their project, and knew planning ahead was necessary. The editing of the film continued under Adam's direction, and Kepstein had time to talk and think prospectively during the interim.

Although the Kepsteins and Jack experienced a kind of reprieve from the hassles that were developing in the States, there was no reprieve for the production crew back in Brooklyn, as the frequency of the surveillance of the house increased. Some of the crew began to feel as if they were in a fish bowl, no matter where they went. This was a great catalyst for a desire to move, and those without families— three men and three women, in total— moved to Dublin when their leases were up.

With this additional staff, Kepstein was now able to direct the project more easily, but he was still concerned that the staff that remained in Brooklyn was taking unnecessary risks and he was worried that, given the increased degree of surveillance, before long he would be confronted with a formal inquiry into his actions.

* * *

There were no sirens coming from the white cars parked outside of the Dublin townhouse, but the meaning of their presence was understood by Jack and Kepstein. The cars were Interpol and Jack knew, as he pressed his nose against the glass of the second-story window, that the time had come for the charade to end and for Bill Kepstein to face the music of a world that would be deaf to his talent. At the first sight of the cars coming over the hill, Jack jumped so quickly, he nearly burned himself drinking his cup of coffee. To prove to himself that what he saw was really happening, he took another peek through the curtain and down the cobblestone street. The cars were stretching around the bend like a funeral procession for a man not yet deceased. In the short amount of time it took the stretch of cars to reach the end of the bank, he had pulled on jeans and a T-shirt and was heading for the door to tell the Kepsteins. When he knocked on the door of the room, he heard no response. Opening the door, he discovered that there was no one there and the only sound he heard was that of the alarm clock radio droning on quietly.

Jack ran back to his room and again leaned against the wall next to the window sill, careful not to disturb the curtains or the plant on the sill. He was shaking like a leaf, sirens wailing in his ears, hot red flashes of heat running across the top of his head and down to his shoulders. After what seemed like an eternity, he finally determined that it was safe enough, and with shifting eyes looked through the window pane, craning his neck to see the road directly below. He could not see any more vehicles outside the house.

Suddenly Jack heard the thunderous sound of feet pounding up the stairs, and before he could react he swirled around to see the Kepsteins staring at him with dismay. They looked to him as if they had seen something insidious.

"Where have you been? Have you seen what's going on outside?' Jack yelled, then dropped his voice to a low whisper. "Of course you've seen it, but what is it? What is going on?"

"It's time, Jack," Kepstein said. "We are running out of time and I think we're going to have to go public very soon. Today — now."

"It's OK, Jack," Rebecca said. "Everything will be just fine. After all, some degree of trouble has always been imminent."

"Those were police cars — Interpol — filing by outside. Correct?" Jack asked, addressing them both.

"Indeed, Jack, those were policemen and they were no doubt attempting to understand the peculiarity of our situation," Kepstein said. "I've taken this into account. We own a house three blocks down from this one, just in case. So, we are registered owners of that house, but not this one. Of this house, we are simply renters and we are not named on the property deed."

"Won't the realtor squeal when they show up at his office, though?" Jack asked, instinctively drawing the conclusions.

"He took a loan for both properties through a bank and the transfer is now in escrow through another bank, that bank being, in both circumstances, mine. So, there will be no trail for a realtor to find immediately, Jack, but yes, for Interpol it will not be difficult. They will no doubt search the houses on this block and will reach ours quite soon."

"It might be a good time to go public with everything," Rebecca muttered again, staring distantly into the floorboards with wide eyes.

"You crafty old fox," Jack said, looking at the banker while rubbing his hands together and grinning, his brain rattled by adrenaline. "Before we go public, though, wouldn't it be wise to contact everyone and find out where everyone is, just in case they are in a dangerous spot abroad."

"Right you are, Jack, right you are. While you and Rebecca do that, I will attempt to conjure up a plan to stave off the financial world when this hits the news. It's not going to be pretty, and I'm guessing we only have this one day before the paper trail — or those curious policemen — leads the dogs to us."

"It is nine a.m. here now, which makes it just after, what, two or three a.m. back in the States? We'd better expect the worst and try to get a real working plan before nightfall, just in case they hit us late."

"Jack's right," Kepstein said. "The worst thing for us in this situation would be to make headline news, with God knows what subtitles, only to be broadcast to a midday America with which we have no contact. If anything is going to happen, we had better tell our side first."

Chapter Nineteen

Kepstein decided there was no other option aside from full disclosure. If he tried to deny any rumors of his project, there was a trail of activities, such as hotel bills and ten-thousand-dollar-a-plate dinners that led back to him as the financier. He decided that he would just have to explain that he'd been involved with the financing of a film for the past eight months and that, while his bank still ran flawlessly, he could understand if the bank wanted to remove him from the Board of Directors.

Although this decision was the best option the Kepstein's could come up with, it made Rebecca nervous. "You are going to have to tell everyone very soon?" Rebecca asked her husband. Jack was in the room with them.

"Yes."

"I thought so. It has been coming for at least a month or so now, and I believe you knew that."

"I did and I expected that it would have to be done while we were here in Ireland. All the same, though, it's not going to make it any easier. What did you guys find out? Who's at the house in Brooklyn right now?"

"Adams is there, but he said he will be unable to make any sort of announcement because if he did they would immediately pull up any left of center project he'd ever worked on and drag your name and the project through the mud as some sort of conspiracy scheme," Jack said.

"God, he is probably right. I wonder how much dirt they could find if they really started looking. The trouble is, if they know I'm involved and I admit this, I can spin it anyway I like when the first media blitz hits. If they find this out without my say, however, then there will be a shit storm to deal with. On the other hand, if no one knows I'm involved, then there is really little to make a fuss about and the production crew would be seen as just another group of New York City film makers traveling the world hoping to be the next Roman Polanski."

"But you are thoroughly involved and this is not just any movie," Jack said matter-of-factly.

"Agreed. Say, what is Milo doing right now?" Kepstein looked towards the ceiling, then at his wife. "Where is he right now?"

"Milo is at Ohio State University interviewing students about the future of the country. We spoke with him last night. He said there was some sort of rally and they were getting swamped by kids wanting to be on camera and wanting to get their opinions out." Rebecca was smiling triumphantly at the notion. "I guess he started talking a little about the project to some of the students too."

Kepstein was quiet for a moment, then he blurted out, "Call Milo immediately, I have to talk to him at once, I — I think I have a perfect idea!"

"But Bill, it's three a.m. there!"

"Oh, yes, of course," Kepstein said, again momentarily lost in thought.

Kepstein decided that Milo was going to be the man responsible for alerting the people of the world to the fact that they'd been recorded during the past year. He was going to have to do this very carefully and he was going to have to do it very soon, especially before the men in suits on both sides of the Atlantic burst down the doors.

The plan he had in mind for Milo required Milo to do a number of things. First, he had to rent, or buy — whatever it took — a minivan. Men from the crew would fit the minivan with as many cameras as possible and, if possible, a large screen on each side. Milo was to show up at the rally driving this vehicle as a stunt aimed at attracting a great deal of attention. When the students approached the van, as Kepstein believed they surely would, Milo would stand on top of the van, or in front of it — whatever he thought best — and deliver a message Kepstein would prepare. The message would be sent to Milo via email, along with instructions that were to be sent to each member of the crew. Telephone calls would follow the emails in order to make sure that everyone had received the message.

* * *

Milo was in the middle of a crowd of about a thousand students when he felt his phone vibrating in his pocket. The roof of his tent was heaving in and out against its fiberglass poles as a strong wind rattled outside. The crowd was stretched across a college square made of concrete sidewalks that zigged and zagged, forming large grassy trapezoids. A park was located between the massive brick buildings of the Midwest's largest campus and the air was filled with an unexpected energy, considering that it was late August and there were no sporting events on this Monday morning.

Most of the students had spent the night in the park protesting a ballot being voted on the next week, a yay or nay to grant approval for the licensing of four casinos in the state. The students had come out en masse to speak against this issue, as well as a number of other matters.

Milo and the rest of his crew were sweltering in the morning humidity and found it impossible to sleep any later than six a.m. They were hurriedly unzipping the doors and windows of their nylon tent when the news came from Kepstein. Milo pulled his phone from his pocket and read the email that he had just received:

Dear friends,

We have run out of time. As expected, there have been certain events that have pushed our project ahead of schedule. We have been traveling the world at a rapid pace and we have been recording every conversation we've been involved in. We have created a vast library of human interactions, dialogues, and emotions.

I, Bill Kepstein, have been traveling the world over the course of the past year with minimal engagement in the financial industry, creating a film based on the notion that humans have lost the ability to communicate and have been driven to silence by their own actions.

Yes, we have the Internet. We have television and telephones that can transmit messages instantly to any corner of the world. We can speak with one another through video messaging, connecting one man in China with another in Alaska as if both were in the same room. With this technological boom, however, has come a degradation of the very use it was designed for, communication. When was the last time you really spoke with another person?

The world seems to have reserved itself into the safety of silence, removing the obligations of real person-to-person interaction. With the advent of constant connectivity, tools that were created to give us more free time have turned us into around-the-clock workers. Tools that were created to share videos and allow people to be socially active across space and time have removed the necessity of being socially active. With only the slightest redirection, these tools can do great things for us, but it is imperative that we remain the talking, interacting, and communicating people we have always been.

We have compiled a collage of conversations from around the world, and when this catalog of human interaction is released, it will change the way we see and think about those around us. The filming — the discussion rather — is not yet finished, and will never be.

Please do not take action against us. Our aim is not political. It is not based on the accumulation of power. We are simply working on a project that has humanitarian aspirations. We hope to present the process of communication in a way that reminds us all that it is necessary to maintain this bond that binds us together.

Sincerely,

Bill Kepstein

Milo closed his phone, then his eyes. He didn't know where to look or what to say to the crew members, but to his surprise, when he looked at them, he realized they had also received the message and were waiting to see what would happen next. In fact, Milo quickly realized that everyone had gotten the same message, as text messages and emails were flooding onto his cell phone screen from Seoul, Mexico City, Dublin, New York City, and other places.

Milo made a weak attempt at gathering another hour or so of rest, but in a matter of minutes, Kepstein's next email made that impossible.

Milo,

This message will most likely be intercepted as was probably the case with the first one — which I directed to a larger audience— but I wanted to address you separately. Please print copies of the last email and distribute it to as many people as you can at once.

You must purchase a van today. There will be a team of AV technicians that will help us refit the vehicle for our purposes. We will need a large working van, white with no windows. Have the men attach as many cameras as they can to every spare surface. On each side of the van also affix a large television screen. The screen on one side will show what is being recorded on the other, and vice-versa. I will send you a copy of a sketch we're working on here as soon as it is finished. This will be the vehicle for advertising the film and spreading the word of its importance.

I understand you are on a campus today. I think it would be wise if we made this your first stop on a nationwide tour of all the campuses you can

manage to visit. You will be generating a running record of people interacting
with one another. Explain to them that what they see on one side of the van is
being recorded and reproduced on the other and that the purpose of the
screens is to capture people communicating with one another. Explain our
position and distribute the aforementioned email if it's necessary and
appropriate. Let them know that many real-life shots will be used for the movie
we are making. If the van does not suit its purposes, or make as large a wave as
we should hope, then perhaps we can offer a taste or two of the footage we
have gathered via the mobile televisions. Go today. Start the explanation and
tell as many people as you can what we are doing.

-Bill Kepstein

Milo and his crew headed for a dealership, then to the audio-visual surplus store before going to a very quiet log cabin located thirty minutes outside of Columbus. In sixteen hours they were able to affix a total of fourteen different cameras and two flat screen monitors to the sides of the van, not to mention a PA system that was hidden atop the van and that was designed to capture any audio that might be chosen for broadcast.

Milo and the crew spent the next week recording. By the end of the week, the crowd had multiplied ten-fold. It was difficult to determine who was there for the ballot protest, who was there to learn more about their project, and/or who wanted to find a place to voice their platform. The crew quickly learned how powerful the suggestion of revolution could become among college students. It was a cursing and a blessing to them, as they saw that anyone with a radical idea could take up a bullhorn.

The concept was a huge success and word of the traveling van and its message spread among the college campuses. Rumors abounded about their activities. The most provocative were those that were closest to the truth: the van was a front for some sort of strange project aimed at toppling countries' status quos. Others said that the band of men and women involved with the project were terrorists and that they were sending the images all over the world with mocking undertones. Perhaps the most flamboyant of all rumors was that the group was somehow involved with a secret society of sex fanatics from New York City and that the only purpose of their cameras was to achieve some sinister form of voyeurism.

The only real knowledge anyone had of their intent and purpose came from Bill Kepstein. His message was spread by Milo, who printed out two hundred and fifty copies of the email — before the school's printer ran out of ink and he was removed from the building — then distributed them to whomever would accept them.

The night of the day they'd received Kepstein's message, and the same night the crew was working on the van, Milo took a cab back to what became the protest sit-in, secured a bullhorn, read the message, and announced that he would be back the following day with a van and the beginning of a long journey. The crowd on that first day was about fifteen hundred, but by the end of the month, when Milo arrived at Tulane University in New Orleans, the crowd was closer to fifteen thousand. Word of something politically important, of secrecy, and of a wealthy financial tycoon had spread like wildfire. The project had gained a life of its own.

* * *

When Kepstein had sent the original email, he'd been fretfully nervous, but what he hadn't foreseen may have been his saving grace. What he hadn't foreseen was that the people who were reading his emails were secretly reading them under the guise of the US Patriot Act. What he did not know, but was delighted to learn, was that there were so many clauses and red tape tied into such an act that even if he were doing something dangerously wrong, it would be nearly impossible to ever say so. His email never made it to the desk of any executives, or to anyone else, but only those who had been standing close enough to Milo on that summer afternoon in Ohio to receive the message.

Kepstein's plan was more effective than expected, and within a few months the names of those involved were becoming common knowledge, not just at college rallies, but within the greater political and media landscape. Milo was mixing past, present, and future as he described the changes that were coming. He was quoting the Occupy Wall Street protests that stopped debit card fee hikes from large banks and the Internet blackout and protest led by Wikipedia and Google that stalled the Stop Online Piracy Act legislation from passing. He quoted events taking place in Europe to combat Internet policing and quoted the Arab Spring that swept through the Middle East. He made a plea to avoid the violence that can result from freedom and said that the point of their film was to demonstrate the beauty of communication en masse. He explained that society was at a point where these wide-scale government coups and political boycotts were increasingly possible due to social media platforms and the ubiquitous videophones that could be tapped into global networks.

"Thank you all for allowing us to broaden our message base," Milo said, standing on a podium as an honorary speaker at the Sasquatch Music Festival in Washington State. Milo's tour had been so popular that the national music festivals had capitalized on their popularity to sell tickets. The concert venues took the camera-van concept and duplicated it on a bigger stage. "Many of you have become aware of the film project we've been working on and you understand many of the technological and social changes that are resulting in a tumultuous world. The question at this point is not whether we can create these changes, but how should we start planning to create these changes properly to ensure positive outcomes? I leave you with that." Then, as he had done in his most recent appearances, Milo walked off the stage amidst a roar of applause.

Naturally the project had its detractors, but their number was fewer at a music festival. General Adams was infuriated by the commotion the publicity blitz was causing. He had a tremendous amount of editing to do and believed that with each new appearance, there was going to be more trouble. One day it would be legal trouble from abroad. The next day it would be another rumor springing up in the American media that would need to be dealt with at once. He was busy editing and couldn't imagine wearing a public relations hat at the same time.

"Have you seen today's front-page headline in the *Los Angeles Times*?" Adams said over the phone, speaking with Kepstein. "It reads — and this is verbatim, 'Big Screen Director Meets Big Money Banker: Financing the Hidden Agenda of America's Enemies.'"

"Wow," Kepstein exclaimed, exhaling a heavy sigh as he slumped in his chair and looked through the foggy windows of his second-story room. He watched the people walking and riding their bicycles along the sidewalk outside and felt a mix of sorrow and anger: on the one hand, these people never got to hear the truth from their news sources; on the other, it was their fault for collectively demanding shoddy news.

"This article goes on to mention the people who've worked on films with me in the past. It calls me 'a potential result from the mixing attributes of an anarchist and film producer' and describes you as a 'gullible banker swayed by ideologies outside of your understanding.' You know, the worst part — the part of all this I have a hard time with — is that I knowingly signed up for this project, but my colleagues from days past did not and do not deserve to have their names tarnished. Old friends have been calling me all morning."

"I'm sorry to hear that, General. All I can offer you is sympathy. I've been under the same scrutiny. I've had some very nasty conversations recently. My replacement at the bank is being threatened with charges of corruption by members of the Board of Directors. I think you know what I know though, don't you?"

"That this is only going to get worse? Yes, I know it very well, Bill. I'm rushing to finish the work, and we've been uploading your hard drives in Dublin on a twice-daily basis, should any of the material be compromised. Time is running out."

The men ended their conversation without reaching an optimistic note. The truth was, the walls *were* closing in on them. General had

213

originally planned on six months for editing, and as it had only been five when Milo made the first announcement, he had been behind on his work ever since then and he felt a great deal of pressure.

When Kepstein's announcement was made and people began to hear about the project, three groups began to vehemently oppose it. Wall Street had already seen the devaluation that a few protestors could cause. Elected officials preferred to operate with a closed-door policy and felt the same threat they'd encountered with renegade politicians going against "Washington" in recent years. And the elaborate hierarchy of influence-pushers, arms dealers, commodities traders, importers and exporters, and the global war machines that kept their structures in balance was at philosophical odds with the project. The one thing they all had in common was the desire to maintain the status quo.

Milo was causing waves months before the American Presidential primaries would begin shaping up. Unfortunately, despite the lobbying and the sway of the media, the politicos were unable to avoid the elephant in the room. No one was able to agree with the movement, but they would denounce it to varying degrees in order to make sure that its supporters were not upset. The process of stump-speech public discord began to create a rift between the young and the old, and the old and the new, much as abortion, stem-cell research, same-sex marriage, or any other contentious subject had done. The more the process exposed the political system and created unanswerable questions, the more people felt duped and switched sides. Still, there was no one brazen enough to condone the film or its aims. The project had led to another polarization of opinion and the taking of sides.

214

Chapter Twenty

"Cheers," Jack said to Lenny and the Kepsteins as they tipped their glasses together for a commemorative pint of Guinness. Lenny had recently made the trip across the pond in search of a reprieve from all the action back home. "It's officially been one year since we started this whole thing, one year since that first night in Brooklyn when everyone got together for the first time. And now here we sit on this August afternoon in Dublin and much has changed."

"Cheers to a successful year," Rebecca said, "with many rewarding changes."

"Well put," Lenny said. "While we've made some new friends, and . . . made a few new enemies, it has been rewarding nonetheless."

Kepstein was sitting at the head of the table, contemplating these comments. He had changed as well over the past year, especially his attire, as he now wore blue jeans and a white T-shirt. He also wore sandals more often and drank less. He thought and wrote more, became frustrated less frequently, and was able to experience a level of clarity that comes from years of heavy meditation, like a monk in some old forgotten tradition.

"It has been both successful and rewarding," Kepstein stated, nodding his head and pursing his lips, "but I'm afraid we've only got an uphill battle ahead of us from here on out."

He didn't mean to be the pessimist of the bunch, but he was a smart man and knew that the writing was on the wall. From constant reports sent by General Adams, Lenny, and a few others still residing in New York, he knew the pressure was getting to the point that something had to give. Many people in the States and many leaders in Europe were upset, but it didn't appear that any of them knew why they were so upset. All different kinds of groups were proponents or opponents of their cause, the project's allies and enemies seemingly so varied and random that it was impossible to determine whom to side with. There was one point, however, that nearly everyone could agree on: the film was attempting to create a change of some sort — a big one at that. The last thing any American wanted was a Middle-Eastern war scene on their soil. They'd heard of anarchy and had seen its results via news reports and videos: far-away lands torn apart by bombing, poisonous gas, hatred. They had witnessed the occasional riots that took place at home. A large portion of the American populace felt that a film seeming to plead for that type of anarchy needed to be stopped at once.

"I've been thinking about something and I want to bring it up to all of you tonight," Kepstein said, feeling the heavy weight on his shoulders. "I have been getting numerous reports from our friends back home. As you can imagine, they're becoming anxious because of all the recent publicity. Some members of the group are hearing complaints from their spouses and families. The very idea of this film is beginning to polarize some groups in America and they worry that by the time the film is released, there will truly be long-reaching and very serious consequences. The media is having a field day with all of us, as you're aware, and both this house and the house in Brooklyn have been under surveillance for some time. I cannot help our

216

friends if trouble arises and I am held captive here in Europe. And I cannot be detained when our masterpiece is released. It's time to get back to the States before anything happens. I'm ready to go back, and I think I need to do this within the next week."

"Are you sure about this, dear?" Rebecca asked softly. She was quickly understanding the seriousness of the risk. "Do you truly feel threatened here — is the threat less severe back home?"

"It's the same threat everywhere, Rebecca, but I've got far less protection here. In the States, I have influence. Lawyers, powerful friends. If we fall into trouble here, I am less sure of my reach."

"How is the crew holding up?" Jack asked, thinking about what Kepstein had just said and about what he'd heard from the group in Brooklyn.

"There's a lot of worry, Jack," Lenny said. He'd just flown in from New York the night before. "Like Bill said, some of the crew have family. There's concern from their spouses about what happens when their bosses find out they're married to members of the crew. This truly is becoming a hot-button issue."

"Right. It's final, I need to get back to New York to pull everyone together. Jack, could you please join me on the trip? Rebecca, I'd prefer you stay here if you're comfortable with it. Lenny, it would be good for you to do the same as well — I know Adams still has some last minute editing to do, and I really think you can get more done, working here remotely without all the distraction. It's completely up to you." Out of habit, Kepstein looked at his watch, then back to the group at the dining table. "Of course, if anyone has different plans, that is completely fine with me. I am just trying to think of the best way to orchestrate everything."

That night, the Kepsteins were lying in bed discussing the recent turn of events and their plans. They felt a sense of finality in the air. "Is there any reason you want me to stay here, Bill?" Rebecca said facing her husband, her head on the pillow.

"I am concerned that if we run into trouble in the airport, you'll also be implicated. I don't want anything to happen to you."

"Nothing is going to happen at the airport, is it?" she asked. with a tremor in her voice.

"I highly doubt it, but it's a chance I don't want to take if we don't have to."

The couple closely embraced in a passionate hug and tried to sleep. Drifting off, the rain outside fell upon summer leaves and they thought about each other and the friends and family they'd met over the past, long year. They thought about the changes that had taken place and the results of those changes in their lives: how they affected them and everyone else associated with the project.

* * *

"I got us seats at separate ends of the plane," Kepstein told Jack as the cab brought them close to the airport. "It's probably unnecessary, I know, but it's become a habit by this point."

"I agree with you. It's better to avoid risks where we can, and I usually sleep on this trip anyhow," Jack answered, wondering why his friend was experiencing so much trepidation. Perhaps it was that Jack had flown back and forth many times, while Kepstein hadn't left Dublin since he moved there half a year ago. Or perhaps Kepstein knew something he didn't.

Because Jack had flown on this same flight so often, he knew several members of the regular flight crew by name. Depending on which time of day he left, he'd either sleep during the entire trip, or spend the first half of the flight drinking cocktails in back with the crew and the second half sleeping. Today's flight was a bit different, however, as it took about six cocktails before he returned to his seat for a quick cat nap. He'd had a great conversation with one of the ladies about his favorite places in Brooklyn and was offered a dinner date should they both be available in the City.

"I will be looking forward to it, Jennifer," he said, taking his luggage from the overhead bin and winking at the flight attendant. "Perhaps this Thursday will work well — I believe we've got some free time."

Jennifer knew who Jack was, as did most of the people on the airplane, and she felt fortunate to get the attention from someone who had become semi-famous. She was following him down the aisle. "The pleasure will be all mine, Jack."

As Jack stepped from the plane into the jet bridge, a tall, very broad-shouldered man shouted, "Jack Shales! You're under arrest."

"On what accounts?" he asked complacently while peacefully turning around to be handcuffed.

"You have the right to remain silent . . ." He was read an abbreviated form of the Miranda Rights.

"Aren't you guys from Interpol? "Jack asked, noting the lack of identification the men had on their uniforms. "Why are you reading me my rights?"

"You'll have time to ask all the questions you want soon, smartass," the lead man said as they took the stairs down to the ground floor of the terminal. Jack was led into an unmarked van. The van drove about half a mile from the terminal to a midsize hangar, the type typically used for small business jets, where he was taken through the empty hangar and past a number of government airplanes to a small set of offices in the far right corner of the cavernous building.

"Why is Bill Kepstein contacting you all of these years after the bribe?" the lead interrogator — Mr. X, as he called himself — asked.

"I'd like to have a lawyer present before answering any further questions," Jack said defiantly while leaning back in his chair.

Mr. X swiftly chopped Jack in the upper chest, causing him to flip backwards in his seat. He hit his head hard on the concrete floor. He felt the room spinning and suddenly become much darker as blood found its way past his hairline and onto his shirt collar. Then he heard the door shut and the number of men in the room decreased from five to two.

"I'll cut your fingers off, I'll knock your teeth out, I'll waterboard you, I will systematically torture you until you're unrecognizable, you little shit.

Do you understand me?" The man was standing above Jack, his boots to the side of Jack's shoulders as he lay on the ground, still handcuffed to the chair. "You do not have any rights here. You are in diplomatic limbo — a grey zone you should be very scared to be in. You blackmailed the police and took a bribe to stay quiet. That is illegal. People want you to stay quiet."

"Is this about the bribe, or is this about the project I've been working on?" he asked.

"Would you be so very kind to give us a little information about both?" Mr. X asked, pulling Jack from the ground so he could sit upright in the chair.

"Yes, I can do that," Jack replied humbly, trying to hold back his anger.

Mr. X punched Jack hard in the face, again knocking him flat against his back. Blood started to drip from his nose. "Oh, sorry Jackie boy. You're a real smart fella from what they say. An intellectual, no? I thought it'd be fun if we did a little experiment with conditioning. If you tell me what I want, I will hit you, or maybe I won't. If you don't tell me what I want, I will hit you, or then again maybe I won't. I am curious to see how that affects you."

Jack lay there in silence, staring up at the ceiling and tried to figure out what was happening. He had no idea, but knew that the way he was being treated wasn't supposed to be allowed.

221

"Bring in Kepstein," Mr. X yelled to the man guarding the door as he lifted Jack back into his chair again and wiped the pooled blood from Jack's nose and upper lip.

A handcuffed Kepstein came through the door and was placed in a chair on the same side of the desk as Jack. Mr. X sat across from them and the guard returned to the door.

"So let's run through the events for a moment, shall we?" Mr. X said as he removed files from the briefcase next to the desk. "Jack, five years ago you blackmailed the Baltimore Police. Kepstein, you and your corrupt friends in the city paid him off to stay quiet. You gave the police a one-million-dollar loan, if I am not mistaken, which you made a profit of two hundred thousand dollars in interest on. Not bad! You still make money when you're bribing cops and fucking justice. You must be proud of yourself. Now about five years later, the two of you find yourselves becoming fast friends. You're even living together and planning to *make a movie*."

The room was spinning around Jack's head again, but this time it wasn't due to a fall. He looked over at Kepstein who was looking down at the table. "Is this true? Were you behind the bribe?"

"Yes," Kepstein said under his breath, still staring down at the table.

"Fuck you," Jack yelled at him with disgust, bewilderment, and betrayal.

Mr. X was visibly confused by their exchange, but neither Jack nor Kepstein noticed him. "Why have you waited so long before contacting Jack Shales? What are your intentions?" Mr. X asked Kepstein.

"Jack was unaware of my interaction with the City of Baltimore. It has been a secret known only to myself and to my wife . . . until you made your superfluous comments just now."

"Bullshit."

"It's the truth," Kepstein replied. "How did you hear about this anyhow, and what is the nature of your questioning?"

"I have never heard of this son-of-a-bitch being behind the police bribe. If I had, I'd never have seen him again. Why are you shaking me down?" Jack said defiantly.

"Shut your fucking mouth," Mr. X said to him. "Do NOT make me tell you this again or I will knock your teeth out."

Kepstein heard this and immediately knew that they were still off the books and under the wings of corruption. While this had its risks, he thought, he still preferred it to the rigidness of the true legal system. His money was significantly more helpful when corruption was a consideration

"First of all, you both are being held on three accounts of conspiracy — one in Spain, one in the United States, and one in Ireland. Kepstein, you tried to run for the Mayor of Baltimore in 2006. The city told you they needed your place at the bank more than they needed you in politics. You inherited some unsavory accounting practices as a legacy from one of your

223

father's friends. Those practices were helpful to the City of Baltimore, and you were instructed to keep quiet. In 2010, Jack Shales was on the brink of exposing the entire police force. The federal inspections would have no doubt implicated you, and you agreed to make a loan of one million dollars, off the books, to keep the issues submerged."

"You're a hypocritical, lying, bastard," Jack said, spitting at Kepstein's feet. Mr. X punched Jack so hard this time that he was knocked unconscious.

"My question to you, Bill, is why didn't you just keep it quiet? Why did you feel the need to ruin your life? Why did you contact Jack Shales!?" Mr. X was standing out of his seat now, but he couldn't strike Kepstein. The man's secrets were too powerful and affected too many lives. He could kill him, but then he'd have to kill everyone else who knew the true story and there was no way to tell how many there were.

"I have not informed Jack of my relationship with the City of Baltimore or my involvement with his bribe. I met him nearly a year and half ago and only learned of his history after a number of months. We had a great deal in common and I enjoyed the conversation. And so, going against my better judgment, I allowed the friendship to continue. What is this all about?"

"Your end of the agreement — a contract written in blood might I add — was to keep your mouth shut about the bribe. Obviously, this meant you were not to inform the recipient, Jack Shales, of what you had done. One of your slimy little colleagues there in City Hall saw the news about you and Jack and your 'project' and got nervous. They thought you were going to come clean and went to the authorities before you went public."

Mr. X interrogated Kepstein for another thirty minutes while Jack lay on the ground in a stupor. Finding out that the State of Maryland thought he was planning to expose the bribery scandal via the film, he realized that he had two choices. He could admit to their misguided accusation and agree to handle it however the authorities felt was appropriate, or he could tell them the true nature of his relationship with Jack and describe the content of the film. Kepstein was not the type of man to make decisions without thinking them through. However, it was clear that he needed to give the cops one story or another and had to determine which choice would most effectively expedite his release.

"You are well aware of what Jack and I have been working on, is that correct?" Kepstein said to Mr. X after Jack was taken away to a separate room.

"Yes, I do read the papers. Why in the hell did you give up your position at the bank anyhow — don't tell me your guilty conscience got the best of you?"

"In a sense. I guess you could say I got tired of doing what I was doing and wanted to change directions."

"You succeeded in that regard, haven't you?" Mr. X said, sitting across from Kepstein and lighting a cigarette. He rested his chin upon his clasped hands as the smoke drifted between them. "You must be one of those types that does everything well. If you want to run a bank, you run a bank. If you want to sell shoes, you're the next big brand. If you want to make a movie, you cause a national uproar."

Kepstein was feeling flattered, but knew he shouldn't be. "Have another?" he asked, motioning for a cigarette.

Mr. X tossed him one, lit it, and went on. "I just wish people like you had more common sense, that's all. You make it very hard for the rest of us. You can't seem to get the big picture."

"Please enlighten me. What is the big picture I am missing?" Kepstein said, getting frustrated with the man's rhetoric.

"The big picture is that I am sitting here," X replied, pointing to his chair, "and you are sitting there."

"And which of us has done anything good with their life? Which one of us will sleep easily at night?"

"I'll sleep very well tonight, I promise you."

"Because some fat cat asshole is paying you to make sure all the wheels are greased and nothing changes? You can sleep well because your existence is to serve as a pawn in some useless corruption scandal?"

"Don't take the moral high ground with me, Kepstein. You've fucked over more thousands of people during your tenure at the bank than I could ever possibly do in all my life. I'm sorry you don't feel the need to work anymore like the rest of us and your time away has given you a chance to feel sorry for yourself, but don't get high and mighty with me. Your little pal,

Jack, said it best. You're a no good hypocrite, and the world's going to turn on you faster than you could ever imagine."

"At least I can understand the benefits of changing . . . everyone likes a change-of-heart story, don't they?" Kepstein replied, half to the man and half to himself. "What's next for us? What are we doing now?"

Mr. X didn't answer, but left the room as calmly as he could. He wasn't prepared for the news he was about to receive from the men on the other side of the thin slab of drywall. He would learn that the arrival of Kepstein and Jack had been talked about and anticipated by quite a few people. Some people in the Dublin airport had seen the men, and word spread fairly quickly through the news and online social networks. The crew in New York had every intention of picking them up in a quick and quiet manner, but by the time they'd reached the airport, there was a small crowd of about fifty people with signs waiting for the men. Airport security was attempting to disperse the crowd, but most of the people there had business at the airport, either coming or going, and couldn't be removed lawfully. Their signs had been impromptu ones, made onsite as the commotion grew. Others had filmed the scene with their cellphones. There was no way to keep Kepstein's and Jack's disappearance hidden and this was a serious problem for Mr. X, the members of Baltimore's police force, and whomever else it was that was pulling the strings behind the scenes.

In an attempt to limit any collateral damage to the project, Kepstein and Jack agreed to keep the bribery issue under wraps and Kepstein agreed to take the responsibility for the three counts of conspiracy upon himself. They also understood that if either of them provided anyone with any information about their prior involvement with the Baltimore city police, Jack would be tried on the same three charges. Kepstein was done for, but Jack could remain free if they played ball.

Chapter Twenty-one

After twenty-four hours, those responsible for detaining Kepstein and Jack knew they'd created a difficult situation for themselves. As there was no easy way to balance their desire to keep the two men in captivity with the need to keep the public from asking why they were being held, the power structure decided it best to provide the masses with some information.

On the second day of their detention, a spokesman from the airport's PR division released a scripted statement that the airport was cooperating with local and international police to review potential breaches of national security and the potential breaches of international laws, and that this would be a "delicate and potentially lengthy review." The public wasn't satisfied with this explanation, and by the third day, an unruly crowd was stirring outside the airport. No one in the crowd really knew whether or not the men were being held there, but it gave them a way to express their frustration.

The day after their separation during the interrogation, Kepstein and Jack were again placed in the same cell. Once their interrogator realized that Jack truly hadn't known of Kepstein's secretive past, he saw the look of vengeance in the younger man's face as an opportunity. He secretly hoped Jack would lash out at Kepstein, or worse.

"You're fine, Jack," Kepstein reassured him. He was in the corner of the cell closest to the hallway, sitting on a dirty orange sofa, one hand on the sofa and one hand on an iron bar of their cell. He was still wearing the same khakis and button-down shirt he'd worn three days earlier when they flew from Ireland to New York.

"There was a time when I would consider your advice and your words of encouragement to be important, Bill — but that time has passed." Jack sat on the opposite side of the room, not looking at his cellmate.

"I understand you're upset, Jack. I understand you're mad as hell."

"You can't imagine the half of it," Jack replied quickly while standing up. "I should have taken Milo's advice the first time we met. He said, 'Jack, you can't trust these kinds of people. They're wealthy, they're in the business of taking advantage of others — he'll use you and toss you aside.' Tell me one part of that characterization that's been wrong, you hypocritical bastard."

"Tell me, Jack, how have I taken advantage of you?"

"Wait until this shitstorm settles, and let's see who lands on his feet and who ends up destitute and imprisoned." Jack turned his back to Kepstein and sat down on the bench opposite him. "Leave me alone. You've done enough damage already. You'd better pray these assholes can keep your bribery scandal hushed up, or you'll be hurting many more people than just us."

Kepstein thought about that unpleasant notion. He thought about everyone he'd worked with and had come to know at the bank. He thought about what was going to happen when rumors about a scandal started to surface. He thought about the repercussions and the depth of those repercussions for a publicly-traded company and about his successor, Kenneth Blackstone, who had gladly taken the position as his replacement. Kepstein started to wonder how many people he'd been lying to, and whether it was all worth it.

"You fellas having a lover's quarrel?" the pot-belly guard said, bringing them their lunches on plastic trays the color of dirt. Neither man said anything. "I imagine you're not going to be crowd favorites much longer, now that it's out . . ."

Kepstein wasn't able to hold back his curiosity. "What's *out*?"

"Uh oh, you haven't heard the news?" the guard asked, relishing the moment. "Someone squealed about your bribery. I'm not supposed to be telling you this, but I couldn't help it."

"Why's that?" Jack muttered quietly. He was staring at the cement floor, completely numb to the new development.

"Hell, I sorta sympathize with you fellas in some respects. You tried to do something big — and unique — and you almost succeeded. Not many folks are doing anything like that anymore. I can't sympathize with your blackmailing the police or paying for the bribery of a man blackmailing the police, however. That's just downright dishonest," he said, winking at Kepstein. "Let me know if you get tired of that gruel they serve here and I'll see if I can find something a bit better on the taste buds."

The guard left and silence returned to the cell, bringing with it a kind of staleness that only an incarcerated man could understand — the penetrating knowledge that his actions were affecting peoples' lives somewhere out there beyond the steel bars that enclosed him.

Indeed, the news had spread almost instantaneously. At first, it came from a few reporters snooping around the county offices in Baltimore, then from a few more reviewing Jack's finances and tax documents. Eventually, it came from a low-level clerk named Margaret Johns.

"Margaret Johns? My name's Peter Talbot and I'm with the Associated Press. I'm working on a story about a man I believe you used to work for before you came to the county offices here. A William Kepstein — does that sound familiar to you, Madam?"

"I'll tell you everything, but I have to have either legal protection or a minimum of fifty thousand dollars," Margaret said, walking around the side of the reporter to shut her office door. She was scared, knew that her situation was vulnerable, and felt that she had no choice.

Talbot gladly accepted the offer and he spun the story like any aspiring journalist would, with bold type face in capital letters on the front page: **CONSPIRACY!**

The story was a goldmine for every media outlet, as it could be covered from any variety of angles, all fascinating. Kepstein and Jack had become darlings of many and enemies of others. Their efforts with the film had turned them into pop-culture sensations and the news of their confinement had made them martyrs. Now, overnight, the nature of their relationship took a sinister turn — a 180-degree turn, some felt. They went from friends to enemies. Some thought Jack had been taken advantage of, while others thought that the two men had been co-conspirators all along. Others found a hero in the story of Jack's blackmailing the police, while others sympathized with Kepstein's being born into a world of corruption.

Within hours of the first leak, Margaret Johns was offered book deals. People wanted to know the real Kepstein — *Did he want to go through with the bribe? Was it true he wanted to run for mayor? Was he really involved with organized crime?* The questions were as varied as were the inquisitors and the entire situation exploded within a matter of days.

As the number of protesters grew, Kepstein and Jack were as distant as ever and Jack was seething with a hatred that worsened with each passing day.

One afternoon, a legal team came to the jail on behalf of Jack's bank to inform him that his assets were being seized until the investigation was over. He knew this meant his money was gone, but it wasn't the money that kept him awake at night. Rather, it was the notion of an "investigation." Bribes were illegal, even when they came from the police. Jack knew he was in trouble. A few hours after the legal team's visit, more men came, each representing a different legal entity that had a different opinion on how Jack could help himself.

"Jack, you simply need to explain the corrupt nature of this Tammany Hall police system in Baltimore. It's in your best interest to make it well known. If whistleblowers do not speak out, corruption and injustice will prevail." Another lawyer said, in a matter of fact I-am-your-best-friend legal representation voice, "I've represented many high-profile men and women in situations quite similar to yours — what do you say?"

It had been seven days since Kepstein and Jack had been locked up and similar conversations took place all afternoon. The lawyers only spoke to Jack, as if Kepstein's situation was not open to the same degree of assistance. Finally, Jack lost control, for, on the one hand, he was getting legal advice, while, on the other, he had also been receiving unwelcome advice from Kepstein, and he now was finding it very difficult to sort out his thoughts or know who was trying to help or hurt him.

"Guaaaaaaaard!" Jack yelled at the top of his lungs. "Guard! Get me out of here! Get me away from this man!" Jack turned quickly to Kepstein. "Don't say a single word, not one word, do you understand — I can't take it anymore!"

Kepstein remained silent, then rose to his feet, hands in front of him as if to plead for Jack to take it easy.

"Stay right where you are, you son of a bitch. I don't know what kind of game you think this is. You don't think I notice what's going on here? These assholes keep coming to give me legal advice. Only I wonder why no one is bothering to instruct the big-whig with the money and connections what he should do next?"

"Jack, I — "

"No." He held up his hand.

The guard came to the cell. "What's going on in here, fellas?"

"I need to get away from this bastard. I need to be put into a different cell far away from him."

"I'm sorry, Jack, we can't do that. We're on strict orders."

"I'll kill him," Jack said with a dead-pan stare, gritting his teeth, but the guard looked unfazed. "No, I'll beat myself to death. No, sorry, I am being unpleasant. Really, I just need privacy to speak with my legal representation. When they arrive, the first thing they ask is if I can have privacy. It would just make it easier — for everyone — if he didn't know what I was going to do next."

After thinking about Jack's request for the next couple of hours, the guard granted Jack's wish.

"You really don't think we should stick together?" Kepstein asked as Jack was being handcuffed prior to being moved to another cell.

"There is no more 'we,' Bill."

"What about the film, Jack? What about all our progress?"

"The movie will proceed, Bill — perhaps it will even be better without you. The only thing you did was pay for it, just like you do for everything else in your life. Your input was minimal anyway."

"I'm sorry, Jack. You have to understand that I believed — I still *believe* — in everything we've done," Kepstein said as the guard took Jack out of the cell into the hallway, the cell door slamming hard behind them.

"Fuck your apologies, Bill. They will not get back the money that I've earned and now lost. They will not keep me out of prison. You can keep your apologies — you'll be needing them."

Chapter Twenty-two

While Kepstein and Jack were being held, Milo was making his way from Washington State through Oregon and into San Francisco. He had a public appearance scheduled for an annual Autumn music festival held at Golden Gate Park, but the city planners cancelled the gathering at the last minute, afraid that its size would invite trouble.

Because Milo's mission was to provide the public with information and updates on the film, he believed that agreeing to cancel his appearance was out of the question. A crowd of nearly one hundred thousand was expected, but it was anyone's guess how many people would show up.

On the way, Milo had made an impromptu stop at UC Davis. The stop had been advertised via Twitter and other social media only for a few hours. It was obvious to the public that something was in the air. News of the bribery scandal and a suspected conspiracy had been leaked the day before, and rumors were beginning to circulate. Milo worried that San Francisco would be a nightmare.

That evening, Milo made his way over the Golden Gate Bridge in the white van. There hadn't been so much media coverage of a vehicle since O.J. Simpson's police chase. News helicopters were circling the bridge, cataloguing his entry in dozens of languages and on multiple channels. Cameras panned to Golden Gate Park. Thousands of people were holding signs and giving interviews to anyone who asked.

Milo's van slowly made its way into the park. The crowd appeared to be as polarized as Jack and Kepstein. He exited the van, and made his way to the stage. While he had a prepared speech, he decided, instead, to speak extemporaneously.

"My goal today was to speak about our project, giving you updates about the film's current status. Obviously, there's a lot going on right now, and Bill Kepstein and Jack Shales have been held in captivity for the past seven days. But there was news yesterday that we need to talk about."

The crowd began roaring so loudly that Milo couldn't speak. Pounding his fist hard on the podium, and showing a sense of exasperation he'd never before demonstrated, he went on, "Please, let me finish what I have to say — it will suit all of your concerns, and is the only way I can get information to you. Please." The noise level declined a bit. "I am not simply going to speak about what we're doing and what is happening, as the level of trust in our project has obviously been damaged. To reestablish that level of trust, we need dialogue. I do not have anything to hide from you. Please ask your questions in an organized manner and I will answer them."

Two members of the crew stood on the stage with Milo. One of them noticed a sign that a younger person in the crowd was holding up with his friend. The sign was large, nearly six feet long and four feet high. It read, "Who does Kepstein work for? Who does Jack work for? Who does Milo work for?"

"You there, with the sign. Why don't you come up here, hold that up, and we can address your questions in the open?"

The two men holding the sign carried it up the steps to the temporary platform. They stood next to Milo and the crew members. Cameras were recording every second of the event. Milo handed the microphone to the sign carrier, saying, "Please tell me what I can explain or clear up in reference to your questions?"

"It's simple. Kepstein speaks as a man attempting to expose the injustices of the world, yet he has clearly been cooperating with the police to hide corruption —does he work for the State of Maryland or the Federal government? Our assumption is that he has created a film attempting to expose state officials, but doing this on behalf of the Federal government."

The crowd reacted loudly after this statement, then fell silent as Milo began to speak. "Bill Kepstein inherited a bank from his father, and he ran it as a bank. News of his financial involvement with the police became known to the rest of us involved with this project only at the time, and to the extent, that it was made available to all of you. I cannot speak about the details of his involvement because I don't have any more information than you do. I can only tell you that he is a genius with a noble dream to correct previous wrongdoings, not only his own, but those of the world over. Perhaps if he'd made his past known to us at the outset, this project would never have left the ground."

"You're telling me that Jack never knew that the man he'd been living with for the past year was the same man that financed his bribe?" the man holding sign asked.

"That is what I am saying. I've known Jack for more than a decade. He spent countless hours attempting to expose the police force and their

239

irresponsible practices. Jack will most likely lose all the money that was given to him to keep quiet, money he has not spent. He has not lived lavishly, and now he is facing criminal charges for nothing more than his pursuit of an ideal — that communication among us needs to be renewed." Milo thought for a moment, looking at the sign. "As for the final question on your sign, I am not working for anyone. None of us are. We've risked a lot to do what we are doing, and now we are facing extreme consequences. While two of our most important colleagues are locked away, I will continue to announce our progress, and I hope you will continue to follow, support, and believe in this project."

* * *

As Milo continued his appearances, the public began to see Jack, not Kepstein, as the project's leader. The details Milo provided about Jack's past and the notion that he'd been duped by Kepstein, losing everything he had in his pursuit of justice and equality, led to Jack's being perceived as a martyr. Crowds at Milo's stops began to chant, "Free Jack Shales." The chants were recorded and heard on a number of news outlets, and became too much for those holding the men in custody to ignore. In order to placate the public, they eventually agreed to release Jack.

When Lenny heard about Jack's release, he felt he needed to contact Milo at once.

"I seriously hope Jack can fix your mistakes," Lenny said when Milo answered his phone.

"What are you talking about, Lenny?" Milo replied, offended by the comment.

"I've seen the videos and read the news, especially what you said in San Francisco. Are there any details about this project that you left out?! Or did you feel it necessary to give all the incriminating information you could? Do you know what you've done to Kepstein's reputation? You've pitted him and Jack against one another. You've painted him as a criminal and Jack as some sort of victim."

"That's not what I meant to do at all, Lenny, you know that — I was just attempting to answer questions to show the crowd that we're not hiding anything."

"There's nothing else to hide now, Milo! You don't know how to speak to these people, and you certainly can't be doing it publicly. The media took everything you said and turned it against us. They've made it sound like we knew about Kepstein's history all along. You've implicated the entire crew in legal matters beyond our comprehension."

"I'm sorry Lenny, I was just trying— "

"Stop trying!" Lenny interrupted and hung up the phone.

Chapter Twenty-three

Milo rented a room in an out-of-the-way hotel in Oakland after he spoke with Lenny. It was a Sunday afternoon, and the world seemed to be getting very confusing for him. The crew agreed to drive the van south of the city as a decoy, where they could get some R&R and Milo could get some sleep at the hotel. He needed to think about what was happening and what needed to be done. He knew that Lenny was right, that he was not smart enough to be answering questions on public television. He couldn't think fast enough to avoid the tricks and word games of journalists. He was in limbo — he felt ostracized by the public and vilified by his longtime friend.

Lying on the smoke-yellow hotel bed, Milo was flipping through the TV stations and downing the last of a beer when his phone rang around eight o'clock.

"Hello?"

"Milo, this is Delores Hamilton, from the University of California, Berkeley, Department of Political Science. We've been watching your progress over the past few months, especially the past weeks and days, and want to extend an invitation to join a panel discussion."

"Hi, Delores," Milo said, taking a deep breath. "We originally agreed not to discuss the project directly with the public, . . . but I guess it depends on the nature of the panel discussion. At this point, what harm could it do?"

"I see," the woman said. "The topic of the panel discussion is the power of social media as it applies to voting, both domestically and abroad. We feel it is so timely you are in town and we couldn't resist contacting you to see if you'd be agreeable to joining us. The discussion takes place tomorrow at five."

"Please give me a moment, Delores," Milo said, setting the phone down next to him. He took a sip of beer and got up and walked to the window, resting his hands firmly on the air conditioning unit as he looked out at the parking lot. He knew he wasn't prepared to join a panel discussion, and knew Kepstein had instructed them to avoid any engagement, sponsorship, or endorsement by any organization. But he felt that this was an open-ended invitation and that he needed to do something — anything — to resurrect the group's importance.

"Delores, thank you for the invitation. Yes, I'll join the discussion tomorrow. If I find that the questioning becomes derogatory or that its purpose is non-academic, I'll walk off the stage. Please remember, unlike many of the students or speakers you're inviting, I am not seeking a career in the field or attempting to build my resumé. I can come and go as I please."

"I understand Mr. Elpmis. We'll be honored to see you tomorrow, and I know the other speakers will also consider it an honor."

Delores emailed Milo the details of the event and asked him to arrive around three o'clock. Before falling asleep, he turned on the eleven o'clock news and saw a brief mention that he'd be attending the University discussion. The reporter went on to list the topics of the panel discussion and what was expected of Milo and the other members of the panel. Milo

243

didn't hear anything the reporter was saying and turned the set off midway through the news story. He slept until late the following morning, his body and mind trying to recover from the past week.

Waking up and ambling to the hotel bathroom, Milo took a long, hot shower then shaved and looked into the mirror. He felt a renewed sense of well-being. He felt that there was an outside chance he really could change things around and present the project in a positive light.

Milo took a cab to the University and was dropped off at a point designated by large plastic signs waving in the San Franciscan breeze. He spoke to a young intern for further directions and was led down a long dark hallway towards a waiting room. The polished cedar of the interior melded well with the pine trees standing solemnly outside the windows. There was more activity in and around the school than he had expected there to be on a Monday. The other panelists were situated around foldable dining tables with attached seats, appearing to Milo to have been there for hours. In front of them were plastic containers containing bits of lettuce and bread, representing the remnants of a lunch that should have been cleaned up hours ago. Milo noticed the other panelists appeared to be older and only two seemed near his age.

"There he is," one of the older panelists said, standing up to shake Milo's hand as he nervously entered the room.

"Milo Elpmis," another panelist said, also standing up. "What a great pleasure it is to have a celebrity among our ranks today!"

Milo wondered, *what's the meaning of all this?*

"Milo Elpmis, indeed," a short woman said, walking briskly into the room and adjusting her glasses, "I am Delores. We spoke yesterday. I cannot thank you enough for coming today, Milo. Your presence has created quite a stir on the campus. Don't tell the others," she said, guiding him to the window and, feigning a secretive gesture by covering her mouth, "but you've nearly quadrupled the expected attendance."

"Quadrupled?" Milo said, somewhat confused. "How many do you expect today then as a final tally?"

"There's already six thousand in the main auditorium," she said. "We had to move them to a bigger venue outdoors and bring in extra cameras and sound equipment to handle the numbers. An overflow crowd is going to be watching us on closed circuit TV."

Milo began to feel like some form of marketing material. He felt like a pawn in some unknown game and thought about Kepstein's guidance and direction in avoiding those kinds of events. Perhaps Kepstein was right, he thought, but it was too late now.

"Milo," came a deep voice from the other end of the table, "come down here, son." The voice came from a bulky man, his accent sounding to Milo like someone from some southern state like Texas.

Milo excused himself and walked to the other end of the table to sit next to the man. "Hello, sir," he said, shaking the man's hand and taking a seat.

"The name's Dr. Fison," the man said, wiping his jaw and reeking of bourbon. "You're going to need to be careful today, Milo. I like what you fellas are up to, but you're pissing off half the country. People in my hometown caught wind you were going to be here. Some of them asked me to give you a punch in the teeth. Others asked me to take you out for a beer. The bottom line is that these folks here get paid big bucks to *talk* about how to change things, but they quit *changing* things a long time ago. That's why they're here today. If they were still pushing new ideas, they'd be getting paid a lot less. You understand, son?"

"Yeah, I get it," Milo said, still a bit confused about all the commotion. "Where'd you get the booze?"

"Always bring it with me, Milo," Fison said, tapping his coat pocket, "but you can ask Delores for a mixed drink. They'll take good care of you."

Milo proceeded to order a whisky neat, finished it, got a refill from the Texan, and read over the discussion outline. He began to feel better and started to jot down notes having to do with how he'd respond to certain questions and prompts. In fact, the more he read, the more he wondered if this panel discussion was a response to the film project or if some of the points their film aimed to illustrate were taking place in a parallel universe.

"Welcome faculty, students, the San Francisco and Berkeley community, and those of you watching live on Channel Seven. Most importantly, a welcome to our distinguished panelists today. We're going to have a great discussion, and before we begin, let's have one big round of applause for all of the panelists." Delores turned to the group seated at two separate tables, facing one another at a forty-five-degree angle. "They're

246

going to be under some intense questioning from one another and from our audience — so give them a big applause now while they're still composed!"

Delores laughed and trailed off to one side of the stage as the audience clapped raucously with sporadic hoots and hollers. On the stage were Republicans, Tea-Party members, Democrats, Libertarians, and Independents. As Delores went down the list of names, the crowd roared when she introduced Milo.

The panel started off with fairly boring questions: "Who felt the House was going to slip toward GOP control or Democratic control after the next election?" "Who felt there should be more curbs on the Super-PAC campaign funding and how should that be done?" and "What could be done to get more younger voters to the polls?" Milo was bored and said very little in response to these questions.

"We have one last question before we move into the second half of today's discussion," Delores said, speaking into the microphone behind the small, wooden podium. "Social media is making communication easier. Officials use it to reach large groups of people, and some claim Barak Obama's first election win was due in large part to the efforts of social media. The question for the panel is, then, 'Could there ever be a context in which social media is *pushed* or *forced* upon the public?'"

"What's that mean exactly, dear?" the Texan thundered into his microphone.

"Let's look at an example," she said. "Twitter users can read posts from their candidates. They can see real-time polls via social media of the public's thinking and how they're voting. Can anyone envision a scenario in which those polls, or trends, or the results of mass communication are at the bottom of every TV screen or every radio channel, for example? And, in this context, can the panel discuss if that would correlate with fair campaigning?"

"Do you mean putting a question like 'Which candidate do you prefer' to the public and displaying the raw results of a poll for the public to see?" Milo asked, holding his microphone tightly in his fingers.

"Yes, Mr. Elpmis. Perhaps not forcing the participation in the polls, but ensuring the results to be seen — displaying them in a more 'open' manner — on all the major news channels, for example."

"Certainly, I think that if you can find a way to democratize the flow of information about what our candidates are doing, or how they are doing in the polls, it will change the way we vote."

Milo's response set off a momentary murmur in the crowd, then another panelist spoke up. "This is already happening. When election time rolls around, there are hundreds of polls taken by all sorts of organizations, and the information is advertised all over the Web, TV, radio, you name it. It's already being done, and it's changing very little."

Milo wanted to ask the man who was doing the polls and where they were being broadcast, if the public had any input on the questions the polls were asking, or if those reviewing the results were in predefined target markets. He wanted to ask a lot of questions, but felt it was time to wait.

The question resonated with the audience, however, and a question from the audience followed.

"My name is Tara Blythe. This is a question for Mr. Elpmis. Thank you for coming here today. I'd like to take the previous question a step further, if I may, and ask what you think will be the result of open two-way communication on the voting process. The cameras you have on the van you've been driving around the country, for example, seem to beget the idea that one person speaks into a camera, and on the other side is another person. Taken on a larger scale, around the country, or world, what do you think this would do for political discussion — and, to my earlier point — voting? Thank you."

She sat down and Milo took the microphone, feeling empowered. "Thank you for your question, Tara. Building on the prior comments, the question is not what would happen if people were communicating more or if there were increased access to information. Indeed, this currently exists. We can talk faster than ever with larger groups of people and, with video, people around the world — it's already being done. The question is, though, through which medium is this being done? What are the factors that influence who is talking with whom, and what they are talking about? You and your colleagues here at the University are having discussions in blogs that are different from the discussions auto mechanics in Topeka, Kansas, are having in their shop rooms, no? And when was the last time you saw news coverage of a Russian restaurant owner happy to be there, or of a successful art gallery opening in Nigeria? Why is that, and how can we take down those differences, is the real question. Once we do that, you will see a plane of clarity that is currently unknown in the political arena. A unified voice to discuss topics, not a voice predicated by preconceived notions, media personalities, or Web-based search algorithms."

"And on the voting?" one of the panelists on the opposite side of the stage asked wryly into his microphone.

"If you take this type of thought process — that communication could be done outside of the usual structures of media, or governmental, oversight, mix it with the speed of the Internet, and apply it to the world, it will change voting forever." He pulled the microphone up from its base, the cord hanging through the small hole on top of the table. He stood up. "Can you imagine if we opened our presidential polls to the world? Imagine asking the world! Asking the world which candidate they thought would be best and why? Can you imagine the power of that information, and the potential ramifications on the American vo—"

Milo stopped talking. He heard a gunshot, then a second, then a third, then a fourth. He always wondered what the sound would be like in real life, and by the time the thought occurred to him, he looked at his chest and saw blood. He saw the people in the crowd blend into one mass, the trees overhead becoming less vibrant and the sky less real. He felt his head become heavy, fell back over his chair, and died instantly.

There was a tremendous amount of confusion and the shooter was easily apprehended. Over one million people had been watching the broadcast and Milo instantly became a martyr. Everything he said during his brief moments at the debate was reproduced again and again all over the world so that, in effect, the domestic film project went viral immediately.

The news of Milo's assassination spread to the members of the film project the same way it did for the rest of the world — big, heartbreaking headlines, subversive undertones, and much commentary. His death led to people picking sides. Some thought that if Milo died for a cause, it must've been a noble one, while others thought that it was a misguided publicity stunt gone wrong and that the project was a farce. Regardless of how it was spun, people were talking about Milo and why the assassination happened. And this meant, too, that they were talking about Kepstein, Jack, and the entire project.

* * *

Jack had been released from captivity the night before Milo's death. He slept from midnight until one o'clock in the afternoon, then walked around the neighborhood in Brooklyn, attempting to get his bearings. He walked past an old coffee shop he and Milo used to go to, wondering how his friend was doing on his tour of the West coast. Stopping a block before his apartment for a newspaper he saw the headline immediately.

At the funeral, all of the members of the film project crew, except for Kepstein, were in attendance. Even General Adams, against the wishes of his past colleagues, made an appearance. He decided it was time to stop hiding from the public. Hundreds of reporters were present and one of them ran up to Rebecca after the ceremony, pressing her for comment.

"Rebecca Kepstein, previously Rebecca Bristle, daughter of Canton Bristle, why have you thrown away the pride of your upbringing and your estate to chase the insanity of a wild, American banker?" the reporter asked with a heavy French accent.

Many questions were asked from many reporters, but this one struck Rebecca. She stopped in her tracks, holding her hands up to indicate to Jack and Adams to slow their pace as they walked beside her.

"I apologize to the world for not making it apparent that my husband had a history mired in things that neither he nor I were proud of. I apologize to the man on my right, Jack Shales, for not making this known to him. It was a marital secret you take to the grave, and when you mix that with friendship, philosophy, love, or justice — whatever you want to believe we are striving for — you will experience heartache. Milo Elpmis is dead. He died because of what my husband did. He died because of the truth that Jack believed in. He died because of the film project.

"My husband held me in disregard for years because I was not an intellectual. What we've learned during the production of this film is that there are no intellectuals. There are only those who are open to learn what they don't know and communicate it to others. My husband created this project — he wants to and he *will* change this world."

Rebecca stopped speaking for a moment. Bright green and orange leaves from the oak trees were blowing in the wind behind her, juxtaposing the mourner's black. She continued, "My husband is being held by the governments. The *governments*. Not my government, or yours, but all governments. He is attempting to change things among them. He is attempting to change the status quos. He needs to be freed from the bondage, my country, your country, and all of our countries impose upon free thinkers! We are not working for any governments. We want to see a more peaceful, and open, world! Please conjure up the strength and persistence to force my husband's freedom — the world needs it. Our film will be released in two months. I beg all of you, FORCE my husband's freedom so that he may see that day and not be behind iron bars. On behalf of anyone who feels things could be better, thank you."

Rebecca walked away from the camera, and the French reporter became famous. The sixty-second interview was broadcast in nearly every language. For those who were against the film's release, the assassination was a nightmare. If they spoke out against the project, their opponents would ask if their stance was worth murder. There was no way to win. The catalytic moment was similar to one seen when one rogue soldier goes on a killing spree in Afghanistan and the people rally for the US to leave: one loose cannon kills Milo Elpmis and the world wonders why it was so important to do so. For those who disapproved of his message, they saw the worst of their brethren take things too far. The moment resulted in people taking sides and expressing widely ranging opinions, an escape on a national level from the status quo.

Chapter Twenty-four

As Jack walked down the familiar hallway to his apartment, he noticed a note on his door. He was being evicted because of poor credit and for disturbing the neighbors. The situation struck him as unfortunate, but hardly a surprise. Nothing surprised him anymore. He'd been forced to forfeit all the money he'd been given by the police and the world was quickly crashing in on him. He felt a great deal of relief when his key still worked and he entered the damp apartment.

No beers were in the refrigerator, only a half-empty bottle of bourbon Milo had brought some time ago for a Halloween gathering. After taking a long pull, he thought about his deceased friend and took another drink. It was hard to bear. He opened the window, letting a little light in, and turned on some music.

The death of a best friend is hard for any man to handle, but when the death is associated with a shared goal, it carries a different weight. Jack felt that this was a notion, along with the sentiment accompanying it, that belonged to soldiers in wartime. He saw the nobility of his life's work evaporate in a matter of seconds when he heard the news of Milo's death. He hardly spoke to anyone at the funeral and refrained from making a statement. After the funeral, Jack took the bus from the cemetery back into the city and that was the last anyone heard from him for a number of days.

Jack remained reclusive for nearly a full week. There were people who wanted and needed to see him, but no one more than his friend Lenny. Lenny was not the first person to knock on the door that week, but he was the first person for whom Jack opened it.

"Hey, Lenny," Jack muttered as he opened the door.

Lenny put a firm hand on his friend's shoulder as he entered the apartment. It smelled of booze and staleness. He sat down on the couch and motioned for Jack to do the same.

"How're you holding up, buddy?"

"Fuck, Lenny. How does it look like I'm holding up?" Jack said, walking past the couch to the living room window. He opened the blinds and looked down with disdain at the street below. "This might be the first day in a week those crazy shits have left me alone. There's always someone out there waiting to bother me. Kids with signs, reporters with microphones, cars with lights and sirens. I'm so sick of it all."

"You know what's going on out there, don't ya, Jack?"

Jack didn't reply. He kept staring out the window.

"Have you watched the news lately?" Lenny asked. When there was no response, he went on, "Have you *listened* to the news, or gone online?"

"No, dammit. I'm not in the mood to see or hear any of this nonsense. Milo's dead, Lenny. Shot six fucking times in the chest. He died instantly — on the spot —because of this project we're all working on, this project we *were* all working on which is tarnished by the lies of an old banker. It has stripped my life of any stability. This project that . . ." He turned away from the window, exasperated.

"Yes, this project we believe in and that is causing a pretty serious shift in society, Jack. People are getting very excited about what we've been doing. You were telling me that when you were flying from Ireland to New York and back again, people were starting to know who you were." He looked up from the couch and met Jack's gaze. "I assure you, my friend, they all know who you are now."

"What does that mean?"

"Jack, this whole crazy fucking experiment has gone into different territory. You need to look at the news online. Everyone is talking about what you're going to do next. Everyone is talking about what Kepstein is going to do next. They want to know if this thing is still on, and they want to know the when, where, and the hows of it all!"

Lenny started to pace the room. "Where's your whisky, Jack?" he asked abruptly.

"It's in the pantry above the fridge. There's three bottles. Grab the one in the back." Jack was looking outside again. "And bring me a glass with a little ice." "Please," he said a half-minute later, almost to himself. There were seconds of silence, then Jack said, "I remember Rebecca's answer to the question from that Parisian man — Jacques, I'd guess his name was. How'd that turn out? Did she ever make any leeway getting the son of a bitch out on bail?"

It was the first time Lenny had heard Jack speak openly about Kepstein with such disgust. It came as a shock, but he knew it shouldn't have. "Yeah man, he's going to be released next week or the week thereafter, if all things go according to plan. You guys really had some falling out, huh?"

"I'd rather not talk about it, but yes, let's just say our time together in the clink exacerbated the gap between the two of us because of the scandal." Jack took a long, slow drink of whiskey. "Let's leave it at that."

"Fair enough . . . So what's next for Jack Shales?" Lenny sat down on the couch, lighting a cigarette. "I strongly suggest you turn on the news, or get online for a second, man. It's going to send a shiver down your spine."

Lenny spoke to Jack as if he were a shaman handing his friend a powerful hallucinogenic, fully aware of what they were about to see and understanding that once they saw the other side, or the "new reality," there would be no going back.

Jack took the drug that was information and coupled it with the other drug, alcohol. Allowing both to work their magic, he began clicking through news story after news story on his laptop. He asked Lenny countless questions about what was happening. He wanted to know if anyone was in danger. He wanted to know if he was in danger. He wanted to know if Lenny had been followed or if Rebecca had been threatened.

After Jack digested a few hours of the news about his life and nearly finished the bottle of whiskey with his long-time friend, Lenny asked, "Will you come back up to New York with me?"

"I don't know, Lenny. I know I need to be there for the project, but to be honest with you, I don't know if this is all worth it. What if you get killed next? Where would that leave me? And vice versa. Think about the consequences of our actions. Can you really say it's all worth it?"

"Yes I can, Jack. What we're doing is bringing about a positive change in society at large. When and how can you ever be a part of something this big again?"

"That's just it, I don't really care anymore how big it gets or how big it already is. I'm not comfortable with the personal toll it's taking. Milo's death is not worth any goal. Not one! I have to admit I cannot feel proud of myself for working on this film any longer. Further, all the money to my name has been confiscated and there will likely be years of legal battles, leaving me with less than I began. Everything is so fucked up right now, Lenny. How can I go to New York with you like this — in this state?"

"Because you are being evicted," Lenny said with a sarcastic smile, pointing to the notice on the coffee table.

Lenny left the following morning and Jack spent the next twenty-four hours thinking about everything that had taken place in the past month. He walked to his favorite coffee shop. On the magazine stand outside the café, he saw a local newspaper with his picture on the front page. People inside the café stared at him as he walked past and two younger fellows asked if they could sit with him. "I'm not staying," Jack said offhandedly, taking his coffee and rushing out through the front door. By this time a reporter had materialized, asking him what he thought about Bill Kepstein and his bank.

Jack turned away, running back to his apartment. He locked the door and poured a few fingers of whisky into his coffee. He realized that his way of life as he had known it was gone. He was now a public commodity and the public needed to see what they owned. They needed their leader, Jack Shales, to take the reins of a film they were dying to see.

* * *

Lenny found Rebecca sitting in the upstairs room of the Brooklyn house, the room where her husband had frequently sat at the small editor's table. "Did you get a chance to see Jack?" she asked, desperation and hope intermingled.

"Yes, I did. He's very shaken up, but I think he'll come around," Lenny replied.

"I certainly hope so. There is nothing worse, nothing anyone could ever dream of, that could be worse than what happened. I've stood by my husband's side this entire time, Lenny, interested in this project as a woman is interested in her husband's hobbies, and little more. But that's changed now. At the funeral, I felt as if Milo was my brother. His loss has stirred something in me. I'm angry."

"I am too, Rebecca. They — and I don't even know who *they* is — have killed a very innocent man. It hurts you, it hurts me. It hurts all of us. We need to get Jack back up here to meet with Adams. Adams is the only one who knows the best way to proceed from this point on. Is he here?"

"He's on his way, actually. He's going over some editing this afternoon and he's afraid of losing the material."

"Losing the material?"

"Yes. He told me that he's followed almost constantly. He has to have a private car so he can avoid the dark corners of the subway. Some of the other crew members can't even leave the house."

"How far along are we now?" Lenny asked.

"Adams has said that the bulk of the editing is done — the story works as is, but the next two weeks will be spent on aesthetics. Then four weeks to get it tooled up for the big screen and distribution to the theaters around the world."

"It's unbelievable we're this close."

Rebecca's phone began ringing. "One second, Lenny, let me see who this is." She jumped to her feet, putting the phone to her ear, and walked towards the second-story window. "This is Rebecca . . . Yes, I'll be right there," she said, closing her phone and turning to Lenny. "He's getting out!" She dove into Lenny's arms for a bear hug. "Bill is going to be released this afternoon!"

* * *

The news spread through the house like wildfire, reigniting the flame of morale that had been blown out a week before. It was perfect timing as General Adams would be arriving that evening and Kepstein wanted to waste no time getting back to business. His wife's heartfelt plea had resulted in his release. When the public saw what had happened to Milo, they knew Kepstein and his project couldn't be as corrupt as the media had made them out to be. And when Jack remained isolated for nearly two weeks, people began to wonder which man needed to be released more. By the end of the first week after Milo's death, petitions were circulating on the Internet and the public started to ask why the government —whichever it was, state or the big house — needed to keep a disgruntled banker so quiet. Kepstein's captors knew they needed to contain the situation before things got out of hand and they agreed to release him before bringing him back for his arraignment.

"Bill, honey," Rebecca said embracing her husband just as he'd dreamt of for the past month. "I've missed you so much. So, so, so, so much."

"I've missed you as well, dear, more than you'll ever know." Kepstein looked over his shoulder at the building from which he was being released and smelled the free breeze that circulated around them. He wasn't allowed to watch television or any other digital form of news while under surveillance, but a kind guard brought him a newspaper on occasion. Kepstein knew how things had changed in a very short time and was happy to see that there were no reporters following his wife. "Rebecca, how'd you get here? We need to make sure we keep you very safe — what are you driving?"

"I borrowed General's private driver. Things are going to be OK — General had to hire a private driver due to the craziness. Things have gotten so crazy, Bill, I — I —" Rebecca started sobbing and threw her arms around her husband's shoulders. "I've been so scared!"

"There, there, Rebecca." Kepstein knew she was hurting and had feared the worst ever since their separation in Dublin. "It's all going to be OK. We're almost done."

They climbed into the dark Crown Victoria waiting for them on the side street and Kepstein asked the driver what precautions were taken to make sure the car hadn't been bugged or booby-trapped. He refused to let his wife, or anyone else, fall into harm's way again on his behalf. He took responsibility for Milo's death.

Kepstein thought he'd maintain his composure for his wife's sake, but as the car drove through the busy city, he started to feel differently. He noticed that New York City hadn't changed and he had a moment's trepidation, wondering if it would ever be possible for something to change on a large scale. Could one man and one group of people change New York City? The US? The world?

"Rebecca, I have something I need to talk to you about before we get to the house," Kepstein said, putting his arm around his wife's shoulder and looking into her eyes. "I know very well that if there was ever a time when we all need a pep talk, that time is right now . . . But I'm so confused. I'm distraught and I'm embarrassed about what has happened. It depresses me to a depth I can't describe. I feel personally responsible for what happened to Milo and I know the members of the team will want answers. They need to know why I've lied to everyone. The lying and the corruption cheapens Milo's death and it makes me sick to my stomach."

A tear rolled down Rebecca's cheek. "Bill, I'm not going to find the right words to make you feel any differently than how you feel right now, but I'm just going to tell you what you're walking into . . . Today, when I told the crowd at the house you were getting out of jail, it was the first time I'd seen anything but sorrow in a week. There was joy on everyone's faces — they all need you so badly. Anyone who wasn't already at the house is coming over today, and they need to see you — they want to see you and we've all missed you dearly. Milo did what he did because he believed in this project so much. He felt like he could save it and get it back on track. No one blames you for what happened. In some way, I think everyone assumed there was some monumental skeleton in your closet that propelled you to change your life the way you have. I knew the truth all along and kept the secret. You need to lead and stay positive."

"And what about Jack? Has he come back to New York?"

Rebecca feared he'd ask the one question she couldn't provide a good answer to. "No, he hasn't yet. Lenny saw him yesterday and said he was doing much better."

As they drove the rest of the way home, Kepstein thought about the recent events that had taken place. He felt disillusioned and unsteady. Lines had been blurred between right and wrong and he was disappointed in himself for betraying millions of people. He felt that his life was a lie and that the lies continued even when trying to right them.

As Rebecca had promised, everyone was very happy to see their leader. "There he is!" Lenny exclaimed, throwing open the front door wide as the Kepsteins climbed up the front stoop. There was a party going on inside, and despite their recent hardships, smiles abounded.

Rebecca was right. This was the first reason in a long time for celebrating and the change in Kepstein's mood was immediate. "Before we celebrate, let's please have a moment of silence for our good friend Milo," Kepstein said as he joined the party.

It was a somber thing to say after being inside the house for only a couple of minutes, but he felt he needed to say it. Everyone stood silently for nearly five minutes before Kepstein looked up and around. "Thank you all. Milo's actions were meant to propel this project, as he believed very deeply in what we're doing. He did not die in vain. He's become a martyr in this country and in others . . . When we talk about martyrs, that stirs up a very strong mental image, doesn't it? The first thoughts that came to my mind the first time I said this word to myself were, 'Is it possible? Is it possible that this simple film we've decided to create could be so profound that it could result in a martyr?' Martyrs are usually reserved for religious freedom and revolutions. . . And for societal change. Martin Luther King Jr. was a martyr for his cause, wasn't he? Do we believe in the societal change that can take place when this film is released?"

Kepstein looked around the room to gauge the response to his now-rhetorical question. "I've decided that I do believe in it. I believe our film is going to make people think a little differently. I hope you all agree we should push on."

Everyone in the room broke into a brief round of applause. They were all behind the film and Kepstein's presence reminded them of that.

Adams announced that the editing was complete. "I know I haven't been able to spend much time here lately," he said. He held up a small, portable hard drive. "But it is because of this. We have the complete film on this hard drive. One copy is in Dublin and two are in other locations. I assure you, there are a lot of people who want to know what's on these disks. In my experience, by the time this is in the theaters, it will already have been released. We may or may not have the technology in place by that time to prevent such a premature viewing, but we'll see. To limit the exposure, what I am thinking is that we display the film in a small number of theaters around the world at the *exact same time*, relative to Eastern Standard Time, regardless of what time it is in the respective location where the film is being shown."

"The film is finished?" Kepstein yelled at the top of his lungs in exasperation. This was news to him.

"Yes, indeed it is, my friend — congratulations, and—. "

"Surprise!" Everyone in the room chimed in at once. It was a silver lining to a dark cloud, and news they'd been eager to give.

Adams explained what scenes they'd kept and which ones they'd taken out, along with those that could be easily replaced in the event Kepstein felt changes were necessary. He explained what the public thought the film was going to be about, based upon Milo's public appearances. In turn, Kepstein explained what he assumed were the fears of those who had held him captive.

After a long night of catching up and drinking, everyone sat down to watch the film for the first time. It was still raw and needed a little polishing, but the grit was there and it was as powerful as they'd assumed it would be. The implications were huge, and Kepstein understood the weight of what was taking place.

* * *

The following morning, Kepstein felt unexpectedly distressed when he awoke. For nearly fifteen minutes, he sat on the edge of the bed. "What is it, dear?" Rebecca asked.

"It's not right, seeing that movie without Jack being here. Everyone knew it. I knew it, you knew it — we could all feel his absence."

"What are you going to do?"

"I know I have to see Jack immediately, no matter what the outcome."

"I agree. You two are so important to this project and to everyone here. And you're important to one another. You need to see him as soon as possible."

"But how? Do you think I should go down to Baltimore?"

"Yes. Lenny told me he's going to be evicted from his apartment very soon."

"I'll call him today."

"I think you should dress and head that way right now, Bill — I really do."

* * *

Kepstein wasn't sure what he'd say or how Jack would receive him, but he knew it had to be done. He found Jack's building easily and made his way up to Jack's apartment. He knocked on the door, feeling more nervous than he usually felt, and waited.

"Come on . . . fuck off, man," Jack said from inside the apartment as he looked through the peephole.

"Jack, just hear me out. I saw Adams last night — the film is done, you have to see it."

"I have seen it. Lenny brought me a copy a few days ago. Go away." Jack sighed heavily. "Please, I'll get up to New York on my own time, I just can't handle this shit right now. Please just go away."

"Jack, there's something I want to show you, from the time we first met." Kepstein took a crumpled piece of paper from his jacket pocket, straightened it out, and slid it under the door. "Do you recall? It was the day of Rebecca's father's funeral — I was not invited and he left a letter for me."

"Yes, I remember it vaguely," Jack said, picking up the letter and reading it on his side of the doorway. "Sounds to me like her dad had you figured out pretty well. I wouldn't have wanted you at my funeral either."

"I'm sorry, Jack, for what happened to Milo. I'm sorry I lied to you for so long. That's really all I can say now."

"Why'd you bring me this letter?" Jack asked, opening the door and walking into his apartment with his back turned to Kepstein. He walked into the kitchen to pour his first drink of the day, assuming his guest would follow him in that direction.

"I brought it because I think it applies to all of us. You're a unique man with a gift of understanding things differently. You have creative talents and a way to interpret the world around you differently. You're able to take that understanding and present it in a way that others will be able to understand and potentially act upon. I think that goes for all of us working on this film. We can either ignore that awareness, we can assume it is the case and do nothing, or we can assume that it *is* the case and do something about it. We can use our collective creativity to attempt — we can at least try — to change things for the better."

"You've known Milo for a little over one year, Bill. I grew up with him. He's dead because of this — perhaps because of you — and I just don't know if it's all worth it."

"If you feel that Milo's death was my fault, say so, Jack, and I will quietly duck out of this project. I'll fund it until its completion, and otherwise remove myself from it entirely, if that is what you desire."

Jack reached into the cupboard and took out another glass. "No, no that's not what I believe and not what I wish. Have a drink. Let's finish this film and change the world."

Chapter Twenty-five

A week later, Jack and Kepstein were walking side by side into a tall and nondescript building in Manhattan. They were well dressed for the occasion, making their way up the grey steps and meeting the concierge on the first floor. "We're here for the press conference," Kepstein said, handing the woman a business card with the suite number marked on the back.

"Yes, of course. Let me just check the directory for a moment to make sure it's the right location," she said, running her hand down the list of names and corresponding floors. "Here we are — yes, I am sure they'll be expecting you."

On the eighteenth floor, the elevator doors opened into another hallway. As they walked down the length of the corridor, they mentally prepared themselves for an interview that would likely shape their lives and the lives of many others for a long time to come.

Jack took a seat on a black ostrich skin sofa, next to the mini-fridge, while Kepstein walked the length of the dimly lit waiting room, looking at the photographs on the walls and the captions below them. "You see that Frost/Nixon movie, Jack?" Kepstein said off-handedly, looking at a photo of Nixon and the taglines beneath. "I remember the day that scandal broke loose, I was in between classes and caught it on a radio in the high school hallway . . . "

"No kidding," Jack said fondly. "Yeah, I saw that movie — it was good. Was it accurate?"

"Yeah, it was. Take a look at this — they did a follow-up interview with Nixon in this very office."

As they were talking, a man came into the room and greeted them. His name was Mars Lampe.

"Hi, gentlemen. I hope you weren't waiting too long and I hope you found the place OK and didn't have any trouble getting up to the suite — it's hard to find sometimes, but that all depends on who's working downstairs and directing traffic, you know. Same as anywhere I suppose!"

Lampe led Kepstein and Jack past the front desk where three people were standing, pens and notebooks in hand. "That's the way it goes around here, anyhow, someone says something's important — someone's important — to talk to and it all has to be done at once and immediately, you know. Like you two fellas for example. Say what is it you do, anyhow, Jack? Kepstein, I know you've got the bank — found you on the Web pretty easily — but you, Jack — what's your story, friend?"

The three men walked into a studio. There was little time to spare and the makeup people and the lighting people arrived at once. Kepstein had his cheeks freshened up and Jack had his hair combed back and spritzed once or twice.

"I'm going to ask you the first question, Bill," Lampe said. "It's going to be directed only at you. Then we're going to have thirty seconds of closure comments and pandering until it somehow rolls into my second question, which will be directed only at Jack. That's really the only hard part. After that you can both answer whatever you want and how often you want. I can only say, though, that it works best for me, the camera crew, and the viewers if it's not one person answering the entire time . . . You see, if it's just one guy answering all the questions, the camera people don't know where to shoot, because one guy looks awkward and bored, and the other looks like a camera hog. What I do in that case is direct my question more specifically at the one not talking. I don't know much about you guys. I'm not Charley Rose, here, OK, and I don't read up on your life's details. If things get dull, I'm going to ask an inflammatory question. I need *you* to lead *me* where you want this conversation to go."

"Where is this going?" Jack asked. "Do we need cue cards, or preplanning of our comments? Is this an interview or is this a conversation?"

"It's a conversation, Jack. You're quick, I can tell, but I can promise you I'm not going to be nice."

"Our mutual friend, Mr. Adams, promised us that," Kepstein said with a smile.

"How I know he'd fret if you called him *Mister* Adams," Mars laughed. "All I'm explaining is what I've been told before you got here, guys. We have one hour together. I've had fifteen minutes to prep. You're intellectuals creating a film that is going to shake a lot of things up, so I know you know how the camera bits work and you know what you need and want to say. I'll be honest and let you know that I wish I had fifteen days, and not fifteen minutes, to get ready for this, as my colleague in Los Angeles

271

called me moments ago and mentioned this could be more important than I realized. I'm sorry for my lack of preparation, but," he held up a finger, "perhaps, this will make today's interview all the more raw and true — Let's see."

The cameras started rolling. "Bill, I'm going to direct this first question to you to get us started," Mars said, leaning forward in his chair, legs crossed. "The world wants to know — why does the head of a publicly-traded bank decide to give it all up for a chance to make a movie of a somewhat secretive nature? Perhaps you're motivated by the notion that we're living in tumultuous financial times, and that this notion has gotten you to the point where you've been arrested?"

"Well Mars, this transition was borne out of a point in my life most of us reach eventually, a point where we look at our life's work and purpose and ask ourselves if that's the place we want to be. My wife, of course, assumed I was having a midlife crisis, as it's often referred to, but my position at the bank and the resources I have available from my position at the bank have allowed me to make radical changes in my life on a more dramatic scale than most people can."

"And you weren't comfortable with your life's work, I take it?"

"That's correct. I was born into the bank and I think the public is well aware at this point that sometimes my position didn't allow me to make decisions I was comfortable with. I've seen and experienced a great deal of what our world has to offer and there were some things I felt needed to be changed. After a chance meeting with Jack and his close friend, Lenny

Manzarec, we agreed that one of the most powerful ways to reach large audiences at this time is through the medium of film."

Lampe turned towards Jack. "Jack, you were — I think the best word is — betrayed — by your friend, Bill Kepstein, for nearly a year and a half. He kept you in the dark about the police scandal that is now common knowledge. His wife even knew of this and kept it secret. Yet here you are together, today. Don't you think that raises suspicion in the public's mind? Some people feel that you two are in collusion, essentially pulling the wool over our eyes, as it were."

"Mars," Jack said with a slight quiver in his voice, "my best friend, Milo Elpmis, was shot dead for this film. I've lost all the money I've ever had. Bill is going back into custody in forty days. I'll answer your question with another one. How much more hardship do we need to endure before the suspicious public trusts us? How many more of us need to be murdered or put in prison before it becomes apparent we're the good guys?"

Mars was not prepared for heavy-handed words like "murder," and there was a silence that only lasted five seconds, but felt to the viewers like an eternity. That pause kept the world watching. Then the interview picked up steam. Mars's prepared questions were thrown away and there was an entire hour of back and forth, philosophical discourse, and bleeding-heart purity of purpose. Towards the end of the interview, Jack looked directly into the camera, stating "When this airs, my face is going to be known to some men and women around the world who realize they're going to be stars of this film. I can assure you, some of them are not going to want that to happen. The interviews and scenes in our film are extremely vivid and will

273

create a mixture of change, dissension, and harmony. To avoid any problems, we're going into hiding. Please keep the winds of opinion from crushing this project before it begins."

"We'll see you in about four weeks," Kepstein said, following Jack.

"You heard it America, world. I'm Mars Lampe. You've met Bill Kepstein and Jack Shales. Thank you and good night."

* * *

A tumultuous two weeks followed the interview. Kepstein called a final meeting at the house in Brooklyn and welcomed the camera vans parked outside. The vans were their safety blanket, as it was assumed that a car bomb or other form of destruction would not happen with so much around-the-clock surveillance. The media was in a frenzy. Everyone wanted to know what the film was about and where and how it was going to be aired.

"Greetings, everyone," Kepstein said to the members of the company gathered in the living room. "We've agreed to spend the next two weeks in a sort of media blitz. No more on-camera activity as we did yesterday with Mars Lampe. From here on out, it's only going to be interviews with radio, magazines, newspapers, and so forth. I think we should all discuss how we're going to present the film from this point on."

"Bill," Adams said, "I was speaking with Lenny about this earlier today and I have created some guides I think might help us."

"You're always a step ahead of me, General!" Kepstein said merrily. "Do you have this guide with you?"

"Indeed! We can pull it up on the projector if you'd like."

The group then generated talking points for nearly any question they'd be asked by the media and set ground rules for questions they wouldn't answer.

* * *

Knowledge of and interest in the film grew rapidly. It seemed everyone, from *National Geographic* to *Cosmo* magazine, wanted an interview with the men and women behind the scenes. Women wanted to know more about Rebecca and the Kepsteins' marriage. Disgruntled college kids wanted to learn more about how Jack had blackmailed the police.

But the media industry found itself in a predicament: while these stories were all extremely lucrative, the characters were hot, the polarizing nature of the film generated excitement, and there was finally something to focus on other than Republicans vs. Democrats, the poor vs. the rich, and the religious culture vs. non-sectarianism, the message of the film was essentially at odds with the industry itself and it took only a few days for this to become obvious to the public. For the film aimed to demonstrate that the media and governmental lenses and mouthpieces through which the world was informed were unnecessary and it aimed to generate interest in the alternative idea that communication between and among the world's inhabitants could, and should, replace the media. The media hierarchies had feared for some time that this might happen, especially with the increased prevalence of blogs and other social media tools, but they were still able to maintain a foothold on the dissemination of what was called news, especially serving as conduits for the agendas of governments and businesses.

In response to this challenge, the media conglomerates came to a secret agreement to downplay the increasing popularity of the film's anticipated debut. They began omitting details of any breaking news that was related to the film. After two weeks of interviews and advertising, knowledge of the project had traveled globally. This curbing of reporting, however, came too late, for the world had *Window fever*, as some put it.

Then the unexpected happened.

"Something big is happening here," Lenny said, crossing the river in downtown Cork, Ireland. He was walking home, briskly as usual, with his phone pressed tightly against his ear and an umbrella in the other hand. "Yes, definitely, something big is happening here!"

"What the hell is it, Lenny?" Jack yelled into the phone, always inpatient with his old friend.

"Sorry, sorry, I was just heading home. I noticed a ton of activity going on in the park next to my hotel, and of course I had to check it out. There was this large group of people huddling around a large object that appeared to be shielded by a tarp from the rain — the rain is coming down in torrents today — and so I approached and it took a while to make my way past the crowd. I finally got to the front of the pack. I could see it. Three or four large wooden sticks — a tripod, buttress type of structure — holding five or six cameras. The cameras were crisscrossed with one another and almost looked like the stamen of a daffodil that had lost its top. Once I was close enough to realize they were cameras, I heard somebody say, 'Look over there' or 'Look way up there.' Large projector screens were fixed randomly to the trees around the park and they were showing real-time images of what the lenses were recording. On the bottom of the tripod was a plank of wood with something scrawled crudely in a foreign language. I asked a rather large woman with a small face if she could translate what it said and she obliged begrudgingly. 'I can't read Gaelic, boy, but someone told me it says *The Windows Around*.'"

The same process was taking place in New York's Central Park and outside of The Hague in Brussels. On Chowpatty beach in Mumbai, cameras adorned the boardwalk. When they were removed by the authorities, they were immediately replaced by others. Cameras were also placed at random in Cairo, Tripoli, Damascus, and Beijing. Europe was abuzz with the idea, with Australia not far behind. No one could contain the momentum. People were mimicking what Milo had done with the van in anticipation for the film launch. The cameras weren't yet connected with each other, but each one took an image and displayed it to the crowd in the area. Variations on this setup soon began to emerge.

The media seized on this phenomenon to try one last time to derail the project. Rumors surfaced that the cameras proved Kepstein's true ulterior motives — he was working with governments to keep a closer watch on people the world over. These rumors were tied in with recent surveillance scandals having to do with the spying on its citizens by the US, and they successfully struck chords of resentment, especially in the European countries that were upset an ally would spy on them. The rumors curbed the spread of the film's popularity to some extent, but too little and too late.

The last media push came when a friend of General Adams called him with an idea for a business venture. "General, I've been reading quite a bit about you in the papers and I think I've got an idea you'll take some interest in!"

"I'm open to anything you've got to say, Chance. It's always interesting!" Adams laughed. "What do you have for me today?"

General Adams and Chance were old friends, and they had helped each other financially over the past few years as business partners for various ventures. "Your film is becoming popular everywhere, and as I understand it, the plot is founded around the process of communication. Is that right?"

"Yes, that's about right," Adams said.

"OK, so out here in the Bay area we've recently finished testing software capable of real-time translation in any medium. For example, if a person is speaking into a camera, or typing in a forum, or reading in a forum, or listening to an interview, etc., the audio and written words will be translated in real-time. There is essentially no lag time between the speaker and the listener. I think there may be a way to utilize this software in connection with your project. Timing is critical, so I'll say right off the bat, I'm willing to give you free use of my software for whatever purpose you need."

"And in exchange?"

"Simply the notoriety, of course. When the technology is used, it's going to take my company from unheard of to world famous within hours."

The men discussed the pros and cons of the joint venture, and eventually took the idea to Kepstein via a teleconference. They decided it was a win-win situation and Chance got his team into full swing. They introduced and hosted the software in a cloud-based forum where people could openly talk about the upcoming film. Whatever was typed was transmitted immediately and the whole world was literally on the same page.

With one week to go before the film's debut, they took things a step further and offered the software to anyone who was interested in the ability to connect cameras through the website, so that whatever someone said into one camera in one part of the world would be sent in real time to cameras everywhere. What seemed like an astonishing feat of technology to most was just a dream of Kepstein's coming to maturity. He hoped people would see the power of the camera and start filming things on their own. Now, with the cameras cycling randomly and ubiquitously around the world, and transmitted in real-time through the website, everyone would talk with everyone else, and no *one* voice could manipulate the dialogue.

Kepstein posted a five-minute video on the site and addressed the world, telling it how important — and difficult — it will be to keep the site up and running and uncensored. He urged viewers to keep fighting for this freedom and bid them farewell, as he would be returning into custody in ten days.

With Kepstein's full disclosure and his support of the website, coupled with the fact he would be a free man for just a few more days, the world trusted him once again. People no longer thought of him as a man that had kept secrets or hurt his closest friends, but, instead, as a man who had a vision, a man who did what he had to do so that he could see his dream realized. They were thankful for his efforts in developing the project, even if they didn't know what to expect, and their anticipation of the film's debut was mounting.

Chapter Twenty-six

"It's *The Windows Around*, Martin. I can't believe you haven't heard of it —everyone's been talking about it for weeks now. It's simply the most fabulous picture of this decade. They've turned down all the major movie festivals and awards shows, darling. That takes a lot of confidence." The middle-aged woman was talking to her husband as she fanned herself in a late spring heatwave. She wore a coral shawl and a long teal dress for the occasion, with pearls and a taste for the delicate to match the tray of caviar beside her seat. To the right sat her husband, a man with small wire-rimmed glasses that he removed occasionally to wipe the sweat from his brow with a silk handkerchief. The couple was sitting in the balcony of an old theater in Montreal, waiting for the debut of the film in less than an hour.

The film's premiere was a nice change of pace for the small band of men and woman who'd led a life of secrecy for the past two years. They watched it from a St. Thomas hotel, high upon the hillside and tucked away above the streets of Charlotte Amalie in a type of 18th century maze of bricks and tropical plants. Their dozen rooms, connected and brightly lit against an otherwise dark and unsuspecting night, resembled a pearl bracelet that had been placed upon black terrycloth. They were celebrating in a way they never would again. They freely moved from room to room to greet one another with kisses and praises, saying things like, "Do you remember what those guards at the Imperial Palace said when you lit a cigarette?" or "How long do you think it will be before they find us" and "What was it that Senator said to you about convincing people with TV ads?" The room refrigerators were filled to the brink with exotic beverages and champagne was chilling in ice buckets.

Kepstein was sitting by a window at the corner of the building that was closest to the harbor streets far below. His eyes were calm, but alive with a hidden fire. He was thinking about his last few days, his last few hours of freedom.

Jack Shales was sitting on the floor in the next room with his feet lying under a coffee table and his back against a couch. He was celebrating their victory and the completion of the strange path he'd been on since that night two years ago when he'd first met Kepstein. He was celebrating the breeze coming through the window from the sea and the alcohol that was entering his brain. But he was also mourning the freedom they'd gained for the world, but had lost for themselves. No longer would any of the crew be able to carry on in the same way, except, perhaps, in quiet, hidden dens such as Betriebsnacht.

Rebecca ascended the stairs to the hotel's rooftop. She'd come there to escape the smells of smoke and liquor and to embrace the glory of the stars. It had been too long since she'd taken the time to thank God for what she had. The last time she had felt like this was the night before she and Kepstein married. Then she had sat on the edge of a steam chimney for thirty minutes without taking her eyes off the stars.

Rebecca knew she and the others in the film company were changing the world. She knew her husband was responsible for it. She thought about the history of their marriage and decided that no matter what had happened in the past, this moment made everything they had gone through worthwhile. She rushed down the stairs, past the telephone booth, the golden lace mirrors, the brass framed paintings, the fading wallpaper, past the elevator, through the door of Lenny's hotel room, and through four more rooms until she found her husband.

As Rebecca rushed by, Lenny set his glass down on a corner table and turned up the stereo. Miles Davis, 1942. He drifted off, feeling a sense of becoming each note played on Davis's horn, then he lit a cigarette and walked through the crowd until he reached General Adams, who was standing on the corner of an L-couch and making a speech. "Hush! Hush . . . Here it is! Here it is!" He was looking down at his watch. "THREE, TWO, ONE!" The sound of cheers and toasts in all twelve rooms was heard in the city streets below.

"Martin, I didn't expect this to be so . . . so . . . confrontational," the middle-aged woman in the Montreal balcony said as she watched the picture with unbelieving eyes. What she was seeing made her feel terrifyingly uncomfortable. She looked at the men and women around her, and for the first time in her life realized that she and her husband were not special. They were no different from those they had always looked down at and she realized that each person was born with an intellect that was cultivated in some areas, not always in others, but that it had the power, nonetheless, of standing out and being important and recognized as important in different cultures. She realized that this human quality was the essence of humanity and it was real. She could sense that sharing one's intellect with another individual created the very fabric of life as she understood it.

The movie was ending with a silent montage of the world's inhabitants living together beneath the glow of a fire burning brightly and streaking across the sky. It was impossible to tell whether the incandescent glow was a missile or a star, a saving grace or a violent threat, as it sailed from east to west through time zones, days, and nights. The camera followed the glow as it circled the globe, passing through nations and over the heads of hundreds of thousands of silent onlookers, then the bright white fire slowly faded out over cities, trees, mountains, and people until it vanished and the screen became dark.

There was an unmistakable hush in the theater as the bewildered crowd searched for something to say, do, or think. Then Martin began to speak to his wife. She did not turn toward him, but kept her eyes focused on the screen. She did not move her head at first, but as she was about to reply, she saw an image of herself and her husband on the screen. She realized there had to be a camera, as they were being displayed in real time.

All across the globe, in each of the three hundred theatres that people had filled, whether at the crack of dawn, the middle of the night, or at other times on this Friday night, there was the same phenomenon: the projection of images on the screen of people who had once been observers and now were actors. Images projected by the cameras in each theater were mixed at random with images taken by other cameras so that the image of someone who was being recorded in a Los Angeles theater, for example, might be displayed in a theater in Seoul, and the theater in Seoul might have its footage displayed in a theater in Sydney. The effect of this event was momentous and generated a sense of togetherness among the audiences in the different theaters. It was as if a social fire had been sparked, an ice breaker in a monumental chain of human silence. Then the people in the theaters began talking to each other, carrying their conversations out into the streets and into their homes, market places, bars and lives. The cameras rolled on, showing what cameras have always shown: that windows work in two directions, allowing viewers to see in and to see out.

After the first twenty-four hours, the film was starting to break records everywhere. Even with around-the-clock show times, lines of people were waiting to see it.

* * *

The crew returned to the US on a private jet commissioned by Kepstein. They would go about their lives as free citizens, while Kepstein would be taken into custody again.

The level of Kepstein's involvement with the police and the level of corruption that had taken place in Baltimore, though, never fully became public. As it turned out, a cover-up was orchestrated by the CIA, allowing Kepstein to remain out of prison under the condition that he was not to mention his — or his bank's — involvement with the Baltimore police force, the City of Baltimore, the State of Maryland, or the Federal government.

"You'll be able to talk, Bill," he was told, "but you're not going to be able to talk to anyone but your wife."

"My wife?" Kepstein asked his lawyer as they shared coffee in the living room of Kepstein's home.

"Yes, the terms they've set require you to be under house arrest. Rebecca will be able to stay here, but you can't entertain visitors and you can't organize any meetings or speak to groups. It's just going to be you and Rebecca, Bill. It's not the best-case scenario, but it's definitely not the worst —they're letting you off very, very, easy, my friend. I think you should accept their offer immediately."

Kepstein accepted the offer, but nearly two weeks later, against his attorney's advice, he decided that he had to speak out to the people who had seen the film and he and Rebecca decided that the best approach would be a letter. Kepstein would write it and Rebecca would read it. He worked diligently on the letter, as he felt it had to accurately express his thoughts. The world wanted answers and the film was breaking records across the globe. People were erecting two-way cameras in major cities as fast as opponents to the idea took them down. Dictators who hated the film's ideas attempted to block any news of it, but their citizens spoke to others from around the world in real-time about the film. A camera in a rural Kazakh town, for example, randomly connected with people in Moscow and Buenos Aires, their words translated instantaneously so there were no barriers to dialogue. And if the film was banned in Beijing, say, stay-at-home moms spoke about it with New York City school teachers in real-time, one lunch café to another. Palestinians who were vehement enemies of Israel spoke to Israeli citizens for five minutes before the cameras switched to another location and they were speaking with Rwandan fisherman. Communication among the world's peoples seemed to have been very quickly turned upside down.

* * *

On a quiet spring afternoon in Baltimore, Rebecca looked out over the brightly colored lawn, its new grass thirsty for rain and sunlight and its perennials blooming in their pinks and yellows, welcoming the change of seasons. She held a piece of paper in her hand, examining the typed black and white letter. She thought about how funny it was that words could be so powerful, depending upon who said them, when, and for what purpose.

She logged into the film's website, with its blogs and comments, its posts, videos, and forums. She could see how many people were currently logged in. It was just a little over two hundred million, double the usual. The rumor was out that the Kepsteins were going to break their silence.

"Greetings all." Rebecca's voice filled hundreds of thousands of living rooms, barrooms, pool halls, hookah bars, and coffee houses. "Thank you for believing in this film. Thank you for going out to see this film and for thinking about it critically. Most importantly, thank you for thinking about the world around you critically. Thank you for believing in yourselves, and for believing in the one thing we all have in common — our humanity.

"It is obvious at this point in history that we live in a global world. We must understand this and work with one another to remove any obstacles put in place to prevent our sense of community — for there is only one community now and we all share it. The emergence of rapid-cycling, randomly-placed, and seemingly ubiquitous two-way cameras is an outcome of this project that I could have only dreamed of. The truth is, that has happened because of you — the people — and not because of me or the film's crew.

"Think of how nice it was to discuss the merits of this film openly with one another and not through the media or your government's version of the media. Imagine for a moment how it is possible to do this with politics and other matters of world importance.

"My dream is that this is the first of many ideas we create together. My dream is that this is the first of many 'global inventions' belonging to all of us and that have the goal of bettering the lives of everyone. Thank you all.

Bill Kepstein"

Rebecca looked at the lawn through the office window. The sun had set just enough to create a shadow across the window pane. She saw her reflection in the glass, readjusting her eyes she could see her husband's reflection in the window as he leaned against the door frame. He was standing behind her, just as he'd always had.

The End

ERC;
I really

hope you

enjoy

(responsibly)

- Co

22511100R00174

Made in the USA
Columbia, SC
01 August 2018